J.J.MAR

GIDEON'S FEAR

AS WRITTEN BY

William Vivian Butler

Hodder & Stoughton
LONDON SYDNEY AUCKLAND TORONTO

British Library Cataloguing in Publication Data
Marric, J.J. *1908 – 1973*
Gideon's fear.
Rn: John Creasey I. Title
823'.914[F]

ISBN 0 - 340 - 41281 X

First published in Great Britain 1990

Published by Hodder and Stoughton,
a division of Hodder and Stoughton Ltd,
Mill Road, Dunton Green, Sevenoaks, Kent TN13 2YA
Editorial Office: 47 Bedford Square, London WC1B 3DP

Photoset by Chippendale Type, Otley, West Yorkshire

Printed in Great Britain by St Edmundsbury Press, Bury St Edmunds, Suffolk
and bound by Robert Hartnoll Ltd, Bodmin, Cornwall.

To Mary with all my love from Bill

Contents

1 Nightmare Conference

George Gideon had battled his way through many, many tough meetings during his twenty-five – now nearly twenty-six – years as Commander of the Criminal Investigation Department at Scotland Yard. But the conference he attended one hot Monday afternoon in August, in the plush mahogany-panelled boardroom, which led off the Chief Commissioner's office, was the most difficult he had ever experienced. And the extraordinary thing about it was that he couldn't, for the life of him, see where the difficulty lay.

From the moment he strode into the room and eased his powerful frame into the chair the Chief Commissioner had indicated, it was obvious that there was something strange in the air. For one thing he had arrived bang on time for the meeting; yet the signs were that it had been going on for quite a while already. It was as though it had been deliberately started early, so that some matter could be discussed in secret before he arrived. Not surprisingly, if that were the case, now that he had appeared everybody seemed ill at ease. Nobody seemed able to look him in the eye – although three of the four other people present were men he had known and worked with for years.

One was closer even than that; Alec Hobbs, the Assistant Commissioner (Crime), was one of the family having married Gideon's daughter Penny some years before. Beneath a polished public-school exterior, Alec could sometimes be awkward and edgy: being both Gideon's son-in-law and immediate superior didn't always make for an effortless relationship, but never had Gideon known him to sit staring down at a piece of paper in front of him, unwilling or unable to glance up in his direction at all.

Chief Detective Superintendent Lemaitre, sitting next to Alec and directly opposite Gideon, was behaving even more oddly. Lem, an irrepressible cockney with an agile brain but a disastrous habit of jumping to conclusions, was not only Gideon's oldest colleague at the Yard, he was also his oldest friend. They had once been detective sergeants together, and despite Gideon's subsequent rise to one of the top positions in the Met, Lem had obstinately continued to treat him with the same frank, cheery informality and Gideon, for the sake of old times, had usually let him get away with it. But there was nothing frank, cheery or informal about Lemaitre now. He was sitting bolt upright, stiff as a ramrod, his thin sharp face almost comically expressionless, his beady eyes darting here, there and everywhere – except within a yard of Gideon's face.

The Chief Commissioner himself, Sir Reginald Scott-Marle, sat chin in hand, reading and re-reading the conference brief, which Gideon had written himself. His manner seemed cold and remote; he acknowledged Gideon's arrival with the faintest nod, and then indicated to the fifth man sitting at the table: a tall bald-headed individual of about fifty-five with one of the hardest, most humourless faces Gideon had ever seen in a policeman.

"This is Commander Naughton, George – Tom Naughton. Joined us from the Liverpool force last week: he's taking over as head of the Drugs Squad."

"Not a job I'd envy as things are these days," Gideon said. "Pleased to meet you Commander – and good luck."

He had heard a lot of things about Naughton, most of them good. The man might look more like a hit-man than a cop but he had hit the drug-pushers of the Liverpool area spectacularly hard; wiped them clean out in many districts. If he could achieve anything like that in London –

"Thanks," said Naughton sharply. "I'll probably need it." His voice was as uncompromising as his appearance. A faint Newcastle accent made it only slightly more human. "Now do you mind if we get on with the meeting? I haven't a lot of time to waste on exchanging pleasantries."

"None of us have," replied Sir Richard, equally sharply, "so I'll ask Commander Gideon to explain to you all his reasons for calling this conference. It's to do with a crisis which according to C.I.D. reports, is developing in the Fletchwood area. Carry on, please, Commander."

There was a pause, during which in the ordinary way

everyone would have automatically looked at Gideon. But still, nobody did.

Alec Hobbs was fiddling with a sheet of paper from a memo pad, first screwing it into a ball with his left hand, then carefully unfolding it with his right. Lem was staring at the carpet one moment, the ceiling the next. Sir Reginald continued to study the typewritten brief. Naughton, arms folded now, seemed wholly absorbed by the covers of some files lying on the table.

Deciding that he had had enough of this, Gideon abruptly rose to his feet, his chair making quite a bang as he pushed it back against the wall behind him. *That* ought to earn him a few startled glances if nothing else, he thought. But even though with his massive frame he was now literally towering over them at the table, not a single eye turned his way.

More baffled than ever, Gideon began to describe what was happening in Fletchwood – a place where, he found himself saying, a "nightmare situation" was developing.

He went on talking about it coolly and calmly, fighting the feeling that – for some reason he couldn't begin to comprehend – exactly the same thing was happening in this very room.

* * *

Fletchwood, he began by reminding them, was a symptom of the extraordinary new London that was coming into existence: a London divided, as it had not been since mid-Victorian days, between the very rich and the very poor.

In this particular area, the rich and the poor lived in such close proximity that an explosion of some sort was, he believed, inevitable. Indeed, he feared that if they could not somehow defuse the situation the explosion would be of an extremely violent and dangerous sort. On Fletchwood Heights, a hill right in the centre of the place, there had recently been built a "millionaire's row" inhabited by young, aggressive tycoons, city whizz-kids and the like. Whereas less than four hundred yards away, at the foot of the hill in Fletchwood Vale, was a trouble-spot inner-city district with the biggest drugs problem in the Met area.

At last, someone reacted. Naughton took his eyes off the files and leant forward, "I can confirm that, Gideon," he said. "Fletchwood Vale is one of the main areas I've been brought down here to sort out. I'd be grateful for any information you have on it."

"Yes, I thought it might be," said Gideon. "That's why I'm glad you're here at this meeting. But drugs is only one of the factors which makes the situation in Fletchwood so dangerous. Another is the way the 'millionaire's row' inhabitants *use* the poor people in the Vale below. They recruit them for jobs unheard of since the days of 'Upstairs, Downstairs'. They've got them working as valets, maids, chauffeurs the lot. They think they're being benevolent but . . . "

This was the cue for Scott-Marle to come to life, "But surely they are being benevolent?" he asked. "They pay them very well, from all accounts. I've even heard of a maid getting £15,000 a year there. What's so wrong with that?"

"I'll tell you what's wrong," Gideon said. "Because they pay so much they think they own them body and soul. They lord it over them and work them like skivvies. Their flashy cars, loud extravagant parties, their arrogant careless manners; everything about them boils up more resentment. And that's not a wise thing to do, when you've got a deprived area like Fletchwood Vale completely surrounding you, only four hundred yards away in any direction downhill."

Lemaitre suddenly joined in the discussion. He was at the meeting as Chief Detective Superintendent in charge of the North London area, in the heart of which Fletchwood lay. It was largely due to reports from his men that Gideon was holding this "crisis conference".

It obviously infuriated him that no one seemed to be admitting that there *was* a crisis. At any ordinary meeting he would probably have launched in with a string of cockney expletives in support of Gideon. Lem was not beyond giving even the Chief Commissioner an earful if he thought he deserved it; one of the reasons why his own promotion had been so slow. But today he was as formal as a sergeant-major around a roomful of field marshals and brigadiers; all of which was very unlike Lem indeed . . .

"I have been over this many times," he began slowly,

"and I agree with the Commander that if there was trouble – a major riot for example, in which the inhabitants of the Vale turned on the people in the Heights – then the latter wouldn't stand much of a chance. At the drop of a hat, they could be trapped in a siege – and – and – " nothing could stop Lem being colourful, " – wiped out before you could say Bloody Sydney Street," he finished in a rush.

Scott-Marle still looked doubtful. Cold and remote as ever, he raised a laconic eyebrow. "But why should there be trouble on such a scale?" he asked. "I take Gideon's point that these rich people may be arousing some degree of jealousy and resentment by behaving like new-fangled Lords of the Manor, but after all, they are paying many Fletchwood Vale people a lot of money, even if they do treat them like peasants. If it's really such a poor district, with high unemployment and all the rest of it, are its inhabitants likely to be so stupid as to bite the hands that feed them?"

"Yes," said Gideon flatly and then found his voice rising to a roar, as he added, "because if the reports Lemaitre's been getting are right, these 'kids' aren't just feeding them – they're half strangling them too."

That did it at last. All eyes in the room were riveted on his face as he launched into the main reason for calling the meeting: the fact that the heart of the Fletchwood drugs problem was uphill not down; the villain behind the drugs distribution was one of the tycoons living in the Heights, literally growing rich on the misery, degradation and tragedy a few hundred yards below his front door.

No longer roaring, but still very grim, Gideon went on: "If only some of the rumours are true, they mean that there's a lot more money going out of the Vale and up into the Heights than the other way round. And it's dirty money – blood money, in some cases – from helpless addicts who have no way of getting it except through crime. Every kind of crime, from mugging to murder, is increasing dramatically in the whole Fletchwood area. Lemaitre has the statistics if you want them. He has some choice stories too. One eighteen-year-old was trapped into the habit when he got a job at the Heights, as a £10,000-a-year chauffeur. The next thing his parents knew, he was stealing to pay for the cocaine to feed his habit. He spent all his earnings on it – and was dead inside a fortnight."

Naughton was concentrating intensely now. "It could be that this tycoon – whoever he is – is the link I've been looking for," he said slowly. "The London contact of the Colombian 'crack' syndicate. They're going to infect all Britain with the bloody stuff unless I can get on to him – quick."

"It certainly could be," said Gideon. "I've also heard a rumour that he's in touch with – and maybe acting under orders from – Jeremy Kemp, the drug-master now in prison awaiting trial."

He found it hard to keep the satisfaction out of his voice as he added these final words. Kemp was one of a quartet of major villains, who called themselves The Big Four. They were caught a year before in an operation which would go down in police history as Gideon's Raid.

Naughton narrowed his eyes. "That's a lead worth following up. If Kemp is in prison, surely he can be kept under close surveillance, with arrangements made to shadow anyone who visits him?"

Gideon glared. No newcomer from the provinces, however brilliant, was going to start teaching him his job.

"We've being doing that for days, but The Big Four are hellishly clever criminals. Kemp wouldn't risk any sort of face-to-face meeting with his man on Fletchwood Heights. I expect he passes messages through a go-between. And don't forget, he's not a full-scale prisoner, only on remand. That means he is allowed unlimited visitors; unlimited opportunities to get word through to anyone he pleases."

The satisfaction had gone from Gideon's voice. Talk of Jeremy Kemp reminded him how hopeful he had been at the time of the raid on The Big Four. Rounding them up would mean, he had believed, wiping out at a stroke eighty per cent of London's organised crime. Well, he *had* rounded them up – with great difficulty and at terrible cost: in the course of the raid, a bomb blast had buried him alive, and he was lucky to have survived.* Others had been injured too. But as a result of all that effort and pain had

---

* *Gideon's Raid*

organised crime in London really been slashed? He doubted it. Certainly the statistics had showed a significant drop in the number of big operations for a while – but already the figures were creeping up again; already the evidence was pouring in that new gangs were forming, major new villains arriving to take over. This mysterious figure in Fletchwood Heights was beginning to look as though he might start operating on The Big Four scale and with the active support of at least one of The Big Four itself. That alone was worrying enough. But add the electrically tense class-war, in the Fletchwood area, with the imminent risk of a bloodbath, it was very clear that catching this master was one of the most urgent tasks he had ever faced.

Gideon turned to the files which had been so fascinating to Naughton, and picked them up.

There were only three of them: a fact which he found heartening, as he explained to the whole room.

"The one good thing about a very grim situation is that it shouldn't be too hard to identify this villain," he said. "All these reports suggest that he is one of the wealthiest people in the Heights – and also a recent arrival there. Because of that, we have been able to narrow it down to three names. There's no certainty, of course – nor can there be as we're relying on rumours, without a scrap of evidence – but there's at least a strong possibility that our man is one of these."

He banged one of the files down on the table with a loud dramatic *thwack*, opened it and pulled out a photograph which he held up so that everyone could see it. There were no gasps of astonishment – not much can surprise hardened policemen, thought Gideon – but it was a face that was known all over Britain from its frequent appearances on news bulletins and TV chat shows. There could be no mistaking those bushy eyebrows, the crinkled, weather-beaten skin, and that tough uncompromising glint in the eyes.

"As I hardly need to tell you," said Gideon, "you're looking at Mr Don Mitchell, newspaper magnate, arch-enemy of the print unions and all the rest of it. Reputed to be worth millions, but he may have lost a few of them lately because of the plummeting circulation of his paper *The*

Sunday View. He's also known to have been involved in shady deals with several dubious people – amongst whom I would certainly include his next-door-neighbour and former business associate – "

Gideon thwacked down the second file, opened it, and held up another photograph. This one was of a man in his middle thirties, fair-haired and strikingly good-looking apart from a smile which was so thin-lipped that it came across as a superior smirk.

" – Mr Fergus Atkinson," Gideon continued, "Conservative MP for West Witchell, Chairman of half a dozen big City companies. He's also incidentally, making a bid to take over *The Sunday View*, which his neighbour, Don Mitchell, is fighting with all he has.

"Not much love lost between *these* neighbours, if you ask me! Atkinson, like Mitchell, has a long record of investment in borderline deals – although nothing criminal has ever been proved against either of them."

Gideon closed the second file, and reached for the third one, he had temporarily tucked under his arm.

"The third suspect lives next door to the other two," he said. "That isn't such a coincidence as it sounds. We've looked for rich, recently-arrived residents, and these three houses are brand new ones that have been on the market only this year. Neo-Georgian villas, they're called. They cost a good half million each and together they make up numbers 1, 2 and 3, Malibu Rise, if you can believe it. Atkinson is at number 3, Mitchell at number 2 and at number 1 is the man who, quite frankly, my money is on." Gideon turned to the last file which was on top of the others, and opened it. This time there was no photograph to be seen. He sifted quickly through the file's contents in search of it, talking all the while.

"His name is Matthew Goddard, which may or may not be an alias. He moved into Malibu Rise only a month or so ago – but that's just about when the rumours started. And according to Lemaitre's informants, they are now hardening around him. Unlike Atkinson and Mitchell, he's very far from being a public figure. In fact we've had trouble digging up even the simplest facts about him. He's fairly young, has an attractive wife named Julie and three small children, two girls and a boy, all under five. He's believed to have come from New Zealand – and to have made his pile through property deals of one sort or – another – "

Gideon broke off, suddenly furious. His search for a photograph had proved fruitless; there simply wasn't one in the file. And yet Lem had positively guaranteed that he'd have one in time for the meeting today.

"For Christ's sake," he growled, giving Lemaitre a glare that was almost as terrifying as the famous Gideon roar. "You're not going to tell me you *still* haven't succeeded in coming up with a picture of this man. They've been useless at digging up anything else about him – but surely a simple photograph shouldn't be beyond them, even if it's only a snap taken through a hole in the bloody fence!"

He expected Lem to reply with a spirited defence of his department, probably turning the air blue in the process. But Lemaitre said nothing, did nothing. He was back to being as stiff and as silent as a dummy.

Gideon looked around at the others. Scott-Marle, Naughton, Hobbs, were all once again studiously avoiding his eye. The uneasiness in the air, back now at a hundred times its old force, was suddenly almost physically stifling. Just as though the room was being filled with some ether-like gas. Gideon momentarily found his senses swimming: the table top seemed to lurch towards him, the windows to veer away, the carpet to heave like a stormy sea.

He took a deep breath, a very deep breath. Everything righted itself abruptly, except for his voice, which seemed to be coming from a great distance as he asked quietly: "Look, gentlemen. Let's stop playing games shall we? Would one of you please have the courtesy to tell me what the *hell* is going on?"

That broke the spell at last. Alec Hobbs, looking up from those papers for the very first time since the meeting had begun, said softly, almost shame facedly: "Lemaitre did get you a photograph of Matthew Goddard, George. But I removed it from the file to show it to Sir Reginald just before you came in. Here it is, if you want to see it."

He produced the photograph from amongst the pile of papers in front of him, and slid it across the table.

"Why on *earth* shouldn't I want to?" Gideon roared, as he picked it up. His question was all too speedily answered. He was staring at what was to him one of the best-known faces in the world. Even though it was twenty years since he had last seen it, there was no possibility of his being mistaken.

Matthew "Goddard" was unquestionably Matthew Gideon, his own son.

2 Day of Days

Gideon had seven children – four sons and three daughters – all now grown up and living away from home. Matthew, he had always thought, lived furthest away. Back in the 1960s he had got a girl into trouble* and followed that by becoming involved in a succession of scrapes which had ended with him being sent down from Cambridge. That had put paid to his dreams of following in his father's footsteps and entering the police force. Though there was no reason why it should have done, as Gideon had repeatedly pointed out to him at the time. "If you really want to follow in my footsteps, what's wrong with starting out as I did – plodding along as a humble bobby on the beat?"

But plodding anywhere wasn't really Matthew's style. Although in appearance he had grown up to be the image of his father, lacking only Gideon's width of shoulder and breadth of chest, their characters had always been poles apart. Matthew had nothing of Gideon's rock-like steadiness in his nature. He was not afraid of hard work – getting that scholarship to Cambridge had been quite an achievement – but he became impatient if it didn't bring quick rewards. At the University, he had made a lot of flashy friends, and his head was full of "get-rich-quick" schemes to make himself as wealthy as they were with all possible speed.

"Look, Dad. All right, I know I've let you down – but if you and Mum could see your way to lending me £2,000 – "

That had been a lot of money in the 1960s, the equivalent of at least £20,000 now. At first, Gideon had flatly refused, but Kate had intervened on Matthew's side, and finally his parents had dug deep into their meagre savings and found the sum. What Matthew had done with the

---

* *Gideon's Fire*

money, Gideon couldn't remember – invested it in some hair-brained property development scheme, he believed. At all events, within months it had gone, and Matthew was back pleading for more. That had led to a blazing row with Gideon and Matthew roaring at each other for half the night. (Matthew could almost – but not quite – equal his father's roar.)

It had ended with Matthew storming out of the house, slamming the door behind him. Gideon remembered yelling "Goodbye and good riddance" after him, but he hadn't meant it, of course. The last thing he had intended was that the remark would be taken seriously; for twenty years, he and Kate would not see Matthew again.

A few days later they received a letter from him saying that he had scraped up the money to emigrate to New Zealand. ("Good news for you, Dad, you're seeing the back of me at last.") Gideon and Kate promptly telephoned to rooms where he was living, only to be told that he had already moved away, leaving no address.

They had heard from him once he had arrived in New Zealand, and for years he had kept more or less in touch even – when he remembered – exchanging presents at Christmas and birthdays. Each Christmas Gideon and Kate had telephoned him. He had always been vague about what he was doing, but usually sounded cheerful and claimed everything was "going great over here – great . . ."

Gradually, though, the letters from him became fewer and fewer, the presents rarer and rarer, he kept moving from town to town and became more and more careless about sending details of his whereabouts. Nearly distraught, Kate wrote letter after letter to Matthew's previous residences, but they all came back undelivered, stamped "address unknown". Finally, there came a time when she and Gideon were forced to face the fact they'd lost touch with him altogether.

"Do you suppose he's not just being forgetful – but has done this to us deliberately?" she asked.

Gideon was silent a long time before saying gruffly: "I don't know love. But I've got to admit it looks that way to me."

Kate's grey-blue eyes, usually so serene, were filling with tears. "He's never forgiven you for those things you said to him that night, has he? Not in all these years. And – oh, George. Do you think it was all over a wretched £2,000!" She was suddenly near to breaking down, and rushed out of the room. Gideon did not follow her. Much as he wanted to, he knew there was no way he could comfort her, because the awful truth was, somewhere inside her, Kate had not forgiven him for that long-ago night either. It was as though he had said "Goodbye and good riddance" not only to Matthew, but to a part of her, too.

* * *

All these painful memories came crowding into Gideon's mind the second he saw that photograph – to be almost instantly crowded out again by feelings that were not so much painful as paralysing.

Mentally, it was the equivalent of being blasted by a bomb again, and buried alive beneath a mountain of rubble.

Now as then, he found himself for a moment totally powerless to move or speak.

Matthew – a criminal? More than that, one of the most dangerous criminals in London? Drugs dealer – accomplice of Jeremy Kemp – taking over the mantle of The Big Four?

There had to be a mistake somewhere. God, there *had* to be –

Somehow, after what seemed to be a Herculean struggle, he pulled himself together, but still found it impossible to speak. Not to utter words, but to think of anything worth saying.

Then it dawned on him that there were none he *needed* to say.

He didn't have to tell anyone round the table whose face was in the photograph. Lemaitre had been a frequent visitor to his house in the days when Matthew was there. He had watched him grow up – given him endless tips on what it was like to be in the Force. Alec had never met Matthew in the flesh, but he and Penny had albums full of pictures of him around the house – Matthew had once been Penny's favourite brother. Alec had said he'd borrowed the photograph to show Scott-Marle so obviously Sir Reginald had been told about the situation. And from Naughton's stony expression, the full facts had been explained to him too.

That was the reason this had been a nightmare conference. They had all been waiting to see his face when –

Sir Reginald's voice broke in on his thoughts, which were rapidly becoming murderous.

"There's something I think I ought to explain, George. That photograph was taken yesterday evening by an undercover man, and developed overnight here in this building. Lemaitre was handed it in an envelope just before he came into this meeting, and only opened it, in fact, when he was sitting at this table, less than a minute before you came in. Hobbs and I noticed his violent start, and compelled him to show it round. I was just going to come and see you and call off the meeting, when you appeared, and the simplest alternative seemed to be to let it go forward, particularly since Naughton had badly needed a full briefing on Fletchwood."

Sir Reginald was actually reddening, and his voice, far from being remote, sounded deeply concerned.

"As a result of that decision, I'm afraid I have put you – and indeed everyone round the table – through an acutely embarrassing ordeal."

He went on, "But if it's any consolation, George, we are all of us as astonished at this revelation as you are, and are hoping as desperately as you must be that this suspect can soon be eliminated from the inquiry."

Not that Scott-Marle could ever stop being Scott-Marle for long. His voice formal and correct, he finished, "Until he is, though, you must appreciate that it would be improper for you, or for that matter, Alec here as he's the man's brother-in-law – to have any further involvement in this case."

Lemaitre suddenly produced a large handkerchief and wiped his forehead. His lean, sallow features looked old and tired.

"I think you'd better count me out of this operation too, sir. Forty years as friend of the Gideons must make me as close as family, almost."

"Point taken, Lemaitre," Scott-Marle barked, and turned to Naughton.

"It looks as if I should make the case a drug-squad baby from now on. Do you think your people can handle it, Commander?"

Naughton stood up and said with confidence, "Leave it to us, Sir. We'll nail the bastard!" Belatedly, he remembered to add, "Whoever he turns out to be." But that was after he had snatched the photograph of Matthew from Gideon's hand and swept up the open "Matthew Goddard" file from the table, leaving behind the files on Don Mitchell and Fergus Atkinson.

How could he blame him? Gideon asked himself. Hadn't he said, less than five minutes before, that *his* money was on Matthew Goddard, and that the evidence was hardening around him? Just because that word "Goddard" had been changed to "Gideon" –

Walking very fast to fight the gnawing fear inside him, Gideon made his way out of the conference room and down the corridor to the lift. He was thankful that Lem and Alec seemed to have been detained by Scott-Marle. The last thing he wanted to do was to talk to them now. The last thing he wanted to do was talk to *anyone*.

He reached his office – a glass-lined cubicle two floors below – and sank down shakily behind his desk. Almost immediately one of the three telephones on the desk-top rang. It was the green telephone: that meant it was an outside call, coming in direct on his personal line. (A new service, made possible by the computerised switchboard now installed at the Yard.)

Gideon had to fight hard to make himself lift the receiver. But finally, just after it had rung for the third time, he succeeded and found himself being swept along on a torrent of words from Kate, who sounded wildly excited, more excited in fact than he'd ever known her in all their forty years of married life.

"George, you'll never guess who's just rung me. It was Matthew! Yes, *Matthew*. He's – you'll never believe it – he's here in London! With a wife called Julie and three children, Richard and Sandra and – and Debbie, I think he said. Imagine it! A daughter-in-law and three grandchildren we never even knew existed. George!" The silence on the other end of the line was beginning to worry her. "George! Are you there? You did catch what I said, didn't you? Matthew – he's here – here in London. Have you ever heard such *marvellous* news?"

* * *

How he did it he never knew, but somehow Gideon managed to convey the right degree of amazement and delight to satisfy Kate. She wasn't really listening to him, in any case. She had so much more exciting information to convey.

"And there's something else you'll never guess. Matthew's living in the most fashionable address you can imagine – Fletchwood Heights, where all the stars are. You must have heard of it."

"Yes, love," said Gideon, and tried hard not to say it grimly. "I certainly have."

Kate had apparently forgotten his many dark mutterings about the place – or perhaps he hadn't mentioned it as often as he'd thought. He didn't always take his work worries home.

"Matthew's been there for weeks," she rushed on, "but he wanted to get the house straight before he rang. Now he's asking us round to dinner – to meet him and Julie and all our brand new family – I can't wait to see them, can you? I wonder if he's changed much – and if he still looks like a half-starved version of you. By the way, he tells me that he's changed his name – he's Matthew Goddard now. He says he did it for the same reason that sons of film stars change their names; he wanted to make good on his own. You do understand, don't you?" Kate was pleading as passionately as she had done all those years ago.

"After all, he has made good – to put it mildly! That house in Fletchwood Heights, he told me, cost half a million pounds – and he didn't even have to take out a mortgage!" Suddenly she was laughing. "Makes it seem funny, doesn't it, all that fuss we once made about £2,000 . . . "

Gideon could hardly believe his ears. On any previous occasion, Kate would have talked accusingly about "all the fuss *you* made". It looked as though with the reappearance of Matthew on the scene, that years-old – it seemed centuries-old – breach between them had been healed at last.

Not that there was much hope that anything could be healed for long, he thought grimly. If Kate had the slightest inkling of the suspicions he was harbouring now – But did he *have* to harbour them?

Suddenly what felt like a blinding shaft of light shone through the menacing gloom inside his head.

Matthew had always had a great respect for his, Gideon's, prowess; at one time, incredible as it seemed now it had come close to hero-worship.

If he was really indulging in large-scale criminal activities, he would surely never in a thousand years, ask him and Kate round to dinner. To him, it would be the equivalent of putting his head not merely in the lion's mouth, but halfway down its neck!

There was another possibility, though, which the stern police side of Gideon's mind would not allow him to ignore. Supposing Matthew had suddenly got wind that the C.I.D. was investigating him? He must have realised that they'd be on to his identity in a moment. In which case, his only course of action would be to play it cool and bluff it out – even if it did mean meeting his dangerous father . . .

Swinging between the two theories with the dizzy speed of a man on a trapeze, Gideon's brain was scarcely able to cope. He concentrated on Kate's farewell remarks.

"I must go now. I can't wait to ring Penny and tell her the news. She'll be over the moon – and I'll bet Alec will be too!"

"Very probably," he succeeded in muttering, adding suddenly; "Oh, and – Kate."

"Yes, love?"

"After you've rung Penny, I'd take it easy for a bit if I were you. Sit back. Have a cup of tea. See if there's a film worth watching on the box. We don't want your heart playing tricks again."

Kate had had mild trouble with her heart for years now, and he hated to think what strain it might be under before this business was through.

Kate, though, burst out laughing again – a bubbly, carefree laugh that took him right back to when they were first going out together.

"Honestly, George, do you really think I'm going to sit and drink tea and watch films on this day of days?" she demanded – and hung up before he could reply.

Gideon was relieved about that. For what seemed the hundredth time since that moment when he'd seen the photograph, he simply hadn't known what to say.

3 War of Nerves

Never in his life had Gideon more desperately needed time to be alone and to think – but that was a luxury which his position at the Yard rarely afforded him, and that afternoon was no exception.

Within a second of replacing the receiver on the green telephone, the black one rang. This was connected directly to an adjoining office, presided over by his Deputy Commander, Paul Barnaby. It probably meant that there was someone out there waiting to see him, although there were no appointments on his pad. He had kept the afternoon clear in case the conference had dragged on.

"Yes, Barnaby?" he asked, as politely as he could, when his assistant came on the line. He was always struggling to be patient with Barnaby, a dedicated but pernickety man who looked as though he would have been happier programming computers than coping with the continual crises of a C.I.D. day.

"Chief Detective Superintendent Riddell is here and very anxious to see you, sir," Barnaby told him, in his usual precise tone. He was almost the only man at the Yard who gave people their full titles, reminding Gideon of a butler formally announcing a dinner guest. Then he dropped his voice, presumably so that Riddell couldn't hear.

"My feeling is that you should see him. He seems very shaken up to me."

"Shaken up? What about?" snapped Gideon – and then could have bitten off his tongue for saying it.

Of course he knew what had happened to Tom Riddell. He had been worrying about it all morning. It was just that that conference had driven everything else so completely out of his head –

Barnaby's precise voice went on relentlessly.

"The file on the case is on your desk, sir, third from the top of the pile, I think you'll find – "

"Never mind about that," Gideon growled. "Just stop yapping, will you, and send Tom in."

There was a pierced and startled silence on the line as Gideon hung up. From that moment, as though to compensate for having forgotten it so completely, he concentrated his attention fiercely on the other nightmare that was facing him that day: the terrible mistake he had made in putting Tom Riddell on to the case of a curious criminal known as the Oxfam Robin Hood.

* * *

The case, in a way, was another reflection of this age of the very rich and very poor. The Oxfam Robin Hood (as a delighted press had christened him) was a skilful thief who burgled wealthy houses all over London, including some at Fletchwood Heights. The thing about him was that he claimed that he was giving all the proceeds to famine relief and left the words "Feed the World", sprayed in red paint on the wall at the scene of every crime. He had been rewarded with massive publicity, and in some circles had become a hero of almost Bob Geldof status. Gideon, though, did not move in such circles, and debated whether such a thing as an altruistic criminal existed outside the pages of fiction. He was convinced that the Oxfam Robin Hood was in reality a twisted drop-out, and had probably not sent so much as one penny to famine relief.

It had seemed at first just the sort of case to give to Tom Riddell. Tom, whom he had known longer than anyone else at the Yard except Lemaitre, was one of the shrewdest and most dependable men in the whole of the C.I.D. Yet long years at the rough end of police work had taken their toll, and for some years he had been suffering from nerve trouble, a far more common complaint among coppers than the public ever dreamed. He was still a brilliant policeman: the success of Gideon's famous raid on The Big Four had owed a lot to him, to give one recent example. As a result of his part in that, he had recently looked like regaining some of his old confidence, a little of that powerful presence he had once possessed. But it could not be denied that he could crack up completely under stress, and was no longer the man to put in charge of a disturbing inquiry – into, for example, a multiple sex-killer. Gideon had thought that tracking a burglar who posed as a romantic adventurer ought to be much more in Tom's line – and if he brought off an arrest, the resultant basking in the public limelight might restore his confidence for good.

On his arrival at the Yard that morning, though, Gideon had received news suggesting that his theory could be very, very wrong. At around two o'clock in the morning it appeared, Riddell had been dragged out of bed by a mysterious phone call, and had gone rushing out of the house on some hoax assignment; the details weren't clear, but obviously the call had been a decoy trick and when he returned to his home, a semi-detached in Wimbledon, around dawn, he had found the place ransacked. His shy, bird-like wife, Vi, was bound and gagged and in such a state of shock that she could not speak, and had to be taken to hospital. "Feed the World" had been sprayed not only with paint this time, but written in bullet holes as well, all along one living-room wall.

Gideon remembered now – God, how could he have forgotten even momentarily? – arranging for a large bunch of flowers to be sent to Vi's ward. He had also left a message for Riddell, telling him to take the day off but to call into the Yard and give him a personal account of all that had happened as soon as he could manage it.

Not that Tom had had much of a day off. He would have had to have spent his time gravitating between his distraught wife in hospital, and a home cluttered up by a scene-of-the-crime "squad" taking photographs and finger-prints – to say nothing of the press and TV men, who would be there in force outside. Hardly the ideal way of overcoming the horror of the previous night.

How were his nerves standing up to it? That was the key question where Gideon was concerned. His invitation to Tom to call in for a chat had not been purely so that he could offer comfort and support. It also had a sterner purpose; to settle once and for all whether he should allow Tom to stay on the case.

The moment Riddell walked in, the issue looked as

though it was settled, without a word needing to be said. Tom was like a man in high fever, sweating and shaking all over. Certainly it was hot outside, the temperature tipping 85° Fahrenheit, and he had perhaps been hurrying through the heat; but that couldn't explain the wild look in his eyes, and the exhausted way he almost tottered towards the chair. He was a big man, in spite of his recently developed gauntness, and it creaked loudly as he slumped into it.

Gideon stood up.

"Something tells me, Tom," he murmured, "that you could do with a drink. And as it happens, that goes for me too."

He dived into the large drawer at the bottom of his desk on the right, and fetched out a bottle of whisky and two glasses. As he was pouring the whisky, he suddenly wondered whether it was the right drink for someone in Riddell's condition. Riddell, though, seemed to have no doubts about the matter. He emptied his glass in two gulps, and sat back, wiping his hand across his forehead, on which the globules of sweat seemed as large as peas.

"Sorry about this, George," he breathed. "Not at my best, am I? Trouble is, I've just come from the hospital. Vi's been under heavy sedation. She's only just woken up and started talking. And *I've* only just realised what that bastard put her through. He dragged her, bound and gagged, into the living-room and sat her in a chair while he fired those bullets at the wall. What's more . . . he positioned her chair so that it was between him and the wall. The bullets went so close that one of them grazed her temple, and two of them passed through her hair. 'It'll be a lot closer next time,' he kept saying, 'if you don't tell your old man to leave me alone.'"

Suddenly his eyes looked not only wild, but dangerous.

"And to think the papers call this brute 'the caring crook!'. By Christ, I'll give him 'caring' – "

He started shaking again, more violently than ever, probably this time more with anger than with anything else. Gideon watched him anxiously. It was obvious that in putting him in charge of the Oxfam Robin Hood case he had done the worst thing possible to Riddell – had pitched him, of all people, into a war of nerves.

"Steady, Tom, steady," he said. "Just keep telling yourself that there'll never be a next time. We'll have a twenty-four-hour watch on your home from now onwards, and you can organise it yourself. Vi's never going to have to go through anything like this again."

He stopped then. That was his cue, of course, for saying "and neither are you, because you're off the case from this moment". But the words stuck in his throat. Riddell, he strongly suspected, was kept from going to pieces by one thing, and one thing only – Gideon's rock-like unchanging confidence in him. Through that, he had not only survived as a copper; he had brought off some of the most brilliant feats of policing in his career. To withdraw that confidence now, at a time of crisis, would be like giving a man who was gasping for air a punch in the solar plexus. It could not only put him down for the count – but for good.

It was obviously essential to soften the blow in some way – but for the life of him, Gideon couldn't see how to do it. To give himself time to think, he sat back and sipped a little of the whisky. His mouth was hot and dry, and the drink felt about as cooling as lava pouring from a volcano. He gasped, choked slightly, and wiped his eyes.

Riddell had got to his feet by this time, and was restlessly pacing the room – hardly normal behaviour for a man being interviewed by his Commander, but quite obviously, his tension was now at such a pitch that it would not let him stay still.

"What a fool I was to fall for that hoax phone-call," he was muttering, as much to himself as to Gideon. "But it was a bloody clever one, just about the cleverest in my experience. The caller said he was the London Secretary of the Oxfam organisation. He sounded right for the part – authoritative voice, Oxford accent, the lot. The only thing was that the voice was a bit muffled, and I should have realised that probably meant the old handkerchief-hand-over-the-mouthpiece trick, to prevent too positive an identification."

"I doubt if I'd have realised that – straight out of bed, at two o'clock," said Gideon.

Riddell was still pacing.

"He told me that *he'd* been dragged out of bed himself,"

he went on, "by a call from the 'criminal popularly known as the Oxfam Robin Hood', as he put it. The man had wanted him to go at once to a secret rendezvous – where he would hand over a large sum in cash to the organisation.

"'My first impulse' the caller told me, 'was to refuse it outright – to tell him that Oxfam does not do business with criminals, no matter how much the starving may benefit. But then I thought this might be a good opportunity to get this man, who is a grave embarrassment to us, put behind bars once and for all. So I asked him where he wanted me to be – and I suggest that *you* go there in my stead, Superintendent. He may know your face from the papers, but it will be hard to recognise it in the dark – and after all, you'll be the last person he's expecting. But you will have to be alone. That is one of the chief stipulations that he made.'"

Gideon grunted in grudging admiration. "So off you went hardly able to believe your good luck," he said, "expecting to bag the Oxfam Robin Hood and collect all his takings in one fell swoop! Yes, you're right, Tom. Clever's the word for that hoax. It's one of the neatest in my experience too. Where exactly was the rendezvous?"

"Three twenty at the junction of Crown Court and Spicer Street," Riddell told him, "right in the middle of Fletchwood Vale." He was pacing – and talking – faster than ever. "Oddly enough, even that address fitted into what I knew of the Oxfam Robin Hood. His first break-ins had been up at Fletchwood Heights – and I had a hunch that he might turn out to be someone living in the Vale. I don't know if you know the area, but it's like Brixton and Tottenham rolled into one, only drabber and grimmer than either. Boarded-up houses – *miles* of closed shops and businesses – graffiti everywhere . . . and what makes it worse, is that wherever you are in that hell-hole, you can look up and see those rich people's homes in the Heights. Even in the middle of the night you get the feeling of millions flaunting themselves above you. There's a luxury hotel up there, floodlit, like some stately home, white lights illuminating the house and coloured lights lighting the grounds. All the time that I was in my car waiting for that bastard to show up, I kept looking up at that hotel and those lights, and thinking that if I lived here, perhaps *I'd* be tempted to be an – Oxfam Robin Hood . . . "

"I can see what you mean," said Gideon gruffly, and found himself gulping down the rest of his whisky. Gideon had always been proud of his ability to force his mind to function in watertight compartments – to concentrate on one thing to the fierce exclusion of anything else. But – at the mention of Fletchwood, it felt as though all over his brain dams were bursting, floodgates were opening; suddenly he was fighting to stop Riddell, the Oxfam Robin Hood and all other considerations being just flotsam on a dark sea of fear about Matthew. The flood became a torrent when the green telephone rang again. It was Kate.

"George, can you come home early? We've both got to put on our finest finery. Matthew's rung about that dinner – and wants us to come over this evening!" She sounded more excited than ever – and on top of that, proud and exultant, "so we'll be heading for Fletchwood Heights – *tonight*!"

4 Other Fathers

However he may have felt, Gideon was far from alone in his anguish at that moment. PC Bert Benton, a stout balding copper in his mid-fifties, one of Gideon's own men, was going through just the same sickening fear for his son.

Benton had lived and worked in Fletchwood Vale for so long that old-timers in the Force still sometimes called the area "Benton's Patch". He didn't think of it in these terms himself any more. When he had patrolled a beat there in the late 1950s and early 1960s, Fletchwood Vale had been a homely, prosperous, working-class suburb. Up in the Heights – where all those toffs, or pseudo-toffs lived now – there had been a de luxe factory, a "Garden Factory", the management called it, turning out buses and coaches for half the world. Just about everybody in the Vale had worked there. Nobody was rich, but most were doing very nicely, thank you, with generous overtime payments. The whole atmosphere of the place, in those days, had been cosy, friendly and cheerful. The crime rate had been one of the lowest in London.

He couldn't remember quite when the rot had started to set in, but gradually, the factory had laid off its workers and people had moved away or given up hope. Street after street became deserted, run-down and vandalised. Around 1970, the factory had closed down completely and from then onwards, *everything* about Fletchwood Vale had become derelict.

It was a different story up in the Heights, of course. The "Garden Factory" site, with its trees and fields and breathtaking view over London, had been the hottest property in years. Luxurious houses were put up; rich people moved in and, down below in the Vale, the atmosphere turned sour. In fact it was so charged with bitterness and resentment that patrolling the streets (usually these days in a police panda car) felt to PC Benton like travelling through a planet inhabited by alien beings.

And what made everything worse – a hundred times worse – was the fact that the most alien of all was his own son, Rod. Twenty-two years old now, he had never done a day's work in his life, and had used the good beginning God had given him to become an unemployed, unemployable rabble-rouser known to the whole community as "Red". Over and over again, PC Benton and his wife Grace had found themselves asking that old, old parental question – where did we go wrong? Not that Grace was really the type to face up to anything serious. A fat, jolly, red-faced woman, she believed in looking on the bright side, whatever the circumstances, and had a genius for finding one to look on.

"Stop worrying about Red," she kept telling him. "I can't help him having a heavy mother, but you don't have to come the heavy father too! He's a bright boy. You've only got to listen to the way he talks to know that. All his friends look up to him – he's really their leader. Shouldn't be surprised if he ends up in politics – and goes to the very top . . . "

PC Benton hadn't tried to argue. He knew from long experience that when Grace stopped looking on the bright side, she could very easily start slipping into depression and end up shaking and sobbing hysterically. That was why he had never mentioned to her his darkest suspicions about their son – that he was not only a layabout, not only a trouble-maker, but actually a criminal, the notorious Oxfam Robin Hood.

He had never mentioned it to Rod either, fearful that the unbelievable would happen and he would admit it to his face. It was only now, now that he had been given an unexpected afternoon off by the sergeant at the police station, and had come home to find Grace out shopping and Rod lounging on a divan in the living-room, unshaven, smelling strongly of drink, and wearing only a dirty old dressing-gown, that he suddenly exploded – and found himself letting the accusations slip out. Rod – or Red, as he liked to call himself – was so startled he nearly rolled off the divan. He tried to laugh his way out of it at first.

Making a joke of everything was something he got from his mother.

"Well, then, Dad. Thanks a million. If you really think I've got the brains and guts – and heart – to be the man they call the Bob Geldof of the Underworld, that's the highest compliment you've ever paid me in my life."

His tone was truculent and sneering – just like those of half the yobs on the streets of Fletchwood Vale. Black, white or yellow-skinned, it didn't matter. They'd all learnt to talk to the police in that voice. From them, PC Benton could take it – just about. But from his own son –

Benton suddenly noticed something: a newspaper which Red had just been reading, hurriedly pushed away under the divan. Moving very quickly for a plump, middle-aged man particularly on a hot summer afternoon, he shot across the room and pulled it out. It was the *Sun*, and a gory headline about the Oxfam Robin Hood, or "ORH" as headline writers now called him, was splayed across the front page.

ORH RAIDS TOP YARD MAN'S HOME

Benton didn't need to read the story. They had been discussing it at the station all that morning, and he knew every detail of it.

"Heart?" he shouted glaring at his son who had sat up defensively. "Is this what you think this ORH character has got? Binding and gagging a policeman's wife, shooting up her home, leaving her so shaken up she can't speak and has to be rushed to hospital? How would you feel if *I* came home and found your Mum – "

Benton broke off abruptly. He had screwed the paper into a ball, and had been on the point of throwing it into his son's face, in a frenzied bid to wipe that sneering look off it, once and for all.

But he suddenly realised there was no need. Something very strange had happened to Red Benton, the tough rabble-raiser of Fletchwood Vale. He was taking after his mother in a way that Benton had not seen for many, many years – since he was five or six years old. He was shaking all over and quite close to breaking down and sobbing.

Gradually he managed to get out his story. Yes, he was the Oxfam Robin Hood – or, at least, he had been.

"And don't think I'm ashamed of what I did – robbing the bloody greedy rich to help the poor bastards everywhere who are starving. I didn't keep a penny for myself – not a penny . . . you've got to believe that, Dad. You've *got* to."

"I do believe it," PC Benton said, suddenly almost as shaky as his son. He had hoped against hope that the suspicions of his had been wrong; he had never really worked out what in God's name he would do if it proved to be true. Instinctively, he found himself moving away from the divan as if it contained an unexploded bomb.

Rod was still talking – but he had turned on to his front now, as though he literally couldn't face his father, and his voice was so low and muffled that it was all but inaudible.

"And there's another thing you've got to believe, Dad. I had nothing to do with the Riddell job, nothing at all. Somebody else is getting in on the act. Somebody who's sick, frightening . . . "

PC Benton heard what his son said – just. But he didn't, couldn't take it in. There was far too much whistling round in his head. He thought he had heard a car draw up outside. That could be Grace, coming home from shopping. What could he say to her? Come to that, what is he to tell his superiors? Could he split on his son? Could he stay in the force if he didn't? Could he – ?

Rod had also heard his mother's car. Quick as an opening flick-knife, he was off the divan and out of the room, before Benton could lift a finger to stop him.

In a matter of seconds – a minute at the most – he'd be dressed and out of the house too. It was, Benton told himself, his police duty to stop him. Christ, come to that, it was his police duty to get those handcuffs out of his coat in the hallway and snap them on him!

What, in front of Grace, whose footsteps he could hear coming up to the front door? No copper could do a thing like that, not even the strictest in the force. Not even a *Gideon*, PC Benton told himself as he went to open the front door for Grace, trying hard not to hear the back door opening and closing behind his departing son.

* * *

Less than a quarter of a mile from the Benton's little terraced house another distraught Fletchwood Vale father was sitting tensely in a corner of a doctor's consulting room.

He was Horace Nelson, landlord and proprietor of The Lazy Fox, a pub in the centre of the Vale. Like PC Benton, Horace really belonged to the Fletchwood Vale of the Garden Factory days, and like him, he had been first bewildered and then bitter since it had changed. It wasn't surprising that the two men had become close friends: each was the only fellow survivor from the good old days that the other knew. Benton had even confided in Horace his dark suspicions about his son, something he had done to no one else in the world. Horace had responded with his own worries about his eighteen-year-old daughter, Suzy, a pretty but slightly mentally subnormal girl who had taken a job as a maid to Fergus Atkinson, the rich MP in the Heights.

"What's there to worry about in that?" Benton had said. "I'd be cheering my head off if Rod had got a position up there."

"You'd be proud if he was a chauffeur or a valet?" said Horace disbelievingly.

"Yes. Why not? Surely any job is better than the dole – and from what I've heard about the rates of pay up in the Heights – "

Horace Nelson had just grunted in reply and turned away to serve another customer. He couldn't explain even to his oldest friend just how uneasy he felt about Suzy.

Horace, a tough bulldog-like man in his early sixties, was a cockney of the old, super-patriotic type, as his very name implied. He had kept a picture of Churchill up in the bar of The Lazy Fox for twenty years after the war, and at the time of the Falklands trouble, had hung a Union Jack across all the doors. He had been known to order anyone who made derogatory remarks about the nation off the premises. But that didn't mean he had no memory stretching back beyond the good old days to the darker Britain of before the war. He had been a boy then, but his mother told him hair-raising stories about what went on below stairs when she was a scullery maid at one of the Great Houses back in the 1920s.

"Thank God those times have gone," she told him, "and neither you or your children will know what it means to be 'in service' . . . "

Frequently during the past ten years, Horace Nelson had found himself asking what the country was coming to. He didn't often ask that question now. He reckoned it was now plain enough where Britain was going – straight backwards, to the days his mother had told him about, when toffs were toffs, and good honest working-class folk had to kowtow to them or else. If that was the country he and his mates had fought for, they could keep it!

This feeling had changed Horace Nelson and made his point of view suddenly very different from PC Benton's. To Benton, the atmosphere of rebellion and resentment and hate was as alien as the air of Jupiter or Saturn. But Nelson was beginning to find he could breathe it with increasing ease. At the thought of his Susan dancing attendance to that bloody Tory MP, he felt as violent and angry as any of those yobbos the other side of his bar . . .

He only hoped to God that dancing attendance was all she did. Maybe his mother's stories belonged to a far-away age, but he just couldn't forget that she *was* (in that dreaded phrase) "in service" in the house of a young man living alone.

Apart from that, every time he saw her, she looked pale and strained. And that wasn't like Suzy. It wasn't like her at all. When she had been home on one of her days off he had made her go and see the doctor. When she came back, she'd looked as white as a ghost – and had refused to say a word about it afterwards.

That was why he was in the doctor's surgery now. Somehow he had to make that quack – Dr Ravi Gharad, an Asian like so many people in the Vale nowadays – tell him what was wrong with Suzy. It wouldn't be easy to get it out of him he knew. But he was *her* father – she *was* subnormal as they called it – and surely, even in this bloody awful Britain of today, he had some kind of right to know.

Although it was now 5.30 p.m., the temperature was in the eighties and the heat in the jam-packed waiting-room was stifling. It was ridiculous that such a large area was served by only one GP – but it was hard to get doctors to volunteer for work in such a trouble-spot. And whatever he might think of Dr Gharad – a fiery little man with black eyes which seemed to stab right through you – Horace had to admit that he worked like a horse. Everyone in the Vale was in awe of him, and that included the toughest of the youths, many of whom he was treating for drug addiction. Some said that without him the whole of the Vale would have exploded into riots long ago.

He appeared on the scene now, his eyes flying from face to face until they settled on Horace's bulldog features.

"Mr Nelson. You are next. This way please."

Horace stood up slowly, and followed the little man into his surgery. What was he feeling so nervous about? He was Suzy's father, wasn't he? Her only kith and kin since his wife Elsie had died five years ago. If something was wrong with his daughter – he had to know. Even if it meant shaking the doctor until those fiery eyes popped out.

It was Dr Gharad, though, who at first called the tune. The moment Horace said he had come to talk about his daughter, his face moved to a cold inexpressive mask.

"There's such a thing as professional etiquette, you know, Mr Nelson. Your daughter Susan – " He reached into a filing cabinet behind him and flicked out a card, his lean delicate fingers moving as swiftly and as smoothly as a conjurer performing a master trick.

" – I see she is over eighteen, fully adult, so it would be very improper indeed for me to discuss her case with you."

Right Tosher, thought Horace, it's time to start fighting. He took the first half of a deep breath to prepare himself but before he could make it a full one, Dr Gharad had put the card back in the cabinet, and was suddenly standing, his black eyes not fiery now but blazing.

"But I am going to be very improper, Mr Nelson, because it may be the only way to save her life. Your daughter, I strongly suspect, is on heroin. From what she has told me, about her periods, it is also highly probable that she is pregnant. Unless *something* is done, the combination of the two will not take long to kill her, or her baby, or both."

He hardly seemed to see Horace's whitening face,

although he was staring straight at it. It was as though he was staring through and beyond it.

"And hundreds of other young people in Fletchwood Vale will be dead equally soon unless we can beat the drugs problem here. Which means one thing, Mr Nelson, and one thing only."

He was suddenly standing at the window just behind Horace. Like so many windows in Fletchwood, it gave a view of the wooded hill with just a glimpse of the roof of one of the plush new houses in Malibu Rise.

"We have to break the power of our new masters – the people in the Heights!"

A man of lightning mood changes, Dr Gharad sat down again, and began calmly explaining the difficulties he had had with Suzy. She hardly seemed to take in half what he said. Asked directly if she was on drugs, she just stared blankly. Asked if she would submit to tests, she shook her head. Told she ought to go into a clinic, she just said, "My job . . . I'll lose my job." It was as though working for this Fergus Atkinson was all she thought or cared about.

"So I'm entirely on your side in this affair, Mr Nelson. If ever there was a need for a father to intervene, this is it."

"Don't you worry," Horace said quickly. "This father is going to intervene and no mistake."

He jumped up from his chair, clenching and unclenching his fists, his face no longer white but an angry red – a very angry red indeed.

Suzy had always been a very quiet girl. She had hardly any friends, and as far as he knew, had never had a single date with a boy in her life. So all this had to be down to Fergus Atkinson. It *had* to be . . .

The handsome features of the young MP complete with that built-in superior smile, loomed up in Horace's imagination. Atkinson might have been one of the villainous "Upstairs" people from his mother's stories. And in fact – in cold, sober fact – he was worse than any of them, Horace told himself. He hadn't just taken advantage of Suzy. He was as good as *murdering* her. Hadn't the doctor just told him that her very life depended on him getting her away?

Horace charged out of the surgery and back into the

waiting-room with a ferocity that left the crowd in there blinking and gasping.

He intended to go striding straight up to Atkinson's house – 3, Malibu Rise – and drag his daughter home, kicking and screaming if need be.

It was only when he had left the surgery far behind, and was striding just past his old friend PC Benton's little home, that it dawned on him just how difficult an exercise that might be.

If Suzy flatly refused to come with him, and Atkinson ordered him off the terraces, maybe even calling in the police, he could end up in the cells with his daughter estranged from him for good, and in more desperate trouble than ever. But there was a worse danger even than that, he told himself: the danger that at the first sign of Atkinson's sneering face, he would lose control of himself and start kicking, punching, trying to kill. It could happen he knew. It could happen very easily.

Maybe it was reaction. Maybe it was the heat, which was making the very pavement under his feet seem to quiver, as though white-hot with anger. Maybe it was the sullen look on the faces of a group of boys who were passing on the other side of the street. Maybe it was the whole mood of Fletchwood Vale getting through to him, becoming part of him. For whatever reason, Horace Nelson could feel a blind fury sweeping over him.

He was momentarily tempted to call in on PC Benton, and tell him: "For God's sake, Benton, lock me up. I'm not safe on the streets – as dangerous as any of your flick-knife-flashing yobbos . . . "

He doubted, though, if Bertie would believe him, or begin to understand. He was, after all, a copper through and through, and had never had an unlawful instinct in his life.

The sensible thing, Horace told himself, was to calm down and head for The Lazy Fox. Peggy, his chief barmaid, would have opened up by now. It would be cool there, cool and quiet and cosy in his little cubby-hole of an office tucked away behind the bar.

What he needed to do was busy himself there for a while

and think. And, perhaps, have a drink or two. He'd think a lot more clearly after that . . .

In the event, Horace was in there not for a while, but for six solid hours. The one or two drinks became pint after pint of bitter, chased by so many whiskies that he used up nearly a whole bottle. Pretty soon, it dawned on him that he wasn't really aiming to think clearly, but to drink himself into a stupor beyond worry, beyond anger, beyond thought of murder. But by then, he was already beyond stopping himself.

Stupor didn't come. The anger didn't fade. The thoughts didn't go.

All that did disappear was the worry and the fear that was in him to kill.

Suddenly – shortly after closing time – when he was left alone on the premises, nothing but dark echoing bars surrounding his little cubby-hole on all sides – the whole situation became shatteringly simple and straightforward.

What was the matter with him? Had he, Horace Nelson toughest landlord in London, become a coward?

Of course he had to go and get his Suzy away from that villain, and if he resisted – if he dared to raise the slightest finger to stop her going – well, he'd regret it.

And to make sure of that regret, he had unlocked a cupboard in the corner of his office, where he kept all the things he'd confiscated from drunken violent customers over the years. Calmly, he took out the most dangerous item – an outsize flick-knife with a blade as big as a butcher's.

He flicked it open just the once to check that it worked, then snapped it shut, and slipped it into his pocket, half shuddering, half rejoicing at the sight of its lethal power.

Then he switched off the bulb in his office, the only light left in the place – and made his way through the hot, beery blackness of The Lazy Fox's public bar and a moment later was out under the stars, making for 3, Malibu Rise.

The walk was only a few hundred yards, but it was straight uphill, and it took him some time to make it.

For one thing, the fresh air, stifling and clinging though it was, mixed with the alcohol in his blood to affect his sense of direction. He kept bumping into things – and people. And they weren't the sort of people who appreciated being bumped into. Twice he was sworn at, once spat at, and once punched in the stomach and sent gasping backwards across the street.

All the gangs of Fletchwood Vale seemed to be on the pavements now that the pubs had closed, which was normal on a Friday night, but unusual on a Monday. There was surely something strange about their manner tonight too. They weren't rowdy. There was little or no fighting going on and not much talking either. They seemed to be standing around in bunches, staring up at the twinkling, coloured lights high above them on the hill.

It was almost as though all of them had heard that angry message from Dr Gharad . . . that it was time to do something to "break the power of our masters – the people on the Heights".

5 Seventh Hell

Up on the Heights itself, at 1, Malibu Rise, George Gideon was experiencing the most curious evening of his life.

Kate, of course, was in seventh heaven – but he couldn't tell where *he* was. Sometimes it felt like the complete opposite if there is such a place: an agonising seventh hell.

He hadn't been there all the time. In spite of everything, it had been heart-warming to see Matthew again. Although he was forty now, it was amazing how little he had changed – he still looked like a thin edition of Gideon himself. What the years had taken away was a certain youthful weediness: a suggestion that he was just an insubstantial copy of his father, a lightweight growing up in a heavyweight's shadow. There was not the faintest hint of that now. A new Matthew was so slick and assured-looking that he might have stepped straight from chairing a board meeting at an international bankers.

At the sight of him in an incredibly prosperous house, with a beautiful wife and three kids, Gideon's fears had been momentarily overtaken by a glow of parental pride such as he had rarely known. Gideon had never been much of a Bible reader, but he had been to Sunday School when he was a boy and biblical phrases, unthought of for years, kept coming back to him now. "For this is my son, who was dead and is alive again . . . was lost and is found . . . "

To his astonishment and embarrassment, there were moments when he was close to tears, especially when he was being introduced to the family. Julie turned out to be a very attractive brunette of around thirty, with large hazel eyes, and hair which, although immaculately coiffured, somehow never lost the windswept look of a girl who had been brought up in, and belonged to, the open air. There was a bubbliness and openness about everything she did and said, too.

"This is a great moment for me, Mr Gideon, though let's face it – also a scary one. Was I right to call you 'Mr' – or should it be Commander, George or Dad?"

Gideon said hastily that George would do, and the next moment was surrounded by an explosion of bouncing grandchildren. The four-year-old Richard regarded him gravely and said: "So *you're* Grandpa Giddyman."

"Quite right," Gideon told him, "and getting giddier all the time."

The five-year-old Sandra already showing signs of being the big sister, advised Gideon not to pay any attention to her brother, he was always being stupid. The three-year-old Debbie just started bawling but stopped instantly when Kate picked her up. Children hardly ever bawled at Kate.

Then, a nanny appeared – the first time that such a person had ever been seen in the Gideon family – and the children were whisked out of sight.

Gideon frowned. There was something strangely familiar about that nanny's face. But before he could think about it, Matthew was bringing round drinks and making profuse apologies for having kept his distance from his mother and father for so long.

"The truth is, Dad, that night we had that row all those years ago, I felt you'd written me off as the runt of the litter. I just had to get away completely and – and some kind of pride forced me to *stay* away until I could give you one hundred per cent proof that I could make good on my own. I hope you can understand that. I'm sure Mum does, anyway," he finished with a disarming smile that came strikingly close to one of his father's own grins. Kate, by that time, wasn't just close to tears, she was openly and unashamedly weeping.

"Of course we understand. We both do – don't we, love?" Gideon's "Yes", although heartfelt, came out as an embarrassed grunt. He was still feeling that golden glow and once again he found himself remembering the Bible. He was like the father in the Parable of the Prodigal Son; this was the moment to start sending for the fatted calf. But then he remembered that *this* prodigal son had returned in a far better position to order fatted calf supplies than his father. The glow began to vanish. The policeman inside him simply couldn't be silenced any longer.

He looked round the spacious dining-room into which they were now being led. Everything here – from the thick pile carpet to the glittering dinner service laid out on the large polished table – spoke of Matthew's new-found wealth. Wealth made from what? Gideon felt a chill through him as he thought of the pale pinched faces of the drug addicts down in Fletchwood Vale.

Just then the nanny poked her head round the door to say the children were ready to go to bed, and Gideon was again certain he had seen her before. His mind was like a card index for facts, especially police ones, and suddenly it started functioning, telling him that Pamela Carter was in reality WPC Pamela Craddock. Formerly in Lemaitre's division, she had been seconded, if he remembered correctly, to the drugs squad.

The chilly tension grew until he felt that he had been transformed into a block of ice. It looked as though Naughton hadn't wasted much time after the case had been made a special drugs squad enquiry. The file he had rushed off with must have contained the information that Matthew and Julie were advertising for a nanny. Presumably he had sent WPC Craddock round to answer it straightaway. A shrewd move, Gideon thought wryly, and he certainly had no right to complain. How many times in the past few days had he roared that it was about time somebody got moving and did *something* about the number one suspect in the Fletchwood scene – Matthew Goddard?

The children apparently requiring no more than a quick good-night kiss apiece – WPC Craddock must be a miracle worker as a nanny, Gideon thought – Julie was back almost before her guests had been seated round the table.

A maid appeared who filled their glasses with wine – a vintage from one of the best-known wine merchants in London, and then served a delicious cold consommé, the perfect starter for a heatwave evening. For the main course there was a beautifully cooked coq-au-vin and for dessert there was a choice of profiteroles or peach melbas, both as rich and sumptuous as if they'd just been sent round from the Ritz.

"Everything prepared by Julie's own fair hands," said Matthew proudly, beaming at his wife. "She won't hear of hiring a cook even though most people do round here.

"You'll find the coffee is something special too." He ushered them into the living-room, continental in style with even more evidence of luxury, including a striking grand piano in the corner.

"So you see, Dad, when Penny comes here," said Matthew, referring to his sister a concert pianist, "she'll feel right at home."

The maid came in, and poured out beautifully smelling coffee from a large silver coffee pot. It *was* special and so were the liqueurs served with it. It was a long time since Gideon and Kate had been wined and dined so spectacularly, and both were profuse in their compliments.

Typically, though, Kate had a last thought for the nanny.

"I thought she'd be joining us," she murmured. "Or do nannies have meals sent up to their room these days?" Julie laughed.

"That's what the nanny wanted done tonight," she said. "I told her that it was a big family reunion, and she said she'd feel in the way. I tried to argue with her about it – but you take it from me, there's no arguing with Miss Pamela Carter." She frowned, then turned to Gideon and said, in her usual frank style: "Quite honestly, I've got the impression that it was *you* that she was scared of meeting. Matthew told me that the thought of you struck fear in the hearts of half the citizens of the UK. I'm beginning to think he's right."

Kate burst out laughing. Gideon found it hard even to smile. He knew well enough why WPC Craddock had avoided being there. It would have been almost impossible for her to sustain her act through a long meal in the presence of the Commander of the C.I.D. – knowing what was suspected about his son.

"But surely she could join us now – for coffee?" Kate was saying. She was still in her seventh-heaven mood and childishly not wanting anyone to be left out in the cold on such a wonderful night. Gideon attempted to nudge her to keep her quiet, but then realised that he couldn't. He would then have to explain that nudge later – and how could he begin to tell Kate that the "nanny" was here to spy on Matthew because – because –

Gideon swallowed hard. Perhaps it was the effect of the liqueurs and the wine, but he was feeling desperately confused. The realisation that this was one of the first times in his life when he couldn't confide in Kate made him feel terribly alone.

In answer to Kate's plea, Julie went to the door and called out to Pamela, begging her to come down for a moment.

She put in a brief appearance – a prim-looking girl with short-cut auburn hair, a prematurely wrinkled forehead, and small brown eyes that seemed permanently narrowed as if she found the whole world a very suspicious place. She was wearing a blue coat and skirt so trim and neat that it looked as though she had changed out of one uniform into another.

She came in explaining that she really couldn't stop, as she had only just arrived here and hadn't even finished unpacking.

Then she made some polite remarks about what well-behaved children Richard, Sandra, and Debbie were, and what an honour it was to meet the famous Commander Gideon; swallowed half a cup of coffee at a gulp, and made a hurried exit from the room – hoping perhaps that nobody would notice that she had been quite unable even to glance in the direction of the famous Commander Gideon, in case she caught his eye . . .

"What a strange, shy girl to be a nanny," said Kate. "You know, it's a funny thing but I've a feeling I've seen her before."

Since she often officiated at police charity functions, it was entirely possible that she had, Gideon realised. Once again he fought off the urge to nudge Kate and instead glanced at his watch and grunted: "Good Lord, look at the time. Half past eleven. I'm afraid we really must be getting along."

Matthew stood up and moved into the centre of the room. He had an air of suppressed excitement about him.

He might have been a master of ceremonies about to announce the high-spot of the evening.

"We can't let you go just yet," he said. "There's a spot of unfinished business on the agenda . . . Something I've been waiting to do for more than twenty years." Julie, her eyes sparkling, moved to the grand piano and played a phrase from Purcell's Trumpet Voluntary. It sounded like a cross between chopsticks and a five-finger exercise to Gideon, but he supposed he had been spoilt by years of listening to Penny. At all events, this was obviously not a time to start quibbling.

Matthew had magicked a bottle of champagne from somewhere and a tray of glasses. He uncorked it with considerable finesse, and poured out glasses – for Gideon, Kate, Julie and himself.

"My goodness," Kate gasped, "after all we've had tonight do you really think I should – "

Then it dawned on her too, that this was no time for quibbling. Matthew had finished passing round the glasses. Now he was handing something else out to her and Gideon – in a hand that was literally trembling. Swiftly, hurriedly, he murmured "Please accept this, Dad and Mum – and – and make your son an honest man again at last."

It was a cheque made out to Mr and Mrs Gideon, for £2,000. Kate was suddenly openly crying.

"Oh, Matthew, you know that there is no need – no need at all to – "

Gideon hardly knew where to look, what to do. This should have been one of the magic moments of his life. In fact, it was one of the most painful, because Matthew, having passed over the cheque, now held out his hand.

How could he take it, posing as the loving, overjoyed father when all the time Matthew was at the top of his suspect list, and a policewoman, more or less at his own instigation, was here in this very house to spy on him?

What sort of a father was he in any case, not giving Matthew a hint of what was really going on – and keeping even Kate in the dark?

The confusion inside Gideon became, for a moment, paralysing. Try as he would, he could not raise his hand.

Matthew's face registered at first puzzlement, then pain, then a deeper hurt.

"Dad – can't you – even after all this time – "

Kate was literally stunned, and reproachful as never before.

"George, what on earth's the matter? Are you all right?"

With a great effort, Gideon regained control of himself.

"Of course I'm all right," he grunted. "Felt dizzy for a moment that's all. Champagne, probably. Not used to all this grand living – " This time he did manage to hold out his hand – but Matthew was not destined to take it. The door burst open, and Pamela came charging into the room, looking – and behaving – very much more like WPC Craddock than a nanny. Before, she had been unable even to look in Gideon's direction. Now she walked straight up to him.

"Commander – er, Mr Gideon," she said urgently, "something's happening next door. The window of my room looks out on the house, and I've heard a shot – some running down the drive – then another shot."

Gideon stood up abruptly. None of those sounds, he realised, could have reached him in here, because the room was both double glazed and heavily curtained. Also until a minute ago, Julie had been playing the piano –

"Next door?" he barked. "You mean number two – Don Mitchell's place?"

He could have bitten his tongue off after saying that. It revealed that he had been keeping tabs on the whole neighbourhood. Not that Matthew or Julie seemed to notice. Julie had burst out laughing.

"Oh, come on, Pamela. All you heard was somebody's telly turned up too high. On these hot nights, with so many windows open – oh, my God! What the hell's that?" Someone had started knocking on the front door loudly enough to shake the whole house. And it was no ordinary knocking. Whoever was doing it was evidently too drunk or panic-stricken to use the knocker and was just battering on the door with bare fists, hysterically trying to break it down.

Gideon was out of the dining-room and halfway across

the hall to answer this curious summons, when Matthew caught up with him and grabbed his arm.

"Sometimes we get gangs of dangerous characters up here from Fletchwood Vale, trying to make trouble. They'll never break down that door – it's doubly reinforced, cost a packet. If I were you I wouldn't open it."

"But I'm not you," snapped Gideon. "And if Pamela's right about those shots the trouble has already been made."

Suddenly he roared at the top of his voice, "For God's sake let go of me!"

It was twenty years since Matthew had last heard the Gideon roar and it obviously shook him. He retracted a full yard and looking strained, uneasy and almost guilty, watched his father angrily turn his back on him and stride towards the door.

6 Heights of Horror

In one sense, Gideon's fears had been right. If "the Fletchwood situation" as he thought of it was not yet exploding into violence, horror was certainly stalking one group of people on the Heights; the residents of Malibu Rise.

At No.2, Don Mitchell, the famous – to some, notorious – newspaper tycoon, had gone to bed early – and alone. It was unusual for him to do either, but he had had a day of blistering rows with everybody – his associates on the board of *The Sunday View*, his editor, his accountant, his secretary, his maid, his chauffeur, and, last but perhaps not entirely least, his current mistress, Georgina. His associates had been verbally blasted until their heads rang. His editor, accountant and secretary had been threatened with dismissal. The maid and the chauffeur had been sacked on the spot. Georgina, so to speak, had sacked herself. One look at the expression of Mitchell's face and she had simply collected her things and ran out of the house, leaving it a luxurious, empty shell, devoid of all human beings except for the owner himself. And Mitchell had hardly resembled a human being since around 8 p.m., when he had received a phone call from his definitely unloved neighbour, Fergus Atkinson. Atkinson's bid to take over *The Sunday View* had now become a major threat, and had, in fact, been the main cause of Mitchell's rampaging fury with all and sundry.

It hadn't helped to hear Atkinson's silky voice murmuring: "I hear from several different quarters that you've not been quite yourself today Donald, my old chum. Why not save yourself all this hassle by accepting my bid? Pop round here and let's talk it over. It'll be a short talk, because I've an appointment at my club with one or two key members of my constituency. When you hear the new offer we're thinking of making – "

Mitchell banged the phone down at that point, so hard that he actually cracked the receiver and ominous crackling sounded from the instrument as he stalked away from it, and headed upstairs to the bathroom, the best place to cool down. It was a magnificent room, with mirrors along all four walls: mirrors which reflected his celebrated face from every angle. It wasn't looking much like the image he projected on TV now. His weather-beaten features were flushed with fury, looking as flurried as a farmer's after a hard night out. His bushy eyebrows were straggled and sweaty. His eyes, which he liked to think of as piercing, were red-rimmed and sunken. He looked not so much a man to be reckoned with as a man about to be wrecked.

He threw cold water all over his face, then an expensive body-splash lotion, but neither refreshed him. He went down to the kitchen in search of some food, only to find that the departing maid had literally emptied the fridge. He proceeded to his lounge, which boasted a large, highly ornamental bar in one corner, and poured himself a succession of double whiskies – but all they did, on an empty stomach, was to make him feel dizzy and tired. Very, very tired. All that anger, all that anxiety, all that tension had drained even his formidable resources of energy, and even though it was hardly half-past eight, bed became suddenly the only place to head for.

Once in his bedroom, he stripped naked, threw himself on top of the duvet – and then suddenly realised that he was being extremely stupid. Number 2, Malibu Rise had one of the most advanced electronic burglar-alarm systems in the country – but it was activated only when all doors in the house were closed, and both the front and back doors were locked. He had not only forgotten to lock the back door: he wasn't at all sure that he hadn't left the glass doors leading from the lounge to the patio ajar. So the house was not only unprotected electronically – there was an open invitation to any passing burglar to wander in. The Oxfam Robin Hood, for instance. It was only two weeks since he had raided Fergus Atkinson.

The thought of his enemy being caught by that ridiculous amateur made Don Mitchell chuckle: it was the first time he had laughed that day. And it was to be the last.

Sleep overcame him before he could take any action about that "open invitation" – and when he woke up, at ten past eleven in a pitch-dark bedroom, it was very obviously too late.

Faint chinks of light coming from round the bedroom door and a succession of muffled noises from downstairs made it pretty clear that the invitation had been accepted. What was even clearer to Mitchell was the fact that the man must be amateur; he was taking absolutely no pains to conceal his presence. Quite obviously, it was the Oxfam Robin Hood, expecting as rich pickings at No. 2 Malibu Rise as he had found at No. 3. Well, he had made a slight mistake, Mitchell told himself, thinking that *he* would be as easy a target as that smooth, slimy Atkinson.

There was a revolver in the drawer of his bedside table, kept there ready for occasions such as this. It was unloaded, and in point of fact he had no idea how to fire or handle it. But what did that matter? He had not had time to read the story in his paper about the Riddell incident, and so did not imagine that the Oxfam Robin Hood would be armed. He pictured him as some scruffy, unmasked, loony leftie, who would cower back into a corner, shaking, the moment he roared: "Hands Up."

Mitchell got out of bed, reached for and donned a dressing-gown and slippers without putting on the light. Then, pausing only to grab the revolver, he crept out on to the landing as quietly as possible and started descending the stairs. Next to the bottom of the stairs was a door leading to the study. This door was almost wide open, and light was shining out of it, shafting across the darkness of the hall.

Mitchell did not have to creep the rest of the way down the stairs. There was suddenly a disturbance from outside: a screaming and scuffling sound, loud enough to hide the slight sound that his slippers made on the carpeting. He was at the front of the stairs in a second. From there, he could see right into the study – suddenly, no doubt about the identity of the burglar remained at all. He had a clear back view of a man in scruffy jeans and a bomber jacket, wearing a stocking mask all over his head. He had a paint-spray can in his hand and was in the act of spraying his trademark "Feed the World" in gory red all over one of the study walls.

At the sight of it Don Mitchell saw red in every sense of the word. He charged into the room, brandishing his gun and yelling – "Feed the World! I'll give you Feed the World, you – "

He had no chance to say any more. The masked figure simply span round and squirted the paint spray full in his face. He dropped the revolver and staggered back, gasping, blinded, clawing at his eyes.

He did not even see the gun appearing in the other's hand, and it is doubtful if he heard the shot as it was fired, once, in his direction.

The bullet hit him in the centre of the forehead, blood and paint combining to cover his face in a hideous mask of red, and he was dead before his body reached the floor.

* * *

It had been a few minutes before that – just past eleven – when Horace Nelson had finally completed his embattled journey from the depths of Fletchwood Vale up to the doorstep of 2, Malibu Rise.

He was breathing hard after all that climbing – hoarse, painful gulps, because his stomach was sore after that punch it had received from that yobbo guy. But he had more than enough breath left, he told himself, for the job he had to do.

The job he had to do?

Just for a moment, his reeling brain went blank on him; he had to struggle to remember even why he was here.

Suzy . . . Something to do with Suzy. Of course, she worked here – as a maid, of all things – for that Fergus – Fergus Atkinson.

At the mention of that hated name, suddenly everything came back to him with the force of a hammer blow on the back of his head, each one threatening to split his skull. Suzy – his little Suzy – pregnant. And on heroin. He had to – to get her away from that bastard. Somehow. Anyhow. And it had to be *now*.

Groping around in the dark, he found the bell-push, put a finger on it, and kept it there until he heard Suzy's footsteps the other side of the door.

Then his brain started reeling again, and when the door was finally opened, he almost fell forwards on his face.

It was Suzy who caught him, and helped him back to his feet. She, Suzy, was quite strong physically . . . It was only . . . only her brain that was . . . weak . . .

Standing, or rather swaying, on the doorstep, he struggled to focus his eyes on her, but the light was behind her, and all he could make out was a blurred silhouette. He could see her fair hair, curly, rebellious, so like her mother's. He could glimpse her large, wide eyes staring at him. But he couldn't see if her cheeks were flushed or pale, if those eyes were wild with a drugged excitement or haunted, strained, afraid.

One thing he could make out was that she was wearing a black dress and a white apron. That shook him. He had never seen her dressed up in a maid's uniform before. Come to that, he had never seen anyone dressed like a maid before – except on TV, of course, in a series like "Upstairs Downstairs". How he'd hated that programme. It had reminded him of his mother's stories so much that he'd never been able to sit through an episode without getting up and angrily switching off the set. And now here was his daughter dressed up as a modern version of those slaves. Taking orders and probably saying, "Yes, sir. No, sir. Three bags full, sir" – from a man who was destroying her –

That was enough for Horace. Although the porch, the front door, the lighted hall – the whole scene – started spinning as though he was on an invisible roundabout, he dived forward and tried to grab Suzy by the arm.

"No – no arguments, now," he said quickly. "Whether – whether you like it or not, my girl, you're coming with – with me."

Suzy ducked away indignantly, evading his grabbing hand with ease.

"Here, what do you think you're playing at, Dad? You're in a shocking state, you know. I ought to invite you in really, for a lie down inside. But I daren't, see. I'm all alone in the house, and if you was to start breaking up the place – "

"It's not the place I want to break up, it's the owner!"

Horace told her, making another attempt to seize her. She avoided him again, this time rather less skilfully.

"What have you got against Mr Atkinson?" she asked just a shade hesitantly.

"What *haven't* I got against him?" Horace shouted.

"I've been talking to Dr Gharad, and the things he told me – "

Mention of the doctor's name evidently shook her. She was quiet for several seconds.

"You don't want to listen to Dr Gharad, Dad," she said. "He doesn't know what he's talking about that man. He had no right to tell you anything anyway. Whatever he says, I'm going to be okay. Mr Atkinson is going to take care of me and – and everything."

So that is it, Horace realised. This evil Atkinson had Suzy so completely in his power that it was almost as if he had doped away what little brains she had. That was why she had acted so strangely at Dr Gharad's; why she simply couldn't take in the fact that she was in deadly danger. How could she be – if Mr Atkinson had told her she was all right?

"Mr Atkinson." God, she was having the man's baby wasn't she? Weren't they even on christian name terms?

Of course not, he thought bitterly. He was a bloody toff, wasn't he . . . An MP, a celebrity, with his picture in all the papers, and she was only . . .

Befuddled though Horace was, he could still feel anger and it raged through him now, indignation at what had happened to his daughter mixing with all his childhood hatred of the toffs, the "Upstairs" people, the toffee-nosed bastards who had made his mother's life such hell. Suddenly he conquered his wobbly knees, mustered his swirling senses, and became Horace Nelson, the tough landlord even drunken yobbos wouldn't trifle with.

He seized hold of Suzy with such a clamp-like grip that this time she stayed seized and found herself being dragged down the gravel path towards the gate of No.3, screaming all the way.

"No, Dad, *no.* Mr Atkinson will be back in a minute – he's only gone down to the club for a drink with his friends. And God knows what he'll do if he finds the house empty – the door wide open – "

"Don't you worry about what Mr Atkinson's going to do to *you*," Horace shouted. "What's more to the point is what *I* am going to do to *him*."

Suzy gave up arguing with him, and started struggling. Horace held on to her fiercely. The scuffling and screaming could be heard streets away.

But it was not loud enough to drown the furious shout which came suddenly from the house next door.

"Feed the World? I'll give you . . . "

And it certainly wasn't loud enough to drown the sound that followed it: a deafening, unmistakable roar of a shot.

Suzy stopped screaming. She stopped struggling, too, even though her father had virtually let go of her, and it would have been easy to break away. She just stood still, shaking, like a frightened child.

"What the 'ell's going on, Dad?"

Before Horace could answer, the front door of No.2 burst open, and a figure came running out, clear for a moment in the light of the bulb on the porch – a man with a stocking mask over his head, in typical Vale outfit – bomber jacket, jeans – and with a gun in his hand. He disappeared into the darkness, but the sound of running feet on gravel left them in no doubt that he was racing down the path towards the gate of No. 2, and since that was just alongside the gate of No. 3, that meant he was coming straight towards them . . .

Horace didn't hesitate.

His brain wasn't too bemused to make out what had happened. It was easy as A-B-C.

"Feed the World" was what Bert Benton's son, Red, sprayed on walls whenever he did a burglary. That shot could only mean that he had been caught in the act and that the bloody fool had turned very nasty to get himself out of trouble.

Well, he hadn't got himself out of trouble. Not if he, Horace Nelson, had anything to do with it.

Suzy yelped in astonishment and horror as the running figure came looming out of the darkness, plain to see now in the light of a nearby street lamp – and her father coldly and deliberately stepped in front of the gate of No.3, completely blocking his path.

"This is as far as you're going, Red, my lad," Horace said, in exactly the tone of voice that had halted many a drunken brawl at The Lazy Fox. "And don't think that, just because your father is an old mate of mine – "

The running figure stopped, pausing slightly, and raised the gun, until it was pointed at Horace's chest.

Nelson, suddenly as heroic as his namesake, folded his arms and didn't move, even though he was swaying now, just slightly, from side to side.

That was when the terrible thing happened.

Either because she was very brave or too dim to recognise the danger, Suzy stepped between her father and the gun.

She knew Red: had known him, in fact, for years and years. They'd even been at school together – before she was sent off to a special school for the mentally backward –

"Red!" she was saying. "Don't be so bloody silly – it's *me* – Suzy."

Horace was on the point of telling her that she was being bloody silly and pulling her out of the way when the gun went off.

The flash was blinding, the roar skull-cracking, the way that Suzy's whole body jerked and then sagged against him was the most sickening and numbing thing that Horace Nelson had ever known.

He hardly noticed the Oxfam Robin Hood shoving past him, scarcely heard the roar of a car streaking up the road behind him.

He was on his knees beside Suzy, seeing the blood pouring out of her chest, her wide sightless eyes –

At the next moment, he was up and half-running, half-staggering up to the front door of the next house in the road and hammering upon it with all his might – bare-fisted, because he was too blinded by tears to see the knocker.

"Get the doctor! Get an ambulance! Get the police!" he yelled to the man who opened it and added half-sobbing, half-screaming: "Not that it'll be much use getting them. There'll be a cover-up as it's a PC's son what done it. Like the bloody toffs, coppers are. Always look after – look after their own . . . "

He collapsed in a drunken stupor, brought on afresh by his terrible grief, before he realised that he was talking to the most famous policeman in Britain, and before the bemused Gideon could say a word in reply.

7 Next Door to Murder

Gideon did not stay bemused for long.

He had seen people distraught with grief before – and needed no telling that someone very dear to this man was in all probability lying out there in the darkness, perhaps dead, perhaps dying.

"You heard him! Get an ambulance here – quick!" He barked at Matthew, treating his son almost as if he was ten years old again. Then, stepping over Nelson's prostrate body, he started racing down the path towards the gate, screwing up his eyes against the gloom, and wishing to God that he had a torch.

That difficulty was soon remedied, from an unexpected quarter. Suddenly he heard running footsteps, and glancing round, saw that Pamela was right behind him, carrying a large rubber torch in her hand.

Forgetting her role of the nanny, she had obviously responded to her instincts as a policewoman, and was determined to accompany him to the scene of the crime.

Gideon took the torch from her with a guttural "Thank you, Constable Craddock." The girl started. It nearly always shook lower-ranking men and women in the Force to discover that the great Gideon knew not just their faces, but their names – and very often a lot of other details about them, too. In Pamela's case, it was doubly shocking. She realised he had been seeing through her performance all that evening.

Before she could recover herself, Gideon was revealing some of his detailed knowledge of her.

Pausing for breath as he came up to the gate, he said over his shoulder:

"You've been on duty in this area for years, one way or another. Do you by any chance know who that man on the doorstep was?"

"Yes, sir," Pamela was very definite. "Everyone round

here knows him, he's Horace Nelson, landlord of The Lazy Fox, the biggest pub in Fletchwood Vale. Susan Nelson, his daughter, has taken a job as maid to Fergus Atkinson, two doors along from here at number three. I know that because as part of my undercover assignment, I'm to try and make friends with her and find out more about Atkinson's habits."

"You might find that just a bit difficult now," said Gideon, in an odd voice, soft, yet grim.

He was through the gate and shining the torch on someone lying on the pavement about ten yards further up Malibu Rise. Even from this distance, it was clear that it was a girl wearing a maid's uniform – black dress, and an apron which should have been white, but was now a blood-stained red.

Inside a second, Gideon and WPC Craddock were kneeling beside her, and Gideon was feeling her pulse. It was faint, but regular, suggesting that the bullet had missed her heart. But it had probably punctured a lung. Her breathing was tortured, gasping, made worse by the fact that she was trying desperately to talk.

To talk: but not to them. It was doubtful if she even knew they were there. Her very young, schoolgirlish face was twisted with anger, and suddenly she made struggling movements, as though she was trying to break free from someone.

"Let me *go*, Dad! I keep telling you, Mr Atkinson will be back in a moment and if he finds the house empty, I'll get the sack on the spot, won't I? *Won't I*?"

Her imaginary father evidently needed more persuading, and she started pleading.

"You've got to believe me, Dad. Don't pay no attention to that Dr Gharad. Mr Atkinson will see me right. He's *promised* . . . "

"I'm sure he has," said Gideon gruffly. "But shush! Keep quiet. Lie back for a bit and rest."

Suzy was coughing now, coughing blood. But even that didn't stop her talking. Her eyes were wide and staring, almost as though she was high on drugs, and she choked out:

"Red! Don't be so bloody silly! It's me – Suzy – don't shoot – "

At that moment, to Gideon's great relief, the ambulance arrived. There was no police car with it. Presumably Matthew hadn't asked for one. And, recognising Gideon, the ambulancemen made no mention of the need to call in police.

As they lifted Suzy on to a stretcher, and rushed her away, Gideon stood up, a dozen questions dancing around in his mind.

"Let me go, Dad," suggested that the drunken Nelson had been dragging his daughter physically away from somewhere – and that somewhere had been Fergus Atkinson's house, No. 3. Now that he was standing, he had a good view of all the houses in Malibu Rise, and yes, the front door of No. 3 was wide open, just as it would have been if Suzy had been pulled, protesting, across the doorstep and down the path to the gate.

But where had this "Red" sprung from and why had the shooting started?

Gideon's eyes suddenly swivelled left, to the front door of No. 2 – and then he drew in his breath.

It was wide open too, swinging eerily in the summer night breeze, with light spilling out all over the front garden.

Turning to Pamela Craddock, who was still beside him, he said tersely:

"Those shots you heard from next door – tell me again what you heard?" As though reading from an invisible police notebook, Pamela repeated almost word for word what she had told him before.

"Shouting, Sir, and a shot, then someone running down a gravel drive or path – and another shot – "

She stopped there, finding herself talking to Gideon's rapidly retreating rear, as he went striding up the path to No.2's open door. She was about to hurry after him, but he turned and waved her back.

"You've done quite enough police duty tonight, my girl – for a nanny!" he said. "I'd watch it if you don't want to blow your cover!"

"Oh, yes, of course, sir. You're quite right," Pamela said, and hurriedly retreated.

To Gideon, the night breeze suddenly seemed glacial as he watched her go. His warning had been an instinctive Commander of the C.I.D. reaction. Telling an undercover policewoman how to do a better job. Only now was it dawning on him that it had been a particularly peculiar thing for a father to do – actually encouraging someone to spy on his son . . .

His misgivings intensified as, at that moment, Matthew himself appeared, striding up the path towards him. With Julie's help, he had carried that drunken man into the dining-room, he said. He was trying to come round from that stupor.

Kate was looking after him, which was good, thought Gideon. If anyone could calm and comfort him, Kate could.

"What's been happening out here?" Matthew wanted to know. "Did you find anyone?"

Gideon only had time to give a hurried answer. "Yes, we found a girl – the man's daughter, I think – badly wounded," he said, adding gruffly: "And she may not be the only casualty, I'm afraid."

They were on the doorstep of No. 2 now. That open gently swinging door, the brightly lit hall, the eerily silent house beyond were all signs that Gideon didn't like at all.

"There's no need for you to come any further," he told Matthew. "In fact I strongly advise you not to."

Matthew's reply startled him. Suddenly years – decades fell away, as he murmured:

"I'll come, if you don't mind, Dad. Always wanted to see you in action . . . Always wanted to be a copper, come to that."

"So – you did," said Gideon, and found it impossible not to say it shakily.

He pushed the swinging door fully open and strode into the hall, with Matthew just behind him.

"Anyone home," he boomed, and listened intently for the slightest sound of life, the faintest cry or gasp, from any direction. None came.

"This is crazy," said Matthew. "Don Mitchell has a

chauffeur and a maid – to say nothing of girl-friends which he changes as often as his socks . . . Somebody *must* be about. Unless – Oh, Christ . . . "

He and Gideon had reached the open door on the right at the foot of the stairs, leading to Mitchell's study. And both men had a sickeningly full view of Mitchell's body, which was lying flat on its back on the carpet inside, its forehead still gaping from the bullet wound, its face still a mask of drying paint, congealing blood. In the midst of all this mess, Mitchell's famous piercing eyes remained wide-open, and staring as relentlessly as ever. If it didn't meet with Don Mitchell's approval, so much the worse for Eternity.

Matthew turned white, and swallowed hard before he could bring himself to follow his father and step over the body into the room.

"Careful you don't touch anything," Gideon ordered. "The scene-of-the-crime boys will be here in a moment, and they won't thank you if you do. Not that there'll be much of a problem deciding who's committed *this* crime."

He was staring up at the words "FEED THE WORLD", sprayed on the wall in brilliant red.

Matthew stared at them too – and lost still more colour.

"The Oxfam Robin Hood!" he breathed. "That figures, Dad, Malibu Rise is a favourite stamping ground of his. He burgled Fergus Atkinson at number three soon after we moved into number one. Now he's done this, I suppose we'll be next on his visiting list."

"Not if we catch him first," said Gideon. His face was grim and stern, reminding Matthew of his expression on that night of the famous row. "And we'd *better* catch him first – because he's getting sicker, bloodier all the time!"

He stopped and nearly picked up the gun he had spotted lying close to the body. Remembering his own advice, he didn't actually touch it but stood up again, glaring down at it.

"I suppose that is what made him murderous. Mitchell obviously caught him in the act of spraying the wall, and threatened him with this gun. He retaliated by trying to spray Mitchell's face and then shot him dead into the bargain."

"But that girl outside," said Matthew. "Why did he shoot *her*?"

"I don't know," Gideon said slowly, "it could be because she blocked his way when he was escaping. It could be she recognised him, in spite of the mask or whatever he was wearing, someone she knew – someone called 'Red'. The girl's father recognised him too, didn't he? You remember all that about a policeman's son?"

Suddenly Gideon's grim look changed. His face took on the expression of a hawk in sight of its prey.

"A policeman's son called Red – obviously known around Fletchwood," he murmured. "With all that to go on we should nab him straight away. Tonight!"

He stepped over the body again, and into the hall and went straight to a slim white trimphone standing on the hall table.

His first impulse was to ring Tom Riddell, but then he remembered Riddell's nerves and his decision to put someone else on the case. Pity he hadn't actually brought himself to tell Tom what he was going to do, but that didn't matter, as it happened, because he *had* given him the day off, and so he wouldn't be officially "on call" tonight in any case.

After a moment's thought, he decided to ring Lemaitre. Lem was the Chief Detective Superintendent in charge of this area, after all, and had been conducting all the inquiries into the Fletchwood situation. Now that the Drugs Squad had taken that case over, it left Lem more or less free – and if (as seemed likely) the Oxfam Robin Hood was going to turn out to be a Fletchwood man, then Lemaitre was the obvious choice for the job of tackling him in Riddell's stead.

Apart from everything else, he knew Fletchwood – particularly Fletchwood Vale – like the back of his hand, and the people too – as he rapidly proceeded to prove.

As soon as Gideon had outlined the situation, he was immediately able to put faces to the names he mentioned – including the key name, "Red".

"There's only one person that could be – Red Benton. He's just a kid – nineteen, twenty, I'd say – but he's a troublemaker with a capital 'T' around Fletchwood way.

Every time there's a riot or brawl in the Vale, you can bet he's involved in it somewhere – and usually leading it. And the tragedy is that his old man – PC Bertie Benton – is a genuine copper-bottomed stalwart of the force. Next thing you'll ever get to a real-life Dixon of Dock Green, old Bertie. Don't tell me that you don't remember the man, GeeGee, your famous card-index memory must want a bloody good reshuffle if you don't."

Gideon did remember the man. Like Lemaitre, he went back to the days when Fletchwood Vale was known to everyone in the force as "Benton's Patch". He had also met Benton on several occasions, a stout man rapidly balding, who had seemed the epitome of the classic "friend of all the neighbourhood" copper. How on earth could such a man have such a son, he wondered – and then stopped himself abruptly. The question he had just put was a little too close for comfort.

Lemaitre was prattling on.

"Horace Nelson – and he's a local legend too. Fletchwood wouldn't be Fletchwood without him being behind the bar at The Lazy Fox. He and Benton are close cronies, by the way. I've often thought that's what makes The Lazy Fox such a good pub to go in, despite its surroundings. The customers know that if they misbehave, there's a very close link-up between the management and the Law . . . " He broke off, whistling. "And you're telling me that Horace, of all people, has fingered Bertie's boy as the Oxfam Robin Hood? Christ, then there *must* be something in it – that's all I can say!"

"Yes, it does look pretty cut and dried, doesn't it?" Gideon said. Then just for an instant some deep instinct whispered caution. "But don't forget – Nelson was in a drunken stupor, and just talked about his girl, Suzy, he may not have known what he was saying, and as for Suzy herself, well, she was in such a state that – "

Lemaitre interrupted him.

"Okay, GeeGee, I get the message. It's the usual one isn't it? 'Cool it, Lem, don't jump to conclusions.' For forty years you've been telling me that. One day, maybe, I'll actually take it in! Anyway, I'll be right over – I'll get the scene-of-the-crime boys along too, of course, and some of my men just in case we can think about making a quick arrest."

"Fine," said Gideon.

"The address is 2, Malibu Rise, as you know. And Horace Nelson's being looked after by Kate at the moment, next door in number one – that's my son Matthew's place." He broke off, startled by the strange, stunned silence on the line.

Obviously, it had only just dawned on Lemaitre that he was in for one of the strangest, most embarrassing experiences of his career. He would not only be conducting an inquiry right under Gideon's eye. He would also have to act normally in the presence of Gideon, Kate and Matthew, although knowing all the time that *nothing* was normal, that there were the darkest suspicions surrounding everything.

What was the matter with him, Gideon asked himself. He should have realised, Lem was the last man he should have chosen in the circumstances. A good police decision it might have been – but he was placing an intolerable burden on one of his oldest friends.

Suddenly, though, Lem seemed to decide that he could shoulder it.

His familiar cockney voice sounding a little hoarse, but otherwise its normal chirpy self, he said:

"Sorry about that, GeeGee. Something wrong with the line, I reckon – we must have got cut off for a moment. As I was saying, hold on to your horses. I'll be along right away."

8 The Two Interruptions

Lemaitre was as good as his word. Within eight minutes, by Gideon's watch, there he was on the doorstep, and looking remarkably spick and span into the bargain. His sparse black hair glistened with just-applied Brylcreem; his shoes were newly polished, and he was sporting what he obviously thought of as the nattiest line in summer suits. It was a brilliant white, and with a bright red-striped tie, made him look like a cockney comedian about to step into the spotlight and begin his act.

A pretty odd outfit for a C.I.D. man, thought Gideon – but not for one who had been brought up in the East End, in the old Petticoat Lane philosophy,

"When in doubt – razzle-dazzle them"; and Lem was probably very deeply in doubt about tonight . . .

"God bless you for coming so quickly, Lem," he said. "But what about your men, the scene-of-the-crime boys, and the others?"

"They'll be here shortly," said Lemaitre. "It could be quite a long 'shortly', though. I've bent the rules a bit, and called them in from some way away. Tottenham and Hammersmith, as a matter of fact."

Gideon stared.

"Why?"

"Oh, come on Gee Gee. Wouldn't be fair to Bertie Benton to use a bunch of Fletchwood boys on this caper, would it? They're all Benton's mates to a man down here – and seeing that we're liable to end up going after Benton's own son, I thought – er – I reckoned . . . "

His voice petered out, his thin, sharp features becoming as uneasy as those of a comic hearing boos and catcalls, and expecting at any moment to be told to leave the stage. He had suddenly spotted Matthew, standing behind Gideon in the doorway, and he had just been talking about going after policemen's sons . . .

Somehow, he managed a fierce, false grin, and stretched out a hand.

"Well, well. Matthew, isn't it? Haven't seen you since you were a nipper. Remember how you used to call me Uncle Lem?"

Matthew was at his smoothest.

He took Lem's hand firmly, and answered:

"How could I ever forget it – all those lessons you gave me about how to handcuff people? There was one Sunday afternoon when you were round to tea, and the two of us even handcuffed Dad."

Lemaitre's laugh was so strangled it was almost a choke.

Perhaps sensing the embarrassment in the air, but possibly not, Matthew muttered something about having to go and see how the family was getting on, and strolled off in the direction of his own front door. Gideon took Lemaitre to the study where the body lay, and then led him on a quick conducted tour of the house.

"I've made a cursory examination of the whole place already," he said, "and I think what happened is pretty clear."

"Including why there's nobody about?" asked Lemaitre. "According to that file on Mitchell I prepared, this place should be seething with people. He had a girl-friend, a chauffeur, a maid – "

"*Had* is the operative word," said Gideon grimly. "It seems as though he had an unholy row with all of them earlier today. There's evidence of hurried packing – wardrobe doors open, wire hangers lying about and so on – in both the servants' bedrooms and even in a corner of his own room."

"So he cleared everyone out, and after that was alone in the place?"

"It looks like it. Alone and doing some hard drinking, as you will see – and smell – in here."

He opened the door of the lounge, and showed Lemaitre the huge, highly ornamental bar. The aroma of scotch still hung in the air, and there was a bottle of Glenfiddich, not quite empty, standing on the counter, with its stopper off.

"No glass beside it," Gideon pointed out. "There's an

empty whisky glass on Mitchell's bedside table, suggesting that he drank himself stupid down here, and then staggered straight up to his bedroom. You can tell the state that he was in from the fact that he never even replaced the stopper in the bottle – and that's not the only thing he forgot to do."

He moved over to the patio doors, which were wide open and admitting a stream of cool air, welcome in the close, clammy night.

"No need to look much further to find out how the burglar effected entry," he grunted. "And there's no sign of forcing whatsoever. It's pretty obvious that the doors were like this before Mitchell went to bed. And the thing is that there's a very sophisticated, almost foolproof burglar alarm system here – see that wire? But it's the type that doesn't react when the circuit's broken. Open and close windows and you automatically switch it off."

Lemaitre whistled.

"He might as well have hung up a sign – 'This is your night, Oxfam Robin Hood'!"

"Ye-s," said Gideon slowly. "But it's still puzzling that the invitation was accepted with such alacrity. These doors aren't visible from the front of the house – and while I can imagine the Oxfam Robin Hood combing the area in a car on the lookout for likely opportunities, it's hard to imagine that he'd be prowling around back gardens as early as ten or eleven o'clock."

"Not if he's a local gangleader like Red Benton," Lemaitre said. "You've got to remember – the whole area's full of Fletchwood Vale youths, working as servants to the new gentry. Any of them could have looked over a wall or out of a kitchen window and seen this place with all the lights on and the patio doors wide open, and then got on to the blower and given Red the wink."

Gideon stared hard at his old friend.

"You're pretty sure it's this Red, aren't you?"

"This case is looking more open-and-shut to me every minute," said Lemaitre. "Isn't it to you?"

"Not yet, not quite," Gideon told him. "Come with me and I'll show you something."

Moving with that famous, highly powerful stride – head

thrust forward, as if nothing, not even a herd of stampeding buffaloes could stop him from going where he wanted – Gideon led the way back into his study. Both he and Lem stepped quickly over the body, Lem slowed slightly as his eyes met Mitchell's sightless ones. It still looked as though the tycoon was ready for a tough confrontation in the other world.

"Well?" said Lem. "What's so special here? It's pretty obvious that Mitchell heard the burglar, came downstairs to confront him here with his gun at the ready. He caught the Oxfam Robin Hood painting his trademark on the wall, and got first a face full of paint for his pains, and then, poor devil, a bullet straight in the forehead. There's no great mystery about that."

"No," said Gideon sternly. "Not about *that*. But look around, Lem."

Lem obeyed – and still couldn't see what Gideon was getting at. The study certainly showed signs of having being very hastily burgled. On a big walnut desk which was set against one wall – obviously an expensive piece – the roll-top lid had been forced upwards, but there was no sign of any of the contents having been disturbed. A stack of neatly piled papers had obviously been left untouched. Out of a stack of nine interesting little drawers at the back, only one had been yanked out of its socket.

"Wouldn't you say," said Gideon, "that this looks like an interrupted job? The burglar got the desk open, but then was stopped before he did anything further."

Lemaitre nodded.

"Sure," he said, "that figures, doesn't it? Red Benton, or whoever it was, obviously – stopped because he heard noises – Mitchell coming down the stairs."

"But when Mitchell got here," said Gideon, "as you've just been saying, all the evidence suggests that the Oxfam Robin Hood was busily spraying his trademark on the wall! Now what sort of burglar is it, Lem, who, abandoning a burglary because he's heard noises, and knowing that he's not going to get any loot tonight, nevertheless hangs about *deliberately making sure that everybody knows he was here*? Unless you can explain that," he finished, grimly, "I don't think this is an open-and-shut case at all."

* * *

Lemaitre was not in the least non-plussed.

"But I *can* explain it. The man's a nutter. All the publicity he's been getting has gone to his head. The money doesn't matter to him – if what he says is true, it all goes to Oxfam anyway. What does matter with him is headlines. He just can't bear to pack up for the night without being sure the press are going to say 'OXFAM ROBIN HOOD STRIKES AGAIN' in the morning. There couldn't be stronger proof that we're dealing with someone who's clean off his rocker – and – " he glanced down once more at the blood-splattered, paint-splattered frame of Mitchell at his feet, " – and a bloody-minded killer. We've got to get him, Gee Gee. Whatever it does to poor old Bertie Benton, we've got to get that sick son of his tonight!"

Gideon didn't reply for a moment. He was finding it hard not to be swept along by Lem's passionate enthusiasm, especially since it was he who had sparked it off in the first place. He, too, would give a lot to be able to close the Oxfam Robin Hood case once and for all, tonight.

"Right, Lem," he said at length, decisively. "If, when we get to see Horace Nelson, he's remembered enough to state positively that it *was* Red Benton who fired at his daughter."

"What do we need that for?" Lemaitre demanded. "He's already raved about a policeman's son and said that his daughter said, 'Don't shoot, Red.' If that isn't enough, at least call the boy in for further questioning – "

A knock at the front door made him break off.

He went to answer it, stepping over the body carelessly this time. Red from the paint, and blood, made a vivid stain on his white trouser-leg.

He expected to find that the scene-of-the-crime boys had made it from Hammersmith at last. But the figure on the doorstep – a tall, blond, handsome man who might have stepped straight out of an aftershave commercial – quite obviously wasn't a policeman. Lem blinked, and then remembered the face from the photograph in File 2 – the one of Fergus Atkinson. Not that he hadn't seen it often enough in the papers and on TV.

It was, in fact, an obviously put-out Fergus Atkinson who confronted him. He had just returned home, he said, to find the front door wide open, and no sign of his maid. He had called to see if his neighbour, Don Mitchell, could shed any light on the matter. He often had servant problems too.

"He's had other problems tonight, I'm afraid, sir," Lemaitre told him. "In fact, I'm very sorry to inform you that he's dead. Shot by an intruder – a burglar – "

Atkinson stared blankly for a second. Then he became even more indignant.

"Good God! Not the fellow who raided me the other night? The Oxfam Robin Hood? I've told the police over and over again we needed special protection here. But would they listen? No! Scotland Yard haven't heard the last of this, I'm telling you. I happen to have the ear of the Home Secretary – and whoever's responsible, no matter if it's the almighty Gideon himself – "

As the almighty Gideon himself turned up that moment behind Lemaitre, for a second, even Atkinson seemed lost for words. Not for long, though. He took a deep breath, and began again.

"Now look here, Commander, as I was telling your man here, this outrage won't be forgotten in a hurry. There'll be questions in the House. I can promise you that, because I'll be asking them!"

Never in his life had Gideon taken kindly to official bullying, and he didn't now.

Folding his arms, he roared, "I hope you get some interesting answers, Mr Atkinson. Because I can promise you, I'll be listening!"

Very much more quietly, he went on:

"That is not to say that I don't very much regret what has happened to Mr Mitchell – and, incidentally, to your maid."

Atkinson stared.

"To – to my maid?"

"Yes. She was apparently leaving your house, accompanied by her father, Mr Horace Nelson, just when the murderer was making his escape. Although I don't know the details, it is likely that she very bravely intervened, perhaps even barring his way. He shot her down, and she is now in hospital, very seriously ill. Once again, I am extremely sorry to be passing on such terrible news."

If it was terrible news to Atkinson, he took it very calmly.

"I see. Well, poor little Suzy," he said. "Rather a stupid girl, but a hard worker. Could have made something of her if I'd had more time to train her." It was exactly as though he were discussing a horse or a dog, not a human being. Suddenly something else struck him. "Leaving my house, you say, with her father? She was on duty – and being paid very well for it. Special night rate. Five quid an hour . . . "

He went, soon after that, still muttering about asking questions in the House.

Lemaitre put in to words what Gideon was thinking.

"Well, Gee Gee, that's one mystery solved, at any rate. We don't have to wonder what Horace Nelson was playing at tonight. If my daughter worked for that man, I'd be up here dragging her away!"

Cars were driving up the road now, a miniature motorcade of them.

Two cars brought a scene-of-the-crime squad from Hammersmith – photographers, fingerprint men and a load of special laboratory equipment. Scene-of-the-crime work was very sophisticated nowadays. A third car contained a uniformed sergeant and four constables from Tottenham. A further one was driven by a police doctor, who turned out to have been dragged all the way here from East Acton. Gideon had misgivings about Lemaitre's policy of bringing all these people from other areas: it was liable to raise far more questions than it solved. In his opinion, PC Benton's feelings wouldn't be spared for long, whatever happened. But Lem was a born rule-bender, and his motives were certainly of the best.

Within a very few minutes, the scene-of-the-crime men were busy all over the house, photographing Mitchell's body from every angle in the study, chalkmarking the intruder's probable route from the patio door across the hall, fingerprinting every possible surface, and so on. Whether they would discover a single fact more than his cursory examination had already shown, Gideon greatly doubted. But after all, one never knew . . .

Lem stationed his own men outside the front door, and down by the gate, protecting the spot where Suzy's body had lain, until it too could be photographed and chalk-marked. There was no difficulty in identifying the exact place: a pool of the poor girl's blood was still visible on the pavement, darkening and congealing, but still sparkling in the light of the policemen's torches.

At the sight of it, Gideon suddenly had a strong urge to find out how Suzy was. He must ring the hospital as soon as he got home to Matthew's: though he would do so with dread. The chances of her being a DOA – dead on arrival – case were tragically high. Perhaps it was just as well her father *was* in that helpless stupor . . .

Gideon had forgotten something – that he had left Horace Nelson in the charge of Kate, and it wasn't Kate's way to leave anyone in a stupor for long.

With the assistance of Pamela, who seemed to have had a wealth of experience of such things, she had raided the back of Matthew's drinks cabinet and concocted a fearful drink, half "hair-of-the-dog" and half-medicinal which they had forced down Nelson's throat. The landlord of The Lazy Fox had turned green and puked all over the dining-room carpet, but then sat up, calm and apparently stone-cold sober.

He had told Kate what had happened to his daughter, and, off her own bat, she had telephoned the hospital, discovering that Suzy had arrived, half-dead but still breathing, and had been rushed into the theatre for an immediate emergency operation.

Nelson's reaction to this had shaken even Kate.

"An operation? Christ. Do they know about the dangers – and the baby? That bloody Atkinson."

Kate had made him tell her everything he knew. She had rung the hospital again, and alerted them to the possibilities of the patient being pregnant and having a heroin addiction. They were not surprised about the latter. The nurses had already noticed the needle marks on her arm.

The hospital had rung back later with better news. Suzy

had survived the operation. The bullet had been safely removed, but she was still weak, and in Intensive Care.

Horace Nelson immediately said that he wanted to visit her. Kate told him that a police car would take him to the hospital – after he had had "a little talk" with her husband.

"Where is he, then?" Nelson had demanded. "I'll talk to him all right – don't you worry!"

It was at that moment that Gideon arrived, on the doorstep, with Lemaitre beside him.

Kate opened the door, and quickly took the both of them into a back room, while she explained what had happened, and what she had learned, particularly about Atkinson and Suzy.

Gideon's relief that the girl was all right – at any rate, still surviving, was mixed with a feeling of fury at Atkinson.

Lemaitre could hardly believe it.

"He gets the girl hooked on drugs, he gets her carrying his baby and when he hears she's dead or dying, all he does is grumble about paying her five quid an hour. Bloody hell, the man's not – not bloody human."

"He was putting on an act, of course. Covering himself by playing the aloof employer," Gideon reminded him.

"But all the same – "

He broke off. There was no denying it, he thought. Atkinson's behaviour had been so abnormal as to be almost pathological. It suggested that, at some level, he was a dangerously disturbed personality. Was it possible that it suggested more than that? Was it possible that –

Somewhere, right at the back of Gideon's mind, an odd theory began to form. A theory so wild, so incredible that his brain began disbelieving it almost before it could take shape. At all events, there was suddenly no time for theorising.

Pamela Craddock suddenly put her head around the door, looking for Julie and Lem, for whom she had worked before going to the Drugs Squad, recognised her instantly – and could not avoid starting violently. Acting had never been one of Lem's strong suits.

Gideon hurriedly made introductions.

"Pamela, meet my associate, Chief Detective Superintendent Lemaitre . . . Lem, this is Pamela Carter, nanny to three of the most beautiful grandchildren any man could have."

Lemaitre was suddenly like he had been at the conference that morning: stiff, nervous, preposterously over-correct.

"Very pleased to meet you, Miss Carter. Bad business, all this, I'm afraid."

Pamela muttered something, reddened and made a hasty escape.

Kate, who rarely missed anything, and certainly hadn't missed any of that, said straightaway: "Anyone would have thought you knew that girl, Lem."

Lemaitre struggled to bluff it out.

"Thought I did myself there for a minute, ma'am. Must be something playing tricks with my memory."

It wasn't a very effective performance, and hardly helped by the fact that never, in all the years he had known her, had he called Kate "ma'am" before.

Kate could obviously sense a tension in the atmosphere, and being Kate, instinctively tried to ease it.

"Look," she said. "Poor Mr Nelson in there is dying to get to the hospital and see his daughter. Can't the two of you hurry up and take a statement from him soon?"

Nelson was in the drawing-room chatting to Matthew and Julie, who both retreated hurriedly when Gideon and Lemaitre entered. The burly landlord no longer bore much resemblance to the drunken monster who had tried to batter down the front door, just an hour or so before. His face had lost all traces of colour, leaving his normally florid cheeks sallow and sagging. His whole body seemed to be sagging, for that matter, as he sat, slumped in the armchair, anxiously clenching and unclenching his huge fists.

Gideon introduced himself and then handed over to Lemaitre, who needed no introducing to his old friend Horace. Very kindly Lem asked him to tell them in his own words exactly what happened to his daughter – "as far as you can remember", he added.

Nelson seemed, in fact, to have no trouble remembering everything. He and Suzy had just reached the gate of No. 2 when he had heard a shot from inside the house: a man's angry voice yelling, "Feed the world! I'll give you feed the world!" The shout had been interrupted by a shot.

"I knew what that meant – Red Benton, PC Bertie Benton's son, up to his nasty tricks again. For months, Bertie had been telling me he suspected Red was the Oxfam Robin Hood. Nearly driven out of his mind by it he was."

"Just a minute," Gideon found himself interrupting. "Suspicions – even a father's suspicions – aren't proof! You can't say for sure that – "

Nelson was beginning to come to life again now. His face began reddening, his eyes glazing.

"Oh, yes, they are, in this case – as bloody well as good as!" he shouted. "Bertie told me he'd kept a diary of his son's movements – and every time, *every time*, there was an Oxfam Robin Hood crime, Red just happened to be out of the house! More than that he'd found a stack of tins of spray paint in the dustbin one morning – the exact colour the Oxfam Robin Hood used – "

"All right, all right," said Lemaitre hurriedly. "You can leave it there, Horace; we'll be taking all that up with Bertie ourselves. Just get back to what happened tonight. After the shot – "

"After the shot I heard Red running down the path towards us," Horace said.

"Red?" said Gideon sharply. "Just how can you be sure it was Red? It was pitch dark – he must have been masked in any case, surely – "

Nelson came leaping up out of the chair and for a moment looked as if he was going to throw himself across the room at them.

Neither Gideon nor Lemaitre needed any telling why. All Horace's suspicions about a police cover-up had been inflamed again. They would do anything they could to stop him naming Bertie's son – and he was determined to beat them at their own game, no matter what it cost.

"Of course I'm sure it was Red!" he yelled. "There was light from a lamppost. He wasn't masked. I saw his stupid face clearly, every detail of it. I shouted out 'This is as far as you're going, Red, my lad' and stepped in his path.

Then Suzy saw his gun pointed at me, and stepped between me and him. I think she said 'Don't be silly, Red' or something. If she didn't say it, she meant it. Both of us knew Red. Neither of us really believed he'd shoot. But he *did*, the shitty little sod, he did – and I'd swear on a stack of Bibles it – it was him and no one else: him, Roderick 'Red' Benton, the son of PC Bertie Benton of 221, Mender Lane, Fletchwood. That clear enough for you – or are you going to trump up some other excuse not to go out and nick the ruddy bastard *now*?"

9 Policeman's Son

That did it, of course.

In the face of such positive identification of the gunman by the victim's father – to say nothing of the girl's own confirmation of it, as she lay bleeding, on the spot – there was only one course open to the police: to spare no effort to bring Red Benton in.

There really wasn't any excuse for not having done it an hour before. The moment Gideon had learnt over the phone from Lemaitre the identity of the mysterious "Red", he should have rung the Yard, and ordered squad cars to head at once for the Benton home. Why hadn't he? What amounted to a dangerous maniac killer was at large, and seconds counted if he was to be caught. Yet he had delayed matters over and over again. First he'd waited for Lem to arrive. Then he'd leisurely shown Lem around No.2, arguing against it being an "open and shut" case, debating over every clue. Finally he'd insisted on taking a statement from Nelson before they moved.

Why?

Was it really because he had doubts – or did it go deeper?

Was it, perhaps, because at some level his brain simply couldn't bring itself to accept ever the possibility that a major criminal could be a policeman's son?

Christ, thought Gideon. If that was so, he was getting so unbalanced that *he* was near to being clean off his rocker. Scott-Marle had not only been right to take him off the Fletchwood case, he should have gone further – suspended him from duty, sent him straight out to grass . . .

Without even a final glance at Nelson, he stormed out of the drawing-room into the hall, with Lemaitre behind him.

"Right, Lem," he said briskly. "You know what to do. You've even got the address to go to. Ring me if the boy isn't there. We'll have to get a murder hunt underway in that case. Probably a national one. He could be almost anywhere by now, thanks to – "

He nearly said "thanks to me", but couldn't quite get the admission out.

"Okay," said Lemaitre, equally briskly. "I'm on my way."

He wasn't quite so brisk as he walked to the front door. Gideon realised why. He was about to undertake the most unenviable task of his career: telling a hardworking honest cop that his son wasn't just a lout, but a twisted killer – and that his best friend had the clearest evidence to shop him.

Ordinarily, Gideon would have caught Lem's arm, wished him good luck. But there was nothing ordinary about the way Gideon felt tonight.

"Get moving, man, can't you, for God's sake!" he growled.

Lemaitre jumped like a startled rabbit, and almost scurried out of the door.

A moment later, he was down by the gate, and Gideon could hear him shouting to his men, and a door slam as he got into a car.

That was when the sudden, uncontrollable impulse came. He couldn't leave it to Lemaitre to confront Benton: couldn't delegate the most detestable job of his, or any copper's career. For some reason, he knew he had to be there when a policeman was brought face to face with the unfaceable truth about his son.

Why, Gideon didn't know, and didn't want to know. He just suddenly found himself hurling his huge bulk at top speed down the path, and shouting in a strange, hoarse voice he hardly recognised: "Hold everything! Wait for me!"

* * *

PC Benton had not had a very good day.

In fact, during the whole of his thirty years as a constable, he had never experienced one like it. From the moment that he had opened the front door to his wife Grace, and had simultaneously heard Red slipping out of the back one, he had found himself sucked into a maelstrom of conflicting emotions and divided loyalties: a situation for which nothing in his law-abiding – and law-enforcing – life had prepared him.

The plain facts were inescapable. Red had admitted to being the Oxfam Robin Hood. True, he had denied doing the Riddell job, but he had owned up to the rest, which was bad enough – and what made it worse, he had then bolted. Scarpered. Made a getaway.

What he, Benton, should have done about it was obvious. He first of all should have taken Grace into the dining-room, given her a strong cup of tea and explained the whole situation. Then he should have rung up the police station and reported his son. To have behaved in any other way was, quite simply, to have become a bent policeman, and given the lie to his whole career.

And yet he *had* behaved in another way for hour after hour.

He had not told Grace anything, except that he and Red had had a bit of a row. And here it was, half past midnight, and he had *still* not brought himself to make that call to the station.

Grace had turned in early. She hadn't been worried in the slightest about Red not coming home for supper. "If we had a pound for every time he stopped out all night, we'd be ruddy millionaires," she'd said, grinning all over her fat face. "And don't worry about that row, love. At least you got him moving off that settee. That's a miracle in itself, these days . . . "

She had gone to sleep almost as soon as she had got to bed – but Benton knew there was no prospect of sleep for him. He'd only got as far as taking his shirt off, so he quickly slipped it on again and started pacing restlessly around the house, drinking endless cups of coffee. His thoughts were whirling round and round: his world was turning with them, and there was nothing to do but pace and pace until he was simply too weary to think any more.

He had almost reached that point when he heard a car pull up outside. Thinking it might be his errant son returning, he rushed towards the front door and gasped when he opened it, and saw who it was on the doorstep.

Chief Detective Superintendent Lemaitre . . . Two constables he didn't know (which meant, of course, that they were from nowhere near Fletchwood) . . . – and – God Almighty, Gideon himself!

Benton had never been more shaken in his life, but all those years of constabulary duty did not vanish in a flash, and somehow – he never knew how – he remained calm, and drew himself stiffly to attention. "G-good evening, sir. Er – that is – *sirs*."

Lemaitre was equally stiff and formal.

"Evening, Benton. Sorry to disturb you like this, but we'd like a word with your son." Benton turned white, but still remained calm.

"My son? I'm afraid he's not – not here at the moment."

Lemaitre swallowed hard, and said: "Normally, Bert, I'd be happy to leave it at that. But he's wanted for questioning – I'm sorry to say about a murder – and I've got to ask you to let me look round and see for ourselves that – "

This was too much for Gideon. All his sympathies were with this legendary police stalwart, whose face had turned from white to grey at the mention of murder, and he wasn't going to stand by and watch a formal police search conducted round Benton's house.

"No, no, that isn't necessary," he barked. "Whatever the circumstances Constable Benton's word is good enough for me. If he says Red is not here – "

"He really isn't," Benton finished hoarsely, "but you're very welcome to come in."

He stood, or rather, almost fell back from the door and Gideon and Lemaitre entered the tiny, neat, flawlessly hoovered hall. Lemaitre signalled to his men to stay outside. They both looked very relieved to do so.

Once they were in the equally neat living-room (Grace had tidied the place up since that morning), Lemaitre pulled no punches. A policeman talking to a policeman, he told Benton everything that had happened – including Horace Nelson's identification of his son as the man who had shot his daughter.

"And," he finished bluntly, "from what I gather it wasn't too much of a surprise to you to hear that your son's the Oxfam Robin Hood, is that correct?"

Benton said nothing but slumped down in a corner of

the settee – the very spot where his son had been lying that very morning.

There was a long, long pause. Normally Gideon would have spent it staring hard at Benton's face. To try and judge what the constable was really thinking. But in fact, he could hardly bring himself to glance in Benton's direction. He was all too painfully aware what the poor man was going through.

Suddenly to Gideon's and Lemaitre's surprise, Bertie Benton showed why he was the police die-hard. Finding some deep hidden reserve of strength, he suddenly stood up from the sofa, calm and even smiling.

"Whatever my son has or has not done," he said, "I can tell you this. He's no ruddy murderer. He's not been within half a mile of a gun in his life, to the best of my knowledge. So he couldn't have killed Don Mitchell. And if Horace says he saw him shooting down his Suzy in cold blood, then he was either raving drunk at the time – or he's the biggest liar in the Universe! Knowing Horace, it was probably the former."

It was Lemaitre, for once, who was reduced to silence. He couldn't deny that Benton had scored a strong point. Particularly since, rather unkindly, he hadn't mentioned to Bertie the condition Nelson had been in when the shooting had occurred.

Gideon secretly felt like cheering. Aloud he said: "Look Benton, no one's claiming there's a watertight case against your son. But it's obvious that we need to talk to him – and fast. If by any chance you can give us an idea where we can find him – "

Benton shook his head. "I'm sorry, sir, but I'm afraid I can't help you there at all," he said, trying – but just failing – to look Gideon in the eye.

So he *does* know where his son is, Gideon thought, and wondered if he could bring himself to try and force it out of him. Every human instinct told him that he ought to leave him in peace; every police one told him precisely the opposite. He was in an agony of indecision when, suddenly, there was an interruption.

Grace Benton arrived on the scene. She had obviously woken up and heard voices, and realising that she and

Bertie had visitors felt that it was her duty to put in an appearance as "lady of the house". She entered the room still blinking and struggling to finish doing up a vast pink kimono which made her look fatter and jollier than ever.

Her eyes widened as she realised just who it was that had called on them.

"Commander Gideon! Mr Lemaitre! This *is* an honour, I'm sure. Wouldn't any of you like a sherry?"

She opened a cupboard and produced a bottle of Harvey's Bristol Cream and a tray of glasses. She was obviously genuinely surprised and delighted to see them, a good policeman's wife awed at the thought of such high-ups condescending to visit a humble PC's house. Either she was a brilliant actress or she hadn't the slightest idea why they had called, which could only mean one thing. Benton hadn't confided in her anything that he had suspected about his son.

Not that anyone would blame him for that, Gideon thought. After all, he had kept Kate completely in the dark about Matthew . . . Grace was passing round the sherries now. Gideon accepted one gratefully. Lemaitre declined, with a "never-drink-while-I'm-on-duty" look.

"No, thank you, ma'am, we're not stopping. Just called in to have a word with your son, but I gather from Bertie here that he's not at home. We'd be very grateful if you could give us some idea where we might find him."

Grace burst out laughing.

"Oh, you'll have to ask Bertie that. He's the only one who knows where Red gets to when he's in one of his sulky 'stop-out' moods," she said, confirming Gideon's feeling that Bertie had a shrewd idea where his son might be.

Bertie, in fact, suddenly looked daggers at his wife. She glanced up at him, startled – and it was then that the terrible moment came.

It began with a tiny frown appearing in Grace's forehead.

"Red's – not in any trouble, is he?"

The frown did not remain tiny for long. Grace looked round at the room – from the glaring Bertie to the grim-faced Gideon, and to the awkward Lemaitre. Suddenly it dawned on her that Red was in no ordinary trouble. With the head of the C.I.D. and a leading Chief Detective

Superintendent involved, it had to be something very big indeed.

Her face did not fall. It completely collapsed, for all the world like a pricked balloon. Her cheeks turned scarlet. Tears filled her eyes. Her triple chin quivered like a three-tiered raspberry jelly as she asked loudly: "You think he's killed someone? *Don't you*?"

She addressed the question to Lemaitre who, embarrassed, made a big mistake. He looked downwards, in the direction of his own shoes. She followed his eyes – and found herself staring at the strange red stain at the bottom of his whiter-than-white trousers. It was as though some instinct told her it was blood: blood from the man her son was suspected of killing.

That was when she lost all control, and started sobbing, shaking and screaming – scream after scream that seemed to rock the eaves and shake the house.

They certainly rocked Gideon. Poor woman, he thought, to be suddenly plunged in the deep end like this, one moment completely unaware that anything was wrong, the next –

He had a horrific vision of the same thing happening to Kate. He had left her wide-open to it. She wouldn't lose control, of course – he had hardly ever known her do that, whatever the circumstances – but with her weak heart –

Benton had crossed the room to Grace, and was putting an arm round her.

"Now then, now then, it's not as bad as all that," he told her, like the classic constable confronting a frightened child – and then he calmly led her up the stairs to the bedroom. The screams stopped; the sounds of sobbing continued for a few moments, but then suddenly everything went quiet.

Benton returned to the living-room. His wife was a bit prone to attacks like that, he explained calmly. The doctor had given him some pills to keep in hand, for these emergencies. She had taken those, and was now much calmer, and almost asleep.

"I told her," he added, with a touch of his earlier defiance, "that Red was no murderer, and that we'd prove it – bloody quick."

Gideon moved forward, and touched Bertie's arm reassuringly. "Please God we do, Bertie," he said gently, deliberately using the Christian name. "Please God we do."

Lemaitre remained very much the Chief Detective Superintendent.

"The boy's only making it harder for himself, though, going on the run," he pointed out. "The sooner we can get hold of him, the sooner we can get some answers from him that might clear him. Is it true what Grace said – you know where he might have gone?"

Bertie's expression had softened at Gideon's words – but at Lemaitre's, all the barriers came up again. He folded his arms, and said implacably:

"I've already told you, sir, I'm afraid I can't help there at all."

Lemaitre shrugged slightly – and gave Gideon a look which said, as plainly as though he had spoken the words aloud: "Passed to you, Gee Gee."

So that settled it, thought Gideon grimly. Lem was trusting in him to do everything in his power to make Bertie tell where his son was hiding, and, of course, Lem was right to do so. It was all very well for him to sympathise with Benton, but what about Suzy, left lying almost dead in the road, her young life ebbing away before his eyes, just because she had dared to challenge this maniac killer? What about Mitchell, blasted by a bullet in the forehead? As long as there was the slightest possibility that Red was responsible for all that, then bringing him to book *had* to take precedence over every other consideration, no matter what the heartbreak involved.

Gideon took a deep breath, and stared long and hard at Benton, until the police constable's eyes were forced to meet his. He could sense the struggle going on inside the man, and was increasingly aware how close it was to the struggle inside *him*. He had to fight that, though; had to concentrate on the hateful job in hand.

Drawing himself up to his full height, and suddenly seeming to tower over Benton, he began quietly, and very deliberately: "Let's face it, Bertie, you and I are two of a kind. For far more years than we care – or dare – to remember, we have been, in that quaint old phrase, servants of the Law. We've been that for so long that it's in our bones and in our blood. The Law is a hard mistress, but she is also a just one – we'd stake our lives on that. In a sense, we *have* staked them on it – and it's too late for either of us to break that now. Do you understand what I'm saying?"

His tone was no longer quiet and deliberate. His voice had risen steadily, until suddenly it was the full, Gideon roar.

"If not, I'll spell it out for you. If you think you know where we might find Red, you have got to tell us. For everybody's sake including his own, if he's innocent – as he well may be. Apart from that, it's your duty as a police officer to tell us – your plain and simple duty, which you've never shirked in all those years, and aren't going to start now. *Are* you?"

For just one second longer, Benton hesitated – but then he gave way. Gideon's voice, when raised to full pitch, had the power to reverberate round every corner of any room in which he was speaking. It sounded to Bertie as though it was coming, not from a single throat, but from all directions, almost as though it was the voice of God. And it was the voice of the man who had been a sort of God – or, at any rate, his idol – since his earliest years in the force. It cut through all his doubts, and suddenly there was only one course that he could take.

"I – I dunno where Red is for sure, sir," he stuttered. "But Dr Gharad runs a sort of hostel for drunks and drug addicts and such, in an attic above his clinic. It's not official, and not thought to be known to the police. Young people in trouble around Fletchwood always head for there – and I also know that Red's often used it as a meeting place for him and his rabble-rousing mates. That's where I'd go if I were looking for him."

"Then that's where we'll go, Bertie," said Gideon, his voice suddenly soft again. "And don't worry about whether you've done the right thing. You can take it from me you *have*."

He managed to infuse the words with such certainty that Bertie visibly brightened. He little dreamed what dark *un*certainty lay behind them. The truth was that rarely, if ever, had Gideon felt less sure about the rights and wrongs of anything.

Could he honestly say that he would have been as keen on duty if he had been in Benton's place, Kate in Grace Benton's and Matthew in Red's?

Unable to answer the question, but equally unable to stop it haunting him, he turned, most shamefacedly, away from Benton and hurried after Lemaitre out to the police car.

Once they had driven off, Lemaitre dropped his former air, and became confidential.

"Thank God you came along. Nobody else in the world could have talked poor old Benton into spilling the beans so fast. Now we've a real chance of nabbing his bloody murdering son."

They arrived outside Dr Gharad's clinic before Gideon could reply.

10 Vale of Anger

The clinic turned out to be part of Dr Gharad's private house. It was situated at the end of a long, dingy terrace which seemed half derelict; window after window in it was boarded-up, and most of the front gardens had become weed-strewn rubbish tips, with rusty cans and broken bottles gleaming sombrely in the light from the radiating blue lamp above the police car. The doctor's house looked in almost as bad a shape as the rest of the row, except that none of its windows were boarded-up, and the front garden was unlittered. It was as though the inhabitants of the area had too much respect for Dr Gharad to chuck refuse away there.

Although it was now nearly one o'clock in the morning, the street was far from being deserted – ominously far from it in Gideon's opinion. A crowd of twelve or thirteen youths were standing talking on the pavement opposite the doctor's front gate. When the police car pulled up, they did not shuffle away. Instead, they stopped talking, and stood watching. One of them – a Rastafarian with white teeth glistening above a jet-black beard – deliberately kicked at a can which was lying on the pavement near his feet. It rolled into a gutter with a deafening clang. One of the group laughed. None of the others did. They just continued staring at the police car, their look suggesting that at any moment knives would appear.

"Ignorant bastards!" said Lemaitre to Gideon as they alighted from the car, followed by the two policemen. He added, "The more I see of this dirty neighbourhood, the surer I am that you're right about it being a powder-keg, Gee Gee. There were guys like these at every street corner when I was driving through here an hour and a half ago – and I reckon they are all still there. Maybe it's just the heat that's causing it – but whatever it is, I've got the feeling that the least little thing could start big trouble tonight. And – "

He broke off there, but Gideon could read the rest of his thoughts easily enough.

If Rod – or Red – Benton was really a local hero, driving him off to the station could count as very much more than a little thing . . .

"We've got to go with it, though, haven't we?" Lemaitre said. "The day we lay off chasing killers because of good community relations is the day yours truly hands in his cards. And it's my bet that you'd be right behind me in the resignation queue."

"You're wrong there," grunted Gideon. "I'd be ahead of you."

Lemaitre gave him the biggest grin that his thin, spider-like features would allow. Then, signalling to his men to follow, he stepped forward towards the doctor's house. Gideon followed.

"Have any of you got guns?" he asked.

It was a stupid question, he realised the moment he'd asked it. Guns were only issued now after a personal order had been made from Scott-Marle himself – and what opportunity had he had to organise that?

Whatever Lem lacked, though, it wasn't guts.

"Not to worry, Gee Gee. I'm the fastest ducker in the business. Being brought up round the Old Kent Road took care of that," he said cheerfully – and suddenly found he had to substantiate his claim straight away. A can came flying by thrown from the direction of the youths across the street.

He caught it haughtily and threw it back, hitting the Rastafarian on the shoulder.

Some choice swear words made the scene bluer than the police lamp – and by far the worst of them were Lemaitre's.

Then the cockney recovered his temper – and his style. Behaving once again like a stage comedian, he shouted across the road, quite genially: "Sorry, lads, but I must love you and leave you now. I've got work to do!"

And the next moment, he was marching up the path to Dr Gharad's front door with his men behind him, and a grudgingly admiring Gideon bringing up the rear. This was not the way he would have handled the situation, but at least no more cans were being thrown, and there actually seemed a shade less tension in the air. Some of the boys were even laughing. Perhaps what Fletchwood Vale needed was more of the Old Kent Road . . .

Gharad's front door was at the end of a small porch, in which a dim electric bulb was deliberately left on all night. By its light, it was just possible to read a white-painted notice-board giving Dr Gharad's name – RAVI GHARAD, MD – Bombay – and his surgery hours. At the bottom it had a simple dramatic line:

"NEVER CLOSED TO ANYONE IN URGENT NEED"

Gideon could not help being impressed. This over-worked doctor, running a dingy clinic in the heart of one of the toughest trouble-spots in London, was providing what amounted to a twenty-four-hour emergency service. Only the casualty departments of giant hospitals normally supplied that these days – and yet there was no other doctor's name on the board. It looked as though the remarkable Gharad was doing it all on his own, fighting a one-man battle against disease, drugs, deprivation – *and* providing a shelter for anyone who was in trouble, with no questions asked. It wasn't surprising that he was respected, almost revered, around Fletchwood Vale.

The little doctor came to the door almost immediately after Lemaitre pressed the bell push, suggesting that he hadn't yet been to bed. He started when he recognised them both and, perhaps because he was dead tired, he greeted them with scarcely concealed impatience. His black eyes flashed fire first at Gideon, then at Lemaitre.

"Good evening. What can I do for our illustrious police force tonight?" he asked sarcastically. "I must ask you to keep it short, whatever your business is. I am extremely anxious to get to bed, having been out half the evening. Three urgent calls in the last sixty minutes; all cases of mugging, one of them extremely serious. No doubt you will be getting reports of them at the station."

"No doubt we will," said Lemaitre hurriedly. "*If* you remember to send them in. But I'm not here to pick a quarrel with you, Doctor."

Gharad's manner turned icy. "I am glad to hear it,

Superintendent. I can assure you, it is not one you could possibly win."

He turned suddenly to Gideon. "The lamentable failure of the police to take action against those monsters in the Heights is a national disgrace. You can't blame the people in the Vale if *they* take action – soon. *Very* soon . . . "

Gideon felt those angry black eyes boring into him. It was uncanny – almost as though the little doctor knew everything that was going on in his mind; had tried him and found him wanting.

Lemaitre hurriedly interrupted.

"Never mind about all that, Doc. What we've come about is something quite different. We have reason to believe you've got a certain young man here – Rod or 'Red' Benton – "

The doctor's eyes narrowed. He made no reply.

Lem got tougher.

"If you're hiding him in that unofficial clinic of yours, you ought to know that you're probably sheltering a dangerous maniac. We want to question him about a double shooting up on the Heights – resulting in the death of Don Mitchell and the near-death of a young sixteen-year-old girl. So stand back, please – unless you're in the business of harbouring murderers, as well as drug-addicts and . . . "

Dr Gharad looked as though he could hardly believe his ears.

"Red Benton – a murderer? Really, Superintendent, that's preposterous. He's a wild boy, some would say a troublemaker, but I have had many a long talk with him, and I know no one feels more passionately for the poor, the hungry, the world's starving . . . "

At that moment, both Gideon and Lemaitre heard faint sounds – a series of odd creaks and scuffles – coming from somewhere at the rear of the house. The same thought struck them simultaneously. Gharad's first instinct, as a sort of father-figure to the neighbourhood, would be to protect his own. He could deliberately be keeping them talking to give Red a chance to slip out by some back way.

Lemaitre swung round to the two men behind him.

"Quick, lads, get running!" he barked, pointing to a

patio leading round to the clinic's rear. The next second, he had pushed roughly past the doctor, and was running across the hall and up a flight of stairs in the direction of the surgery.

Gideon, left alone on the doorstep, was about to follow Lemaitre when suddenly there was a resounding thud followed by shouts. Then the two constables returned from the patio, dragging a young man with them.

He'd just climbed out of the attic window at the back, they told Gideon, and had been shinning down a drain-pipe when Lemaitre's head had popped out of the window above him. He'd been so startled at the sight that he'd let go – and had fallen right on to the constables arriving beneath.

It was a comically ignominious end, thought Gideon, to the exploits of the famous Oxfam Robin Hood. But then he remembered about Suzy Nelson and Mitchell, and there no longer seemed to be a vestige of comedy in the situation at all. He peered hard at the youth as the constables dragged him on to the dimly-lit porch and then through the front door into the slightly more brightly-lit hall. He saw a mass of tousled hair, a youthful, freckled face, eyes that were sullen and resentful – like a spoilt boy's – but no trace of viciousness or madness.

"I suppose I should say that's a fair cop," Red told the world at large. "But since it is my old man that split on me, I reckon it's a bloody unfair one!"

Dr Gharad suddenly found his voice. "Don't blame your father or anyone else, you stupid boy. When I heard you'd committed murder, I was about to split on you, as you call it, myself!"

Red Benton's eyes stopped being resentful. They stared – with a blank astonishment.

"Murder? Who am I supposed to have murdered, for f---'s sake?"

Lemaitre appeared at that moment, panting from his run down the stairs, and heard the question.

"Who do you think?" he shouted. "Don Mitchell, for a start. And – unless you're bloody lucky – poor young Suzy Nelson, who's fighting for her life in Fletchwood Hospital. Have you frisked him?" he asked the constables.

One of them nodded.

"Yes sir – no gun on him at all."

"Of course there isn't," Benton shouted. "I've never had a gun – or used one in my life."

"Just a sweet innocent babe in arms, aren't you?" said Lemaitre, with a sneer. "I suppose you're going to tell me that for the past twelve hours, you've been lying here tucked up in bed, being read Jemima Puddleduck stories by the good Dr Gharad."

"The last twelve hours? I can do better than that, copper. I've been here the whole day. Ever since bloody lunchtime. Just went out once, around six o'clock, for beer and sandwiches down at The Lazy Fox – "

Lemaitre became even more sarcastic.

"So you've been skulking here since lunch? Why? Afraid you'd get sunstroke in all this heat or something? Pull the other leg, son, it's got bells on it. And it'll start ringing like Big Ben before I believe a word of all this rubbish."

Red's cockiness abruptly evaporated. He was suddenly red-faced and not far from sobbing, Grace Benton's, rather than Bertie's son.

An odd, half-stuttered answer, was all he could manage.

"From my – my old man," he said. "He's got a bee in his bonnet that I'm – I'm the Oxfam Robin Hood. Said he'd got watertight evidence against me. I thought I'd lie low until I was sure he hadn't reported me. Don't you see? If he hadn't, I was in the clear. If he *had*, half the bleeding men in the Met would be after me. It's a bastard, having a copper for a father."

For some reason, perhaps coincidence, perhaps some obscure instinct, he addressed those words directly at Gideon. Never knowing how he succeeded in keeping his voice steady, Gideon growled back:

"I shouldn't think it'd be much fun for a copper having a criminal for a son."

That threw Red into even more of a panic.

"Who said I was a bleeding criminal? I didn't. I haven't admitted anything. I'm demanding to see a lawyer – "

"If you aren't a criminal," said Gideon, "then where does all this watertight evidence that you're the Oxfam Robin Hood come from?"

"It isn't watertight. It's – what's the word? – circumsical."

"Circumstantial, you mean," said Gideon – but Red was hardly listening.

"Whatever. One thing, though, I'd swear on a stack of Bibles a mile high. The real Oxfam Robin Hood has nothing to do with this sick weirdo who's been muscling in on his act. I swear, the man who tortured that Superintendent's wife – Mrs Riddell. Christ, I felt for her. I can imagine what could have happened if he'd tried a filthy stunt like that on my Mum. And – and those shots. How can anyone imagine that *I'd* been involved?"

Suddenly he was close to hysteria. "Did – did someone say Suzy Nelson had been shot? Why should I have done that? I know Suzy. Went to school with her. I know her father too – old Horace Nelson's my Dad's best mate – "

Lemaitre had heard enough of all this.

"Sorry to break up the friend-of-all-the-neighbourhood act," he said harshly, "but you might be interested to know, laddie, that it was Horace Nelson himself who identified you as the man who shot his daughter. And you did it even though she stepped in your path, and was actually calling out to you 'Don't be silly, Red.' "

That shook Benton more than anything else he had been told.

He was reduced once again to staring blankly, struggling to take it all in.

"Horace – said – that I – "

Gideon found himself feeling sorry for him. More important, he was very nearly convinced that the boy's story was true. He looked a truculent, turbulent youth, hysterically emotional one moment, tough and cool the next. It was quite possible to imagine him setting out to be a hero, as legendary a figure as his father, and carrying out one reckless burglary after another as the Oxfam Robin Hood. After all, he had proved himself extremely adept at sliding down drain-pipes that very night. It was even possible to believe that he had been that hitherto unknown criminal species: a genuinely quixotic thief. If he had kept a tenth of his takings as the Oxfam Robin Hood, he would hardly have any need to skulk in a shabby clinic barely half a mile from his own front door. He would have been in a position to take a suite at a West End hotel and book a seat on the next flight to Rio de Janeiro . . .

At the same time, it *was* difficult to picture him coolly shooting Don Mitchell through the forehead, or blasting Suzy Nelson. This wasn't only because of Bertie Benton's stark denials that his son could be a murderer. Gideon had met more than his share of murdering psychopaths in his time, and they had all had a certain maniac look, a streak of coldness in their make-up, which he could not see in Red Benton. Moreover, there was independent evidence that the person who had murdered Mitchell was not the real Oxfam Robin Hood, but an imitator: an imitator who had demonstrably been far more interested in spraying the Oxfam Robin Hood trademark on the wall than in committing a theft! Surely that showed all the signs of a clumsy attempt to frame.

One big question remained, though.

Why in God's name should anyone want to get in on the Oxfam Robin Hood act, first terrorising poor Vi Riddell and then committing tonight's bloody and motiveless atrocities in his name? Gideon's imagination couldn't begin to find answers.

Lemaitre's thoughts obviously hadn't been travelling remotely along the same lines. He still imagined himself dealing with a dangerous young killer who was also a pathetically inept liar.

"So don't try and come it with me any more laddie," he was saying sharply. "You're in it up to your dirty little neck, and there's only one place you're going to – and that's right down to the station. I'm booking you for Mitchell's murder – and for maliciously wounding Suzy Nelson too."

That was all too typical of the impulsive Lemaitre thought Gideon, deciding not just to pull in the boy for questioning but to go straight for an arrest. He did not have one of the best conviction rates from his arrests in the C.I.D. although arrest was probably justified on this occasion, on the Oxfam Robin Hood case if not on the grounds of murder.

Red was nearly hysterical again, and struggling wildly to

escape from the policeman holding him. The inevitable happened: handcuffs were brought out and snapped on him. His eyes filled with tears as he stared down at them – tears of frustrated disbelief.

"But this is crazy!" he blurted out. "I told you – I've been here in this place since lunchtime. Dr Gharad, you can swear to that – "

Gharad seemed about to speak, but hesitated. His black eyes for once were not filled with fury. They registered a helpless uncertainty and loss.

"The Doc's already told us, he's been out half the night on urgent calls," Lem answered, with heartless relish.

"But there've been other patients up there with me in the attic. *They'll* testify – "

"Will they hell, laddie!" said Lem. "I took a gander at them when I was upstairs just now. Blundered in by accident. Three junkies, doped or sedated or something and all out to the world. If you think *their* evidence is going to be worth half a can of baked beans, you're even barmier than you look!" Contemptuously laughing his answer, he turned to the men holding him. "I've no more time to waste, even if he has. Let's get him into the car!"

While Gideon and Lemaitre followed watching, the boy was dragged out through the front door, across the path, down the tiny front garden, and on to the pavement to the waiting police car.

As they recognised their local hero, a mixed sound – half an angry roar, half a cheer – came from the gang of youths on the opposite pavement.

Red Benton looked up – and at the sight of an audience, an extraordinary change came over him. Suddenly it was clear why he had such a reputation as a troublemaker and rabble-rouser. He was suddenly no longer a sobbing boy, but a man born to control mobs.

He startled his captors by stopping struggling, and standing for a moment, completely still. Before they could recover their balance, he threw back his head and yelled to his supporters: "Stop this! They're arresting *me* – for murder!"

He made it sound the most preposterous absurdity in history. Then, suddenly, his voice rose to a high frenetic pitch, reminding Gideon of all the Hyde Park orators he had heard rolled into one.

"And it's my guess they're acting under orders from the real murderers around here – the bloody drugs kings and villains in the Heights! The rich bastards who kick us in the balls and then expect us to polish their bloody furniture – "

That was as far as he got before the constables dragged him into the car. But that was as far as he needed to get, thought Gideon grimly. That single word "Heights" transformed the youths on the opposite pavement from a lounging mob into an attacking force.

Suddenly they weren't on the opposite pavement any longer. They were everywhere in the street, collecting cans, bottles, bricks, anything and everything that could be thrown . . .

Lemaitre was just climbing into the back of the car when the first bottle came. For once he didn't duck fast enough and it landed somewhere on the side of his head.

He gasped, grimaced and half-fell inside – but Gideon knew he was all right, from the string of swear words that came flowing back through the window.

One of the two constables had opened the front door of the car, and was on the point of climbing into the driver's seat. A brick landed in the small of his back. He stopped and spun round almost as though he'd been shot.

"*Get in*, now!" roared Gideon. "For God's sake, *get in*!"

The constable pulled himself together and somehow managed to stumble inside the car. Gideon was now the only one outside the car, his tall massive frame an easy target for any missile; and yet he did not hurry to climb in.

He glanced around him, coolly, almost as though he was daring the mob to attack.

"I'd just like to tell you people this," he roared, his deep, powerful voice in striking contrast to the high-pitched tones of their young leader. "We aren't under orders from anybody in the Heights, or in the bloody depths for that matter. If Red Benton here, turns out to be innocent – and you may be surprised to know that I hope and pray he will – he has nothing to fear. And finally, if there's a drugs king in Fletchwood I give you my word that we'll get him –

whoever he is, wherever he lives, and – ", his voice hardened slightly as he finished – "whatever the cost."

Perhaps because of his passionate sincerity, or perhaps because of the shock of being faced by so fearless an adversary – the mob held off long enough for Gideon to slip into the car behind the driver, and close the door hard behind him.

But as the car set off the barrage of missiles began again, bricks and bottles pounding at the toughened-glass windows, until they felt like astronauts passing through a storm of meteors. The driver, still grimacing from his battered back, had to swerve wildly to avoid the bricks and bottles littering his path.

In the back seat, Lem was still swearing continuously, which meant that his head was still hurting. Red Benton, sitting between him and the remaining constable, was staring down dolefully at his handcuffs.

Within seconds, they moved clear of the street – but not of the atmosphere of anger and menace, which seemed to be pervading the whole of Fletchwood Vale. During the three-minute drive to the police station, they seemed continuously to be passing groups of yobbos. Some of them shook their fists. Some spat. Most glared – with looks that said, "Just you wait, pigs, just you wait!"

For weeks, Gideon had had a sense that the people of Fletchwood Heights were living above a time-bomb – but now he had a feeling that was far more unnerving: a deep, growing conviction, becoming almost a certainty, that *it was timed to go off tonight.*

11 Gideon's Walk

The worst of it was, Gideon realised with a sickening sense of dread, that there was nothing more he could do to alert anyone to the mounting danger.

On a hot night like this, inner city areas all over London would be showing much the same signs of tension. Restless gangs prowling the streets, sporadic outbursts of bottle-throwing, even the odd knifing incident, were nothing out of the ordinary in these violent times.

Nobody at the Yard would think such things enough to call red alert, and he was hardly in a position to order one himself, since both he (and Alec, for that matter) had been specifically ordered off the Fletchwood case by Scott-Marle.

And yet unless a major emergency was signalled – unless hundreds of men were rushed in from all surrounding districts – there was nothing to stop the nightmare that had haunted him for weeks becoming terrifying reality. The anger around him would mount and mount until suddenly – perhaps spontaneously, perhaps in response to a pre-arranged plan – an army of louts would head for the Heights, which could so easily be cut off, laid siege to, or even burned to the ground, with a loss of life unheard of in London since the days of the Blitz.

True, nothing like this had happened before but couldn't they see that *London had never been like that before*, with whizz-kids earning hundreds of thousands a year deliberately choosing to live where they could flaunt their wealth in the faces of the very, very poor, and attempting to lord it over them as well?

Here there was of course a deadly extra aggravation: the widely-held belief that the problems riddling the area were caused by someone living in the Heights. And it was clear now *why* it was so widely held – within the past half-hour both Gharad and Red Benton had been propagating it – the voice of the area's wildest rebel and its revered doctor combining to urge action against "the masters on the Heights".

The master on the –

Gideon tensed, a wave of fear sweeping over him. It was close and clammy in the crowded car, but suddenly the air seemed to be freezing.

The latest reports had said that most people around Fletchwood believed they had identified the master – and that Matthew was the drugs king. If that was so then Matthew's house would be the number one target for the besieging mobs.

He had a nightmare vision of Kate, Matthew, Pamela and the children being at the heart of the holocaust, the focal point of the bloodbath, and he came suddenly as close to panic as he had ever been in his career.

What in God's name did he think he was playing at? It wasn't his usual policy to stand by watching while experienced officers like Lemaitre went about their business. He had allowed himself to be transfixed like a mesmerised rabbit by the whole sad saga of Bertie Benton and his son. He ought to be back in Malibu Rise, getting Kate home, warning Matthew – whatever he had or had not done – to get himself and his family the hell out of the Heights without a second's loss of time.

At that moment the car pulled up outside Fletchwood Police Station – and was immediately surrounded again, this time not by a mob of youths but by a crowd of journalists, including cameras from the BBC and ITV. Gideon was startled to see them! He had not authorised any news release – but then he realised that he didn't need to. Fergus Atkinson, a darling of the media if ever there was one, would have lost no time spreading the story of the murder – and the news that a top newspaper tycoon had been shot by the Oxfam Robin Hood, was, of course a sensation to beat all sensations from the Fleet Street point of view.

Red Benton brightened visibly at the sight of them and was obviously all set to make the speech of his life – but Lemaitre was too quick for him: "Sorry lad, but the only public appearance you're booked for is a nice little chat show with the magistrate tomorrow morning."

Whipping off his own white jacket he threw it over Benton's head and shoulders and a second later, with the help of a constable, he was expertly whisking the startled youth, hooded and handcuffed, through the crowd of newsmen. "Nothing new to tell you boys," he called out as he went, "except that as you can see, a young gentleman has been arrested and is very kindly agreeing to give us a hand with our inquiries."

The newsmen stood back and let Lemaitre and his party through. Then they spotted Gideon and they closed in as he stepped out of the car.

"Do you really think you've got him George – the Oxfam Robin Hood?"

They were obviously relishing an even more sensational headline – "C.I.D. CHIEF ARRESTS OXFAM ROBIN HOOD" – which would hardly be fair to Lemaitre.

"Who do you think I am, the ruddy Sheriff of Nottingham?" Gideon growled. "Chief Detective Superintendent Lemaitre is conducting his inquiries. I've gone along for the ride."

They didn't believe that, of course – they knew as well as he did that he never went along for rides – but as far as he was concerned, they would have to take it or leave it. Without another word, he led his constables through the crowd, and the next thing they knew, the doors of the station were being shut behind them.

In the entrance hall, Lemaitre was already embarking on the rigmarole of formally charging Benton. Under the hard bright strip lighting, he looked haggard and exhausted, and kept dabbing at his head with a blood-stained handkerchief. It couldn't be clearer that as far as he was concerned the case was swept up and he was heading as soon as possible for bed.

Gideon didn't stay to watch the scene. He went straight to the counter, and asked to use the telephone. After a minute of messing about with Directory Enquiries – the number was too secret to be found in the phone book – he was through to 1, Malibu Rise. Matthew himself answered the phone.

"Listen," Gideon said quickly. "Tell Kate I'm sorry I have been away for so long, but I'll be back in around five minutes. Before I arrive, I want you to have the whole family dressed and ready to leave. You're all of you spending the night with Kate and me."

"Wh-what?"

Matthew, for once, sounded totally taken aback. Kate, who had been sitting behind him suddenly came on the line.

"George, I heard all that. Look. What on earth are you talking about? We can't put Matthew and everyone up – not at this short notice. The rooms aren't ready – we haven't enough sheets – we . . . "

"Never mind about all that – this is an emergency," Gideon told her. "There's trouble building up here – really big trouble, and Fletchwood Heights is no place to be in tonight."

Kate didn't argue any longer.

"Right, love," she said, very calmly. Then, not quite so calmly, she added: "Get here soon, won't you?"

"Quick as a flash," Gideon promised, and put down the phone – to find the desk-sergeant and a constable both looking at him in blank astonishment.

"Excuse me, sir – but did you say trouble was building up? Here in Fletchwood?" the sergeant asked.

Half the men in the entrance hall were now staring at him – with equal amazement.

"We've had special patrols covering the area all night," a puzzled inspector said, "keeping in constant touch by radio. But no one reported anything out of the ordinary, sir. Could you tell us what you mean?"

Very much at a loss – for the men knew Fletchwood Vale far more intimately than he did, and were far more familiar than he was with its moods – Gideon tried to spell out the reasons for his fear, the anger in the air, the youths at street corners . . .

He was met with weary shrugs and sighs.

"These yobbo groups are around most nights when it's hot like this, Sir," the sergeant said. "They're mostly boys on the dole, with no jobs to get up and go to in the mornings. So they kip down during the day and spend the night on the prowl with their mates. It's unnerving when you first come across it but we get used to that sort of thing round here. I hear you had cans and bottles thrown at your car, Sir. I'm afraid that's pretty common around here too."

"If you'd radioed," the inspector added, "we'd have sent a police car to the spot, of course, sir – though the yobbos would probably have scarpered before we got there."

Gideon had one last try.

"But surely there's an unusual tension in the air tonight? Can't you sense it? The hatred in the air – it's so thick you could almost cut it with a knife."

"It's always like that in Fletchwood Vale," the inspector told him. "And we get a double dose when the temperature rises. But believe me, sir, it's not anything special tonight."

Gideon felt dazed, confused. Could he really have been so mistaken? Was it possible that, under the extra stress of the most fraught of all days he had allowed a bee in his bonnet to develop into a killer swarm? It was possible, he supposed. But deep down inside him urgent alarm bells were still ringing – perhaps a little muffled now but far from switching off.

Just then something happened to deepen his sense of foreboding.

On the other side of the entrance hall, Red Benton was being made ready to be marched down to the cells. He had been deprived of the contents of his pockets and even his bootlaces, but decidedly not of his spirit. Between the sobbing and shouting, he was protesting his innocence in a series of fiery harangues. The best and most violent of them he addressed directly to Gideon.

"You're not only arresting me for a murder I didn't commit. You're letting the bloody maniac who *did* commit it go free – to kill again and again and *again* in the name of the Oxfam Robin Hood – "

"All right, laddie. We get the message. Now get him out of sight, for God's sake," commanded a weary Lem, and Red was dragged out still protesting, down to the cells.

The hall became mercifully silent for a moment after

he'd gone – but there was something embarrassing about the silence too. Then Gideon remembered. This was Bertie Benton's station: all those men were his colleagues and friends, anxious and unhappy about his son.

Gideon himself was silent – but for a rather different reason. Another alarm bell had started ringing in his head – this time telling him that what Red Benton claimed could very well be true. A "bloody maniac" was at large, he could kill again and again . . . perhaps tonight.

Whoever could be persuaded to do anything about that, though, it certainly wasn't Lemaitre. His old associate was striding to the door, quite obviously heading for home. His wounded head had stopped bleeding, but he still looked all-in. He managed, though, as usual a cockney grin. "Okay, gang, that's yer lot, as Jimmy used to say," he informed the room at large. "I will be back first thing to introduce young Benton to the beak. Reckon he'll keep till then. There's nothing else is there?" he asked anxiously with his eye on Gideon.

There was a lot else, in Gideon's private opinion. Red ought to be interrogated some more, his story checked and re-checked, and an intensive new hunt for the real killer started if there looked even the remotest chance of his being innocent.

But Lemaitre had done enough – and more than enough – for one night, and he himself had no time to organise eighty men.

So he just said: "No, Lem, good night. Look after that head – and you'd better put in some more ducking practice. They'd be ashamed of you in the Old Kent Road."

Lemaitre groaned, smiled – and left. And then what seemed like a miracle happened. Gideon was still staring at the space where Lem had been when – the big swing doors at the entrance opened again – and of all people, Chief Detective Superintendent Tom Riddell walked in.

Tom had heard a news report on the radio that the Oxfam Robin Hood had shot Don Mitchell at Fletchwood, and that an arrest was imminent. Imagining that he was still in charge of the inquiry he had come rushing round to see what was going on. He did not look so wild and sweaty now, but seemed highly incensed that no one had contacted him.

"I knew you'd given me a day's leave," he said. "But not to be notified of such a key development – it sounds almost as if you'd taken me off the case for good and all. Have you?"

He stared hard at Gideon, half resentful, half fearful.

Gideon decided to walk a diplomatic tightrope.

"If Lemaitre is right, there's no case left to be in charge of," he said. "But I'd like a second opinion on that, Tom – and you're the very man to give it. Your appearance at this moment is heaven-sent."

Riddell brightened. It was almost comic – yet at the same time almost tragic, thought Gideon, how quickly he could raise Tom's spirits by showing a touch of faith in him. The man, for heaven's sake, had one of the shrewdest brains and fastest minds in the whole of the C.I.D. He shouldn't be in such persistent need of confidence-boosts. Gideon gave him a rapid rundown on all that had happened, and Riddell seized the key point at once.

"So Benton's virtually admitted being the Oxfam Robin Hood but insists he's not the bastard who used Vi for target practice or shot Mitchell tonight. I reckon he could be telling the truth. I've been stalking the Hood for months, but never felt I was up against a maniac till now."

"Well, if he *is* telling the truth," said Gideon, "you know what that means, a very dangerous murderer is out on the loose – "

"And it'll be up to me to nab him – quick. Right. Leave it to me, George. Leave it *all* to me!"

Riddell went striding off down towards the cells, brisk, commanding, over-bright, as if determined to show that the real man in charge of the case had arrived to take over. It was a mood that would last as long as his nerves held out. Gideon could only hope that they would see him through the night.

"Tom," he called suddenly just before Riddell disappeared down the steps.

"Yes?"

"After you've seen Benton, you may feel you want to

visit Mitchell's house – 2, Malibu Rise. The scene-of-the-crime boys have probably just finished there."

"You're right. I may."

"Well – " Gideon hesitated, then went on. "If you take my advice you'll wait for the scene-of-the-crime reports instead. I have a hunch things may not be too friendly around the Heights tonight – although it's only a hunch, I must confess," he added lightly, sensing the amused looks of the men behind the counter, as he passed them as he made his way to the door.

Five minutes later, a police car had dropped him at 1, Malibu Rise, and he was astonished to see very much the same amused looks on the last faces he expected: those of Matthew and Julie.

They had made no attempt to pack, or get the children up and dressed.

"I've begged them to listen to you," said a despairing Kate. "But they say they can't see any reason to leave – and just won't go!"

"Sorry, Dad," Matthew drawled, "maybe it's the Gideon in me asserting itself – but I'm not going to be driven out of house and home by threats of marauding yobbos, and that's that. I've told you we've got a reinforced door here. We've also installed over fifteen thousand pounds worth of electronic security equipment – reinforced locks on all the windows, steel doors in the garage, even a special device that activates a light at the police station if a burglar gets in."

Gideon glared.

"Don Mitchell had all that, remember – but it didn't exactly help him tonight, did it?"

Matthew laughed.

"You're forgetting I came round that house with you. We assumed he'd gone to sleep leaving the French windows open, and all the electronics switched off. Well, that's just asking for it."

Gideon came close to losing his temper.

"And *you'll* be asking for it," he roared, "if you stay here in this house a moment longer tonight." Suddenly he found himself playing out the whole of his private nightmare – how the vulnerable Heights could be laid siege to, cut off, set blazing.

"And what good would all the electrical equipment in the world be to you then?" he shouted, and because he could not stop himself, added: "Especially since I've reason to believe that this very house will be the number one target for the mob."

He broke off there, abruptly, wondering what in God's name he could reply if Matthew picked him up on that.

WPC Craddock intentionally or otherwise, suddenly intervened.

"It's not for me to say, of course, Mr Goddard, but I believe you should listen to Commander Gideon. He's had more experience of crime and criminals than anyone else in London, and if he believes that you're in special danger here tonight – "

But Matthew simply laughed.

"Special danger?" he said. "*What* special danger? All this sounds like something from an old Tarzan movie – 'the natives are restless tonight'. Well, I've been living with these particular natives for some weeks now, and I can tell you all that they're pretty quiet this evening. Many is the night I've heard far more noises from the direction of the Vale. I reckon the sight of all those police cars up here has scared them off, and they're keeping well away. And whatever Dad says, if it comes to a fight, I'm sure we'd be more than a match for 'em. From all I've heard, they're not too bright, the inhabitants of Fletchwood Vale – and with all the drugs they're taking, poor sods, they're getting a lot less bright every day."

Gideon stared hard at his son. Would he dare to mention drugs so casually? It was the attitude he displayed that shocked his father. His heartlessness, his laughing contempt – Gideon had experienced them both earlier *that* night in Fergus Atkinson. If that was how the majority of people in the Heights regarded the inhabitants from a hundred yards below, then he could understand the latter's hatred and resentment all too well. In fact, it was all he could do not to show it: to keep his voice calm and friendly and be kind to Kate.

"Well, love, it looks as if there's nothing more we can do except say good night and go."

"We can say thanks for the lovely meal," said Kate. "And

what a really, marvellous evening we've had – until it was interrupted, of course . . . "

She looked a little tired, but her eyes were still sparkling as she eyed her long-lost son and brand new daughter-in-law, and kissed them both good night. She was obviously still not far from that seventh heaven, thought Gideon, in spite of all that had happened: and he was now deeper than ever in that "seventh hell", prey to a hundred hateful suspicions and what seemed like a thousand dark forebodings.

They all seemed to press in on him as he climbed behind the wheel of his Rover, and with a serenely smiling Kate beside him, drove out of Malibu Rise and down towards the emphatic darkness of the Vale.

They had rounded only a couple of corners by the time he had realised that he had misjudged Kate. Her smile vanished and she suddenly seemed as anxious as he was. Perhaps she had been anxious for longer, but hadn't let her feelings show, once she saw that nothing she could say or do would persuade Matthew and the others to leave. He was always forgetting that Kate didn't miss much, and now he realised that she hadn't missed anything.

"Are they really in such awful danger?" she asked in a quiet voice, adding sharply: "and why in the world should *Matthew*'s house be in the biggest danger of all?"

Before Gideon could think of a reply, she went on, still more shrewdly: "There's a lot I don't understand about this evening. You ate that dinner as if every bite would make you sick. Then Lem was in a queer mood – he kept looking at Matthew as though he suspected him of something. And that nanny woman, Pamela Carter. I kept getting the feeling that I'd seen her before somewhere – at some police do – and she certainly behaved as if she was somehow in league with you. What's going on, George? And whatever it is, if it's to do with Matthew – don't you think I have the right to know?"

* * *

For perhaps a minute, Gideon was tempted to fob Kate off with evasive answers. She had had a day of hectic excitement – could her heart stand the cold truth of horrific facts that he would have to tell her, once he started to be frank?

As against that, as he knew from long experience, once her suspicions were aroused Kate couldn't be fobbed off that easily, if at all.

There was another thing: he had a sudden vision of Grace Benton shrieking hysterically as she was confronted without warning with the truth about her son. Hadn't he decided that he would never leave Kate as unprepared as that?

There was nothing for it he realised: the whole truth had to come out now.

And so, step by step, as gently as possible, he told Kate everything that had happened, right from the moment when he had been shown that photograph of Matthew at the Yard conference that afternoon.

When he finished, there was a lengthy pause of such total silence that he glanced anxiously round at Kate, wondering if perhaps she'd fainted.

She hadn't. On the contrary, she was sitting as bolt upright as her seat-belt permitted, staring at him with an expression he couldn't make out at first because her face was in darkness. Then he turned into a main thoroughfare – Fletchwood Vale High Street – and bright street lighting lit up those grey-green eyes. He was startled to find when he looked in them that they were icy with anger and contempt.

"You mean, you've been playing at being a friendly, forgiving father while all the time Matthew's being spied on, and a police net closes round him?" she asked. "With – with a policewoman posing as a nanny reporting to you at one moment and having drinks with him the next? Sorry, love. But whatever Matthew has done or is doing, that's too cold and calculating for me."

Never before in his life had Gideon been so completely taken aback. Fletchwood Vale High Street seemed to swim before his eyes: the heat inside the car seemed to reach oven temperature, and so did his own feelings.

Before he knew it, he was suddenly roaring – and it was years since he had roared at Kate. "What the hell else could I have done? Written him a note saying 'Sorry, Son, you're a suspected drugs king. See you when you've cleared your name, and not before?' Is *that* what you'd call behaving like a loving father?"

Kate's eyes lost not one whit of their cold fury.

"That would be just a little more human," she told him. "But you'd never have done that, would you? It's against C.I.D. rules for a suspect to be told he's suspected. It might give him a chance to get away. And Commander Gideon always sticks to the rules, doesn't he – even if it means setting traps for his own son – and bringing me along as part of the bait!"

"Oh, for God's sake, love, pull yourself together and see sense," Gideon snapped. "We weren't setting any sort of traps for Matthew tonight. I've been taken off the case, so's Alec. We were just – "

"We were just going along to reassure him that he has nothing to worry about, and no one at the Yard suspects anything," said Kate. "That's worse than setting traps – that's playing cat and mouse with him!"

"Then what do you want me to do?" said Gideon. "I can't just have it out with him, can I, as though he was twelve years old again and I'd just caught him stealing Penny's pocket money!"

The icy look vanished from Kate's eyes. Suddenly they filled with tears. "Why can't you?" she said. "That's how you've always handled it before now when any of the children have been in trouble. And – and I know that you'll find Matthew's got a complete explanation for everything. He's – he's our *son,* George. He just – he just can't really be a villain . . . "

Gideon said nothing. His feelings at that moment were so strong that he had momentarily lost control of the car, and nearly swerved into a passing lorry. He pulled up at the side of the road, braking hard.

"Can't he?" he said softly. "I'd give everything I have in the world, love, if only I could be sure of that."

"You will be," said Kate, "once you've talked to him. And you're going to aren't you?" Then very calmly, she presented her ultimatum. "Because if you don't, at the first opportunity I am going to ring him and tell him everything you've told me tonight!"

"You – wouldn't," Gideon was about to say, but stopped, realising he'd be wasting his breath.

Kate wasn't bluffing him – and in any case, half of him didn't *want* to argue with her and was shrieking at him that she was right. Her way was their way, the human way, the *Gideon* way.

He had to see Matthew and have it out with him, man to man, father to son. But there was only one time when he could possibly do it and that was *now*, before the morning, when the cold light of reason would remind him that he'd be acting as accessory before and after the fact, risking prison as well as jeopardising his whole career.

Scarcely knowing what he was doing, he slipped off his seat-belt, opened the door beside him, and stepped out of the car on to the pavement. It was as hot outside the car as in; the night being as airless and suffocating as a vast marquee.

"You take over the wheel and get home as quick as you can," he told Kate. "I'd rather do this alone."

12 The Second Opinion

Tom Riddell was still in his bright "real expert taking over" mood when he arrived down in the cell to talk to Red Benton – and he had not been in there more than two minutes when he arrived at the conclusion that it was *time* a real expert took over the Benton case.

Red himself was now freely admitting that he had been Tom's long-term adversary, the Oxfam Robin Hood. But he was denying as strongly as ever that he had been responsible for the "nerve-war" raid on Riddell's home, or the murder of Don Mitchell, or the attempted murder of Suzy Nelson.

"As for that attack on you, Mr Riddell," he finished with a cheery grin, "it don't make any f-----g sense that I should have done it. Why should I have wanted to score you off the case. As far as I am concerned, you were my favourite copper. You'd been chasing me for weeks, and got bloody nowhere!

"I tied you up in knots and stitched you up in the middle. You've got to admit it!"

"You gave me a run for my money, lad, no doubt about that!" he said, ungrudgingly.

Red Benton suddenly remembered where he was and plunged into a bout of defiant oratory. His face reddening, his voice rising to its highest pitch, he yelled:

"I gave the world a run for its money. I hit the bloody rich where they were asking to be hit, and every penny's gone where it deserved to go – to feed the starving! And no matter how this f-----g sick society persecutes me, 'come dungeons dark or gallows grim' as they say, I'll always be proud of what I done! *Always*!"

It was an impressive, if also a deafening performance. Riddell found it hard not to warm to this extraordinary youth, who seemed at that moment to deserve all the attention the press had given him.

"The Bob Geldof of the Underworld". "The caring criminal". "The hero of the dispossessed – "

Then suddenly, he was no hero, but a shivering, sobbing wreck.

"But it's what I've *not* done that I'm in here for, Mr Riddell. And unless somehow – God knows how, I can make you in *some* way believe me – "

Riddell, who had been sitting on a bare wooden chair facing the prisoner, abruptly rose.

"Cheer up. I'm halfway to believing you already," he told Red.

This was no less than the truth. He found it hard to picture this fanatically flamboyant Red – skilful though he must be at breaking into houses – having the sophisticated cunning to pull off that decoy trick on him, still less impersonating an Oxford accent on the phone. It was equally hard to picture him sadistically using Vi for target practice. In any case, Vi had described her tormentor as being at least six foot tall. Benton was shortish, barely five foot nine. And his voice, she'd told him, had been deep and thick. Benton's was high and thin.

"But what's hard to see," Riddell went on, "is what *reason* anyone would have for impersonating you."

At that Red calmed down and became desperately eager to help.

"If you want my guess, Mr Riddell, it's one of those rich bastards up in the Heights. They've all got it in for me up there – because they know I've got it in for *them*. My first success as the Hood was to lift a load of stuff from Fergus Atkinson in the house right next door to where Don Mitchell was topped tonight. Funnily enough I was, in fact, planning to make Mitchell my next target. He is – or was, I should say – as evil as tycoons get. Made millions out of his gutter newspapers."

"Isn't he being taken over at the moment?" Riddell frowned, searching his mind. "I read about it this morning. Yes, by – by Fergus Atkinson!" He stared into Red Benton's eyes, his head whirling with possibilities.

"I reckon there's no love lost between those two, Mr Riddell," Benton replied slowly. "In fact, sir, if you were to go into it I should think you'd find that each of 'em had bloody good reason for murdering the other. This takeover bid, for instance – "

"If Don Mitchell was the only person blocking the deal," Riddell couldn't help interrupting, "that would give Atkinson a motive." He laughed. "We're clutching at straws, laddie, and you must know it. Why in the world would Fergus Atkinson carry out the raid on my wife and me? Unless – "

Benton was not to be put off now.

"Don't you see? He had to do it because, if he was going to frame me for murder, he needed first of all to give the Oxfam Robin Hood a different image. I had to stop being the gentle criminal who never hurt a fly. And so the cunning bastard deliberately staged all that to make it look as though the Oxfam Robin Hood had turned vicious and trigger-happy. Doesn't that make sense?"

Riddell folded his arms, and stood very still.

"As a matter of fact, son, yes, it does," he said softly.

He could remember that hoax telephone call – the muffled voice speaking with a cut-glass Oxford accent, which had fooled him into thinking he was talking to the secretary of the whole Oxfam organisation. That wasn't the sort of stunt that Red Benton could have pulled off, not in a million years. But it would have been child's play for Fergus Atkinson, MP, a director of a dozen City companies. And a daring decoy trick was just the type of scheme that might have occurred to a sophisticated political brain. Whether Atkinson had carried out the actual raid on his home, or paid some thug to do it, was immaterial. What mattered was that it looked as if the Oxfam Robin Hood had been the man behind it.

But then he saw a glaring flaw in the whole argument.

"Why should Atkinson, after killing Mitchell and so clearly putting the blame on you, have gone berserk and shot that poor girl Suzy – his own servant?" he asked.

Red Benton had no trouble answering that.

"From what Mr Lemaitre was telling me, Suzy was at that very moment being dragged away from Atkinson's house by her own father. I reckon Horace could tell you a thing or two about what was going on between her and her employer. Filthy Fergus. That's what he was known as in the Vale. Although they are all pretty filthy up there in the Heights."

Riddell frowned. Gideon had given him such a rapid run-down on what had happened that he had hardly taken it all in; but he did remember something about the girl being on drugs – perhaps pregnant.

Seeing her suddenly in his path, had Atkinson coldly seized the chance to rid himself of a source of scandal that might otherwise threaten to ruin his whole career?

That was enough for Riddell. He turned and walked to the door of the cell, banging on it for a constable to let him out.

Benton watched him in despair.

"Don't you believe me, Mr Riddell? It's God's truth I've been telling you. I swear it. It's Atkinson you should be talking to, not me – "

Riddell turned back with a grin.

"As it happens, I quite agree with you. That's why I'm off to have a little word with that gentleman – now."

The constable opened the door, and Riddell went striding through it almost jauntily. It was years since he had felt such a flood of self-esteem. He had not only taken over the inquiry. In ten minutes, he had transformed it, seeing through and seeking out all the errors of that fumbling idiot, Lemaitre!

As he went, he repeated over his shoulder what had become his catch-phrase of the evening.

"Leave it to me, Red, my boy. Leave it all to me."

* * *

The shrewd side of Riddell's brain did not stop working as he climbed the steps from the cell into the entrance hall of the police station.

His case against Atkinson at the moment was only a conjecture, it told him, and most people would consider it a wild one. Atkinson was almost as much a celebrity as Don Mitchell had been. The whole thing needed to be handled with kid gloves, and his first step ought to be make sure of his ground.

The place to start doing that was, obviously, the scene of the crime, Don Mitchell's house. There might be documents there relating to the takeover bid, or failing that, scribbled memos about it in wastepaper-baskets. He could also look at the "Feed the World" scrawl on the wall. He had seen so many of the Oxfam Robin Hood's scrawls over the past few months. He believed he would know at once if this was an imitation . . .

Somewhere at the back of his mind Riddell remembered Gideon warning him against going to the scene of the crime tonight – but he was too excited to pay any attention to that. Looking almost as commanding as Gideon himself, he marched through the entrance hall and out into the station precinct. The reporters were still there, and so were the TV newsmen, who recognised him immediately as the Superintendent who had fought so long and so unsuccessfully against the Oxfam Robin Hood –

In fact, one of the reporters had been at his house earlier that day asking him how he felt about the ordeal Vi had undergone.

"Hello, Tom. How is Mrs Riddell?" he asked now.

"Getting along fine," Riddell answered briskly, and tried to stride on.

Camera bulbs flashed, a TV spotlight was shining on him, and then the awkward questions began. "We thought you'd been taken off the case. Isn't Superintendent Lemaitre handling it now?" "How do you feel about him being the man who finally captured the Hood?"

The lights glared blindingly; the sea of faces was bewildering. God, Riddell thought. Surely his nerves weren't starting to play up again.

"I'm very grateful to, to Mr – Mr Lemaitre for helping me out. He's – he's done a great j-job," he said shakily, painfully aware that he was stuttering badly. "But who's in charge now – Lemaitre or you?" someone persisted. "*I* am," Riddell said adding with a smile and a worse stutter than ever: "F-f-for the m-moment, a-a-anyway."

At that, they at last allowed him through – and a second later, he was in his car, driving at full speed towards the Heights.

He'd been silly to think that his previous nervous-tension trouble was returning, he told himself. It had just been those torrents of reporters' questions and there was nothing extraordinary about the sweat that was suddenly breaking out all over him. It was the sultriest of city nights. No air anywhere. Hard to breathe, let alone think . . .

He felt calm again by the time he reached the Heights and drove into Malibu Rise. There were no lights on inside No. 2 which meant that the scene-of-the-crime boys had packed up and gone. But a constable who was on guard duty by the gate had a key in case anyone from the police wanted to go over the premises.

Riddell took the key from him, and went into the house. His first act was to find the room where the body had lain, a spot now identified by chalk marks, and to examine the scrawl on the walls. Sure enough, it looked different from any he had previously seen. The real Oxfam Robin Hood had never put such a flourish into the "F" of "Feed". And the capital Es were so curly that they looked as if they were part of a royal cipher. It was all in great contrast to Red Benton's style of handwriting which had been bold and crude. There could hardly be a stronger indication that someone new *had* taken over, someone with a very different background and probably a far more expensive education. Riddell wondered what school Atkinson had been to, probably somewhere like Eton . . .

So far so good, he thought, for Red Benton.

He walked through into the lounge, switching on lights as he went. The double windows on to the garden were closed now, but he remembered Gideon mentioning that Mitchell had gone to bed drunk leaving the windows open and that that was how the intruder had come in. He opened the left-hand window and peered out thoughtfully. The night was as dark as it was airless but he could see one thing: the dull glint of a window pane on the house next door as it reflected the light streaming out from behind him.

From there, Atkinson would have had a good view of these windows. He could have seen that they'd been left open and immediately decided to seize the opportunity and commit his crime right away.

So far, Riddell told himself, even better for Red.

He went back into Mitchell's study and this time turned his attention to the bureau desk. It was going to be easy to search, because the intruder had already broken it open, forcing the roll-top upwards.

"Thank *you*, Mr Atkinson!" murmured Riddell.

He pulled a sheaf of envelopes towards him, and picked up the first of them, which was large and bulky. It contained, he discovered, a collection of press-cuttings, some of the most recent about the takeover bid threatening Mitchell's newspaper, *The Sunday View*. Fergus Atkinson's company, Worldwide News, was making the bid – and cutting after cutting made it very clear that only one thing was preventing *The Sunday View* Board from accepting it: the obdurate stand against it being made by the chairman, Mitchell himself.

As one of the cuttings – from an eminent City columnist – put it "Fergus Atkinson's company stands to gain millions if only his erstwhile partner Don Mitchell would be kind enough to walk under a bus tonight!"

Riddell's hands were shaking as he put the cutting back into the envelope. He had just seen all he needed, the clearest motive for murder anyone could ask for. As far as he was concerned, the case against Atkinson was now overwhelming. He certainly *had* been put in charge of the case again just in time!

A worrying thought suddenly struck him.

As he had told the newsmen, he was in charge "only for the moment". For all he knew Gideon would take him off the case in the morning; and in effect, there would be no case once the magistrate had sent Red Benton for trial. The triumphant Lemaitre would be congratulated on his catching the killer, and the file would be closed. His "second opinion", as Gideon had called it, would probably be politely listened to, but then disregarded as too far-fetched to be worth considering. Poor old Tom – those nerves have sent him round the twist at last. That's what they'd be saying.

His only hope was to take action now, while he was indisputably in control, and the only action he could think of was to live up to his promise to Red – and confront Fergus Atkinson straight away.

What did it matter that it was the middle of the night? If Atkinson had committed these crimes, he had no right to be peacefully slumbering anyway. And two o'clock in the morning was, psychologically speaking, not a bad time for asking straight questions. Slick answers didn't come quite so easily then – and even the most cunning minds could be caught off guard . . .

Riddell turned away from the bureau, paused a moment to switch off all the lights in the house, and then went out through the front door, handing the constable back the key.

The constable looked curiously tense.

"Be glad when I've finished here tonight, sir. Don't like the sound of things down in the Vale," he said. Riddell paused to listen for a moment, but couldn't hear anything except a vague shouting from seemingly a long way away.

"Two or three yobs having a set-to somewhere, I suppose," he said, casually.

The constable was not reassured. "A moment ago it sounded like two or three thousand of 'em," he said.

Riddell laughed. "Must be the heat playing tricks with your imagination. Or your concentration," he told the constable and went off in the direction of 3, Malibu Rise.

It was just as he was reaching the gate of No.3, and starting down the long garden path to Fergus Atkinson's front door that he realised what the man had been talking about.

More sounds of shouting came – and this time it was no ordinary shouting. It was a continuous, intensifying roar of hate, still distant, but becoming louder, nearer second by second. Interrupting it were the noises – dozens of objects being banged on the ground; hundreds of people jeering, chanting, or stamping their feet: one or two women screaming: someone laughing hysterically – and, suddenly, above it all, a booming voice obviously from a police loudhailer. "Listen to me, everyone, for God's sake have some sense," it resounded.

Riddell stood stock-still, halfway down the path to the door.

The voice was unmistakably Gideon's. His spirits rose. Well, if anyone could restore order down there, Gideon could, he thought – and then gasped as he heard the roar swell up into a shattering crescendo of hate, following up and silencing all other sounds with the force of a tidal wave engulfing a microscopic sea shell on the shore.

Had Gideon just been silenced, Riddell wondered, or overpowered and swept under by the crowd! It sounded very much like the latter. In which case –

But Riddell suddenly had other things to think about.

The front door ahead of him opened. Light from the hall of No. 3 poured out all round him, blinding after the darkness, dazzling and dazing him. Then he made out the tall elegant figure of Fergus Atkinson, familiar from his TV appearances. He was fully dressed in flannel trousers and a blue blazer and with his handsome, regular features and slick blond hair, might have strolled straight out of the pages of a Sunday magazine supplement.

His manner, though, wasn't as smooth as his appearance. It was extremely curt.

"Well, which are you?" he snapped. "A marauding yob or a murdering thief! They're the only visitors we get in this neighbourhood."

The roaring noises had temporarily died down. It was as though the crowd had been momentarily satisfied by letting blood – and Riddell needed no telling whose blood it would have been.

He felt sick and dizzy, but summoned up every ounce of his sagging confidence and managed to reply, quietly and formally. "Good evening, Mr Atkinson. I'm Chief Detective Superintendent Riddell of the C.I.D. Sorry to disturb you so late – but I think it's important I should talk to you. Very important indeed."

13 Breaking Point

Atkinson stared at him so frostily that for a moment Riddell was sure he was going to slam the door. But then a yell from below – very close now, it seemed less than a couple of hundred yards away – made him change his mind.

"All right, I suppose you'd better come in. Won't be too safe out here for much longer from the sound of it. Things are obviously getting out of hand down there due, no doubt, to the usual incredible incompetence of the police."

He stood back, and Riddell walked into a spacious, elegantly furnished hall. The walls were of imported, polished pine, with modern paintings hanging on them, each meticulously spotlit. It looked almost like some corner of an art gallery – an expensive Mayfair one, of course.

Atkinson closed the front door, secured each of the three reinforcing safety locks on it, and led Riddell into a large dining-room, quite exquisitely furnished. The sounds of uproar outside did not penetrate into here, probably because of the thick red velvet curtains covering the windows, which would in any case be double glazed. Despite all the curtaining, the room was cool, due no doubt to the total air conditioning. Expensive cigar smoke hung in the air. Soft music was coming from stereo speakers built into the walls, another factor cutting out the slightest sound of any mayhem going on in the Vale below.

Atkinson strolled over to a drinks cabinet disguised as a large illuminated globe, and poured himself a double whisky. He pointedly refrained from offering Riddell a drink, and made no attempt to wave him to a chair. Nor did he sit down himself, but stood, peering down at the global cabinet as though it fascinated him. The reddish glow from it gave his face a flushed, rather fevered look.

"Before you start, Chief Detective Superintendent

Riddell," he began, "I hope you do in fact, have a good reason for intruding on me at this time of night. I happen to have the ear of the Home Secretary, who is especially concerned these days about the conduct of the police. I wouldn't like to have to tell him that such a high-ranking officer as yourself showed total lack of consideration — "

Riddell found himself beginning to lose his temper. He found himself replying with cold police formality.

"I have already said I believe it was very important for us to have a talk, Mr Atkinson, and I can assure you that it is. There is one fact I must know which is vital to the inquiry I am pursuing into the murder here, and it is something only you can tell me."

Atkinson moved away from the globe; his face did not quite return to its normal colouring. Perhaps the drink was putting a genuine flush on to his cheeks.

He smiled faintly.

"All right, what is so vitally important that you need so desperately to know that it can't possibly wait until morning?"

Riddell folded his arms, and said, as calmly as he could: "Just this, sir. Where were *you* between 10.30 p.m. and midnight last night?"

He did not take his eyes off Atkinson's face, looking for the faintest sign of a guilty start. From his experience, he knew that the moment when a murderer first realises he is seriously suspected can be the most revealing one of all.

Atkinson did not start; but there could be no doubt that the question jolted him. He looked up sharply and there was suddenly a dangerous glint in his eyes: a glint which said more clearly than any words that the gloves were off between them – if, in fact, they had ever been on!

Aloud, he said, more coolly than ever:

"Heaven knows why you should consider *that* so important, Superintendent, but as it so happens, I can give you an immediate answer. I spent most of last evening at my club – Twentieth Centurion, in Jermyn Street – attending an informal meeting of my fellow-directors in Worldwide News. Would you like the names of them? Lord Clinton-Smythe was there, for a start. Then there was Sir Robert Paignton, Right Honourable Michael Beardsley . . ."

He went on and on, and Riddell felt his spirits sinking. It seemed as though he was listing one of the most gilt-edged alibis in history. He should have known that a smart operator like Atkinson would have arranged nothing less. It was probable that, if he questioned these illustrious gentlemen individually, he might be able to break it. The problem was that each and everyone of them probably had, like Atkinson, "the ear of the Home Secretary", or, at any rate, enough pull in high places to make it very difficult for him to take a case against Atkinson an inch further – not, at any rate, without some sort of hard evidence to back him. And he had to admit that he hadn't a shred.

The gleam in Atkinson's eyes had become a triumphant one. He obviously expected this impertinent copper to shuffle off, muttering apologies. Riddell looked for a moment, as if he might just do that. He nervously crossed and uncrossed his arms, and seemed to be almost shuffling his feet.

"Have you any more vitally urgent questions, Chief Detective Superintendent?" Atkinson demanded, again deliberately giving Riddell his full title. "If not, I would strongly advise you to stop bothering me – for the sake of your future in the force!"

Riddell stopped shuffling abruptly. Mounting anger suddenly overcame his nervous tension, and all the people at the Yard who had written him off as a spent force would have been astonished to see how powerful and determined he suddenly became.

"It's *your* future I'd be concerned about, Atkinson, if I were you," he said quietly and deliberately. "It looks to me as if you'll be spending a great part of it behind bars. So many suspicious facts have come to light about you in the past half hour – "

This time there was no doubting that Atkinson was rattled. He looked away quickly, obviously to hide the alarm in his eyes, and hastily poured himself another whisky.

It is probable that no one, least of all a policeman, had talked to him in that disrespectful tone before, and like most bullies, he couldn't take even a second of the treatment he himself dished out.

The glass trembled in his hands as he turned back to Riddell, his face not just flushed now, but crimson with a peculiar mixture of nerves and anger.

"*What* suspicious facts?" he shouted. "And watch what you say, Superintendent, or this'll be your last night in the police force as sure as there's a law of slander!"

Riddell decided that the time had come to play his whole hand. It was the only way to get Atkinson to crack, and there were more chinks appearing all over his armour now. "Fact one," he said as abruptly as before. "It's public knowledge that your company, Worldwide News, stands to gain millions by Mr Mitchell's death at this – for you – very opportune moment. Fact two – I strongly suspect that Miss Nelson's father will confirm that her death will free you from a very serious situation. Fact three – I am prepared personally to swear that it was you who impersonated the secretary of Oxfam in a telephone call to me last night. Which means that *you* are the man responsible for that cowardly and despicable attack on – on my wife – which is all part of an ingenious plot to pin your murders on the Oxfam Robin – "

He stopped there, for a very simple reason.

Atkinson suddenly dropped all pretence, and made a full confession of guilt. Not in words, but in a single dramatic act.

He reached into the side pocket of his blazer, and brought out a revolver, which he pointed at the dead centre of Riddell's forehead. The spot was his favourite target to judge from what had happened to Don Mitchell earlier that night.

"You'd be prepared to swear that *personally*, would you?" he said softly. "How very interesting. It shows me that there's a lot that's very personal about what you've said tonight. I haven't been able to sleep and I've been listening to the radio – all-night news bulletins on LBC. They've been saying that you're off the Oxfam Robin Hood case. The great Detective Superintendent Lemaitre has taken over – and he's had the good sense to arrest a local boy, Red Benton, for the murder of poor dear Don next door. That somehow leads me to think that what you're doing is somewhat – shall we say – extra curricular.

You're carrying out this little inquiry purely off your own bat. And you're dead scared that no one is going to believe your crazy story in the morning. That's why you've barged in on me at this ungodly hour. It was a desperate attempt wasn't it, to make me do or say something incriminating – well, you're in luck, Chief Detective Superintendent. I am going to do something very incriminating. I am going to silence you once and for all."

Riddell reacted to that with magnificent, almost majestic, contempt.

"Fergus Atkinson," he barked, and it was almost the full-blown Gideon roar. "You are under arrest for threatening a police officer with a dangerous weapon. And I'd advise you now to hand over that gun. Even you couldn't get away with blowing a police officer's brains out – not without an Oxfam Robin Hood to blame it on. And he's in a cell at the moment down at Fletchwood police station. A better alibi than all the members of the Twentieth Centurion Club put together. And if you need any more convincing of how helpless your position is, take a look outside that window. You'll see a constable on guard at the gate of number two. He watched me come in here, and is under instructions to radio to the station for help if I am not out of here within a quarter of an hour. A time limit which, I might add, is very nearly up . . ."

It was a masterly performance, one of the best of Tom Riddell's long and intermittently brilliant career. He looked confident, totally assured and he did not give the merest outward sign that in reality he was gripped by nothing short of terror.

He'd been reckless to the point of insanity, he told himself, coming here alone to confront a dangerous murder suspect. For all he knew, Atkinson might not be amenable to reason: he could well be a homicidal maniac. In which case, his situation was desperate. Shouts for help were no use: the soundproofing in the room's windows worked two ways, and the constable was too far off for even the loudest bellow to reach him. Making a sudden dash for it wouldn't be any use, either. The front door was triple locked – he could be riddled with bullets before he had undone one of them. His only hope was to stand his ground and keep Atkinson talking – but that depended on his nerves holding out – and already, there were alarming signs that at any second, they might give way. His mouth was dry: his heart was pounding painfully. There was so much sweat under his armpits that his shirt felt wringing wet. It only needed that giddiness to return – the room to start whirling round and –

Miraculously, though, Atkinson seemed impressed by what he'd said. At all events, he suddenly pocketed the gun and turned to the windows, drew back one of the long curtains and peered out, presumably to confirm that there was a constable outside No. 2. And at that moment, the whole situation was drastically altered.

Parting the curtains broke the sound insulating barrier surrounding the room, and immediately, shouts and yells and chanting became audible from outside. Although they were obviously coming from very close, the music playing from the stereo – vaguely instrumental music now – still somehow distanced them: the effect was something like background music on the sound-track of a film. Riddell moved forward until he could see out of the windows over Atkinson's shoulder – and drew in his breath sharply.

The room faced front, and the windows looked out to a large bushy front garden, with Malibu Rise beyond. The garden was in darkness but the Rise was brilliantly illuminated by tall street lamps – and their eerie orange light showed what looked like an advancing army of thugs, pacing down the road in their hundreds. Not that there was anything military about their progress. They were coming in disorganised bunches, screaming insults, kicking cars, and hurling aside everything and anything in sight in the direction of 1, 2 and 3, Malibu Rise. This included bricks, odd bits of metal, branches yanked from trees, lids scavenged from dustbins – and altogether more sinister objects that they had brought with them: bottles full of petrol which exploded like incendiary bombs.

"Christ Almighty," breathed Riddell, as he suddenly spotted the constable outside No. 2 retreating under a shower of missiles back up the drive to the front door.

"I rather think," said Atkinson, "that your man, Chief

Detective Superintendent, is a little too preoccupied to bother about what's happening to you."

He seemed blithely unconcerned about their own predicament, although the danger was now acute. Rioters were pouring all over the front garden. Bricks and cans showered viciously against the glass in front of them. The thick, double-glazed glass was more than proof against them, but that was only the start. As the volume of the music over the stereo rose, strengthening the feeling that all that they were watching was part of some superior stereophonic film, a couple of louts – one black, one a white youth with a head shaved bald as a billiard ball – came right in front of the window. The white boy yelled something like "F – filthy Fergie," and spat at such close range that his drops of spittle showered on the window. They both turned and ran – throwing something into a big rhododendron bush just beneath the window. It was one of the "Molotov cocktail" incendiary bottles. It burst, with a crack that was deafening even through the double glazing – and the next moment the bush, dry as timber as a result of the hot summer, burst into flames.

Other youths were in the garden now and one of them had a can of petrol. From a distance of only a few yards, he was throwing its contents towards the blaze. A sheet of flame shot across the front garden, so close that it singed his hair and eyebrows. He dropped the can and ran, but the fire was now perilously close to being out of control. It was probably leaping up the wall of the house. Choking smoke began to fill the room.

Forgetting that his only audience was a dangerous enemy, Riddell instantly started barking orders. "Quick, get a fire extinguisher, water, anything," he started. "And for God's sake, where is the phone?"

Not that there was much need to use one, he told himself. With a riot like this going on, fire services were probably already rushing here from all over London. Riot squads, too –

He tried to head for the door, but with a lightning movement, Atkinson barred his way.

"No one uses the phone in this house without my

permission, Chief Detective Superintendent. And I'm not going to give it to you just now." Riddell almost gasped.

"Good God, man," he yelled. "Do you *want* your house burnt to the ground?"

A slow smile spread across Atkinson's handsome features.

"With the amount I have paid in insurance, it's a hardship I can bear with equanimity," he said. "As I can the thought of your death, Chief Detective Superintendent, if in spite of all my heroic efforts, I am unable to rescue you from the flames."

He produced the gun again, this time holding it menacingly by the barrel and plainly intending to use the butt as a cosh. Riddell needed no telling what was in his mind. If his main object was now to get rid of this troublesome copper, then the fire was quite simply a godsend to him. The body of the Chief Detective Superintendent found shot through the head, even amidst the debris of a burnt house, would raise unanswerable questions. But if he kicked Riddell unconscious, the bruise would be undetectable in a charred corpse. And he would have a very plausible story to explain his presence. The busy-body Superintendent had come banging on his door in the middle of the night, asking a lot of irrelevant questions about the Oxfam Robin Hood case. Then these rioters had appeared, starting a fire. The Superintendent had collapsed, overcome by fumes and smoke – and before he, Atkinson, could do anything, the fire had –

Riddell backed hurriedly to the door, suddenly painfully aware how high the odds were against him. Powerfully built he might be, but he was in his late fifties, nearing retirement, whereas Atkinson was probably in his middle thirties, and had kept himself in pretty good trim. He proved this now by lunging across the room with the speed and power of a jungle beast.

Fortunately, at that moment, the lights blacked out, and he blundered heavily into a low coffee table and some chairs. Before he'd had time to regain his balance, Riddell was out in the hall, and had groped his way across to the front door. His fingers had already closed around the first of the three bolts – but they were slippery with sweat, and the rising panic inside him made his efforts to pull it back little more than feeble fumbling.

Worse, smoke from the burning garden was now pouring in through the letter-box slot, streaming into his nostrils, eyes and mouth, so that it was impossible either to see what he was doing, or breathe while he was doing it. Choking, spluttering, gasping, Riddell staggered back.

He heard – or thought he heard – Atkinson's footsteps right behind him, and swung round – but the gloom in the hall, combined with the scalding smoke in his eyes, made it hard to discern anything except a blurry shadow with an upraised right arm. Riddell raised his own right arm to shield himself – and then the thing that he had been dreading most of all happened.

His nerves, tautened to breaking point, gave way. In fact, it felt as though they were exploding inside him.

Saving Atkinson the job of knocking him out, he thought ironically – and that was his last thought before he blacked out and fell, right at his enemy's feet.

14 The Circle of Hate

When Gideon began his walk back up to Matthew's house, it seemed as though he had the whole of Fletchwood to himself. He was soon nearing Fletchwood Vale High Street, an oddly but aptly named thoroughfare, which led through the centre of the Vale, and then right upwards through the Heights, changing its name to Fletchwood Heights High Street when it got there. Malibu Rise was on a turning off it at the uppermost end.

At the moment he was in a sordid-looking approach road to the High Street, where half the shops were boarded up and the rest sleazy-looking take-aways. The place seemed to be devoid of any living soul. The only sound to be heard was that made by his own footsteps, echoing eerily round the doorways of the shops he passed, and taking him back to those distant days when as a young constable, he had spent night after night ponderously pounding his beat.

Not that there was anything ponderous about his progress now. He was suddenly striding so fast that he was quite close to running. It was the only way to stop himself from thinking too much about the task that lay ahead.

Confronting Matthew with the full facts about what he was suspected of being was, without question, the toughest job that he had ever faced, either as a father or as a policeman. And it placed him in a situation where he could not win. If, as he hoped and prayed, Matthew was completely innocent, he would be indignant, perhaps bitterly aggrieved which could lead to an even bigger row than the one they had had all those years ago – and this time, to an estrangement that might last the rest of their lives. If, on the other hand, Matthew was not innocent – if he tried to bluster, or give unsatisfactory answers to his questions –

Suddenly that freezing dread was back, so powerful now that it seemed to paralyse his legs, slowing his pace, almost to a faltering halt. With an iron effort of will, he mastered his emotions, and was striding as fast and purposefully as ever when he turned into Fletchwood Vale High Street – and made a disturbing discovery.

He was no longer by any means alone.

As though in answer to some secret signal – or more probably, following a pre-arranged timetable – gangs of youths were pouring on to the road through every side alley. Like gutters in a downpour, filled to overflowing in seconds by countless rivulets of streaming rain, the pavement on both sides of the street suddenly became packed with them. What added to the strangeness of the sinister influx of humanity was the fact that there was little or no noise: the youths, still very roughly grouped in gangs, stood silent, waiting and watching, as Gideon calmly moved into the centre of the road to continue his walk.

Then somebody somewhere gave an order – it sounded more like a jungle war cry – and the next thing he knew, the yobbos were off the pavement and on to the road, ahead, behind and both sides of him, going the same way that he was, and mockingly matching his own strides.

They were far from silent now. Shouts and jeers, amid deafening shrieks, rang out all along the street. Then came the rattle of kicked dustbins and cans – and suddenly deadly objects were being brandished everywhere, gleaming evilly in the light of the street lamps: chains, bottles, hacksaws, knives. Gideon's experienced eyes registered others, still more destructive objects at the moment being concealed behind bushes or hidden under coats: bottles had been converted into incendiary bombs, cans of petrol, jagged bits of metal, heavy enough to kill or maim if thrown . . .

He needed no telling that his worst forebodings about the Fletchwood situation were being fulfilled. The bomb that he had sensed all along to be ticking away under the people of Fletchwood Heights *had* been timed to go off tonight – and the explosion was taking the form he had most dreaded: a mass attack by fire-raisers.

"Mass" was the word for it, he told himself grimly. There must be hundreds of armed thugs and yobbos in the High Street by now, and still more were pouring in from all sides, joining the wild, disorderly procession that was now relentlessly rolling towards the point where the street turned upwards and climbed sharply for four hundred yards to the very heart of the Heights. Gideon had pored over maps of the area for hours, and knew that this was the only road that led up there; the only connecting-link between the two halves of Fletchwood, the only escape-route for the inhabitants of the Heights in an emergency. Already it was too crowded for vehicles to *use* easily. It only wanted a couple of cars to be overturned in the middle of it, and it would become totally impassable, creating the siege situation that he had foreseen and feared for so long.

Anxiously, he glanced up at all that could be seen of the Heights from here: those twinkly fairy lights on the trees in the gardens of that luxury hotel. On a hot dry night like this, a few well-aimed petrol bombs could set those trees blazing like an Australian bushfire, he thought. A few more in the bushes of the luxurious Fletchwood Heights front gardens – and the whole area could be swept by what amounted to a miniature fire storm. And it wouldn't be a miniature one for long, if the rioters stopped the fire engines getting through . . .

As if to spell out their evil purpose, someone started chanting: "Kill the bastards in the Heights!" Suddenly almost everyone was joining in, knives flashing, chains rattling, even half-hidden petrol cans being banged in time to the menacing rhythm of the chanting, that grew louder and louder until every building in the street seemed to be echoing with it. "*Kill the bastards in the Heights*".

To make the situation still more nightmarish, someone on Gideon's right – that sinister Rastafarian he had encountered outside Gharad's surgery – was spitting out the names of their targets during pauses in the chanting. "Matthew Goddard! Fergus Atkinson!" he shouted. "And Don Mitchell – he's the worst one of all," he muttered.

Gideon was suddenly aware of the sickening irony of his situation. Here he was, in the midst of this terrible procession, hell bent on causing the most hideous bloodbath, and he was to all intents and purposes marching with it! Or, to be absolutely precise, it was marching with him. He had no idea whether or not he had been recognised by anyone, but the toughs around him knew well enough that he was some kind of authority figure, and unlikely to be on their side. He was moving too fast, though, to be easily surrounded and his apparent total unawareness that he was in personal danger – not one sideways glance did he throw at any of them – seemed to fascinate them. Perhaps, at some level, it frightened them. At all events, they maintained their distance, but still continued mockingly to keep in step with his powerful, purposeful strides, which abruptly slowed as he realised that the last thing he wanted to do was set the pace. The road was already beginning to climb. In ten minutes – no six or seven, more likely – they'd be within slinging distance of their targets.

What in God's name were the police doing, he wondered. The police station was in a turning just off the High Street, and they'd be passing the end of it at any second. It was true that all this trouble had blown up in a matter of moments, but the men at the station must be aware of it – they were easily within earshot of the shouting and swearing. Why weren't police cars turning out by the dozen?

A moment of reflection told him the answer. There were only a handful of men at the station. Remembering the relaxed attitude of the Inspector-in-Charge and the sergeant there too – this whole thing was catching them completely unprepared. Obviously they'd have contacted the Yard, and were radioing for help to all surrounding stations. A full-scale riot squad equipped with all the latest riot shields, protective helmets and hoses was probably on its way – and would arrive a damned sight too late, he thought despondently. Now was the time when something had to be done – now, in these precious few minutes before the Heights was reached, and –

Gideon stood stock still. He was suddenly aware of the whole terrible situation and his own complete helplessness. The men at the station would be skulking in terror of the mob and he had no right to blame them. They were a handful against hundreds.

Just then he heard the most welcome sound of the night, the wha-wha wail of a police car siren immediately to his left. It was followed instantly by the sight of the flashing lamp on top of the car as it attempted to come out of the turning on to the packed High Street. The faces of the marchers around him were suddenly lit up by a single shaft of blue from the lamp; but there was nothing welcome to Gideon about what it revealed. He had never in all his life seen faces of such concentrated hate. Everywhere, manically glinting eyes – hysterical, gaping mouths reflected their common purpose, and actual readiness, even eagerness, to murder.

Suddenly there was an empty space in the road all round Gideon. The marchers who had been mockingly pacing alongside him held torches in the direction of the car, totally surrounding it and – it seemed to Gideon – submerging it in a sea of swearing comments, spitting faces and heaving fists. The car was forced to a halt. Still with the occupants inside, a gang of youths was rocking the car and trying to turn it over.

Somehow, a man in the car – the sergeant who had been behind the counter in the station – managed to get one of the doors open, sending a couple of youths flying in the process. He had a loudhailer and was about to shout something through it when abruptly he was seized and dragged out bodily by the mob, to the accompaniment of whoops and roars of triumph that seemed to split the sky.

The sergeant resisted bravely, but fell to the ground, where he was kicked and punched from all directions.

In a second, worse would happen, Gideon knew. Knives would flash and –

At all costs, he had to create a diversion – and suddenly what seemed a heaven-sent opportunity came his way. The loudhailer was wrenched away from the sergeant, and eventually tossed through the air. It landed less than a yard from Gideon's feet.

Gideon grabbed at it, snatched it up, and switched it on.

The next moment, a new sound was filling the street – a sound that silenced everything else, and even brought the whole procession to an abrupt halt.

It was the sound of Gideon's roar, shattering enough at normal volume but deafening when electronically magnified to ten times its normal force.

"Listen to me, everyone!" he called. "For God's sake, have some *sense* – "

Just for an instant miracles started happening. The mob surrounding the police sergeant drew back. The other policemen in the back of the car started to clamber out, actually grinning with relief. It was obvious that they thought the old Gideon magic had all its former powers. He had quelled rioters single-handed before. Incredibly – he was doing it again.

But very rapidly, it became clear that that was too much to hope for in this day and age and, of all places, in Fletchwood Vale.

It was true that the mob was initially awed by the realisation that the most famous policeman in Britain was in their midst. The name "Gideon" was murmured on all sides but soon there were other murmurings, proving how fast news travelled in the Vale, passed by word of mouth.

"Gideon! He's been up at Goddard's house all evening – had his bloody dinner there! He's one of the Heights' bastards himself!"

The Rastafarian who had crossed swords with Gideon earlier that evening added, "*And* he was the one who nicked Red Benton! Let's get him!"

The crowd suddenly turned on Gideon, but did not rush into the cleared space around him. Enough of the magic remained to make them, momentarily at least, still nervous of touching him. He found himself in the centre of a circle of staring, menacing louts – a circle that steadily closed in on him, as screams and shouts from all sides grew into a crescendo of murderous hate.

Gideon raised the loudhailer to his lips again, though even with its help he doubted if anything he said could be heard above the din. Then someone threw something – a strip of metal guttering it looked like – which crashed against the loudhailer, knocking it out of his hands and sending a shock of jarring searing pain along his jaw and all over his face. He reeled back, just as a shower of objects – chains, bottles, jagged-edged cans hit him at what felt like a dozen points of his body, neck, elbow, right calf, head –

Suddenly – dazed – he found himself literally on his

knees, as if begging for mercy. Not that anyone would have thought it if they could have heard what he was yelling. "You bloody f---"

The rest was lost in the ear-splitting, seemingly earth-shattering roar of triumph as the circle broke and the mob closed in.

* * *

What happened next Gideon was never able to remember very clearly. More objects landed on him, or on the back of his head, and the darkness round him suddenly became red and misty, though a fire was raging somewhere in the depths of his brain. Then he was vaguely aware of a ton weight lying on top of him, a heavy writhing weight, representing a mass of struggling people. Kicking began, one blow landing in his groin, another in the pit of his stomach. The red mist intensified; he might have been running into a solid wall of scarlet fire . . .

Then, suddenly, it cleared. The weight on top of him vanished. The blows and kicking stopped. The ear-splitting yelling and shouting died away to be replaced by a much quieter sound: a single voice talking very softly, but somehow carrying an unquestionable note of command.

"Do you hear me, all of you? It is insanity to harm this man. He is much loved, much respected. Touch a hair of his head, and you will raise the anger of the whole nation. Then *no* one will have sympathy for your cause. Do you understand? *No* one . . . "

The voice went on and on growing and fading, growing and fading on Gideon's battered senses swinging to and fro between consciousness and unconsciousness. Finally it stopped fading, and became, in fact, so strong and clear that the speaker was obviously kneeling over him.

"Try to sit up, Commander. The rabble have gone. I didn't think they liked me giving them a piece of my mind."

Gideon opened his eyes and found himself staring into a face that was instantly recognisable, even in the gloom. It was that of the little doctor, Ravi Gharad. The only man in the world, he thought, who *would* be listened to by an angry Fletchwood Vale mob. He tried to thank him for almost certainly saving his life, but Gharad would not listen.

"It was a pleasure to help, Commander," he said, and then added, softly: "Where I come from, it is not the custom to visit the sins of the children upon their fathers."

Then he was gone, his slight frame walking witch-like into the darkness, before Gideon could take his advice and try to sit up.

When he did manage it, every muscle in his body screamed its protest by contributing its own particular spasm of pain. He found that not only the space around him, but this whole part of the High Street, was now completely deserted, except for the police car and the policemen who had occupied it. All, heavily bruised and shaken, were standing by as if awaiting instructions.

They were not long in coming, once Gideon had glanced up the hill. That told him all too clearly where the crowd had gone. The procession – if the collection of rowdy, can-kicking yobbo groups could really be called that – had rolled on up the road, and the holocaust in the Heights was beginning. As he watched, a petrol bomb was sent flying and one of the trees with fairy lights caught ablaze.

The sight dragged him to his feet in a flash, all pain forgotten in his horror of what was going to happen – and his fury at his own powerlessness to prevent it.

Yet whatever he could do, he must . . . for the sake of everyone in the Heights.

A second later, he was striding towards the police car – just a little slowly, but with most of his old purposefulness and drive, barking orders as he went.

"I still want you and all your men, sergeant. We may not be able to drive all the way up – but by God, we'll go as far as we can. And heaven help any of those marauding yobbos who try to stop us. The road looks clear at this end, at any rate. If we can get up enough speed, there'll be no question of anybody stopping us – they'll have to scatter, and be quick about it. What are you hanging about for? Jump to it, for God's sake!"

He was only dimly aware that he was asking the men to embark on the most reckless, suicidal manoeuvres since the Charge of the Light Brigade – and the men weren't aware of it at all. They were so awed by the sight of Gideon on his feet and in command after all that had happened to him that anything seemed suddenly possible, and they "jumped to it" with enthusiasm, climbing into the car behind and beside him as he took the front seat next to the driver.

In seconds, the car was crackling and creaking its way up the hill over the cans, bottles and other bits of menacing debris that littered the road. Nobody was in sight – but as they neared the top of the road, close to where Malibu Rise led off it, the air was full of the sounds of the crashes and yells of the marauding gangs – and the screams of the panic-stricken victims.

Here the road, now Fletchwood Heights High Street, had suddenly a tree-lined residential look: big houses with large front gardens lined it on both sides, beginning with the de luxe hotel. Not that much could be seen of either the hotel or the houses. Thick smoke was billowing right across the street, so that the constable behind the wheel was forced to slow down. They might have been in the middle of an old-fashioned pea-souper fog, except that it was red, not yellow, suggesting that a large blaze had been started somewhere beyond: a suspicion confirmed by a dull, earthquake-like roaring that seemed to be coming both from ahead and all round them. Adding to the roaring was the continuous cracking of trees and shrubs being set ablaze, and the even more alarming sound of breaking glass as windows were smashed in . . .

Suddenly a strong breeze whipped the smoke away from in front of them, revealing in gory detail what lay ahead. At the very end of the High Street two luxury cars, just recognisable as a Bentley and a Jaguar, obviously dragged from a nearby garage, lay on their sides, blazing and totally blocking the road. Beside them barricades had been made out of what looked like two yanked-off car doors, from behind which a deadly hail of bricks, dustbin lids and other objects were being hurled in the direction of the police car. Worse still, a couple of bullets suddenly knocked against the toughened glass of the windscreen. Then the breeze dropped and the curtain of red smoke returned, blanketing off the scene and streaming into the car with the blinding stinging power of an unleashed canister of tear-gas.

There was only one word that Gideon could say – and he said it in a manner that was half a gasping splutter.

"Back!"

The driver reversed with alacrity and it was only when the car was fifty yards back down the hill that they were able to breathe properly again.

Gideon radioed to Fletchwood Vale police station and, in a moment, was through to the inspector and giving him a report on the situation which was one of the bleakest he had ever had to make.

Half the houses in the Heights could by now be in flames, and their fleeing occupants would be forced through a hail of missiles from rioting gangs now in a mood of hysterical, murderous hate. The only road out was blocked by two blazing vehicles flanked by barricades.

"So the fire engines can only get through if the Riot Squad gets there first – and if that squad isn't here bloody soon, there'll be nothing for them to do except count corpses. Tell 'em that from me," he bellowed.

The inspector stammered something about the squad being on its way, and due to arrive within minutes. "We're under orders from its Commander to sit tight here until then," he said. "Of course, if you wish to – countermand them – Sir . . ."

Gideon's impulsive reaction was to countermand them with emphasis but then he thought better of it. How many men were there at the station? Ten, fifteen at the most. What good would it do to send them up there like lambs to the slaughter? Police lives were too precious to be risked in futile gestures in his book, too.

"No," he said gruffly. "Those orders stay." Turning round to the sergeant in the back seat he added, "and they apply to you and your men too. Just sit tight till the right people arrive, and keep praying that it won't be long before they do."

He was out of the car by now, and standing in the road.

The sergeant stared dazedly.

"You're not going back there – alone?" he gulped.

Gideon's only reply was a grunt. He was already striding in the direction of the hotel gardens and was too far away for it to be heard.

It had occurred to him that on foot, by keeping to the gardens, he could by-pass the barricade, and perhaps get through to Malibu Rise.

Matthew and his family, as the number one targets of the mob, would by now be in a desperate state of siege. Whether he could help them or not Gideon had no idea but every instinct told him that he ought to be with them.

It was not long before he was striding past the first of the hotel's blazing trees.

15 "What Else Can I Think?"

At that moment, up at 1, Malibu Rise, Matthew was only just beginning to realise the perilous situation he was facing.

He and Julie had gone to bed almost immediately after they had seen Gideon and Kate drive away, and both had been fast asleep when the first signs of trouble had developed outside. By the time they had been fully roused, a mob yelling "Kill the bastards in the Heights" was rampaging all over the front garden and bricks and other heavy missiles were crashing against window after window.

Not a pane of glass was even slightly cracked, though: the expensive double glazing saw to that. And Matthew's first reactions had been anger and a lofty contempt. As he had told his father, with costly security locking on all windows, a specially reinforced front door, and steel doors protecting the garage, he thought he was well equipped to see off any attack by marauding yobbos. It might be an idea to inform the police though and, donning a bath robe, he strolled downstairs to the phone.

His composure began to vanish when he realised that the phone was dead. Wondering if someone outside had cut the wire, somehow he doubted if a Fletchwood Vale lout would have the intelligence to do so, he walked over to a front-facing window – and received the shock of his life.

Just about everything in sight seemed to be ablaze – the whole front garden of No. 2 next door, the trees lining Malibu Rise, yes, and the telephone pole too. Smoke was pouring into the house now and, most menacing of all, there was an overpowering smell of petrol. It was as though rivers of it were being poured somewhere close by.

An object the size of a car door came hurtling towards the window as he stood there, thrown by two shadowy figures crouching on his lawn. Even that did not break the glass, but it landed with a crash that shook the house, and

Matthew's confidence, to its foundations. The children were up and crying. He could hear both Julie and Pamela, the nanny, trying to soothe them.

"There's nothing to worry about," he heard Julie say in a voice which sounded as though she was stifling sobs of fear as she spoke.

For a moment Matthew felt panic welling up inside him and then, almost as if in answer to a prayer, came a thunderous knocking on the back door – and a familiar voice shouting: "Hurry up, can't you. For God's sake, let me in!"

Matthew rushed into the kitchen, opened the door which faced the rear garden. He was knocked back on to his heels by the sight of his father, bruised, dishevelled-looking as though he had done battle with a whole yobbo army.

"Dad – What the hell – ?"

But Gideon had no time for explanation.

"Listen," he growled. "I've just dodged my way past dozens of evil youths as murderous as those in your garden. They're all out to get you and make no mistake they're going to send the house up in smoke any second. That creeper you've got all round the house – they've probably soaked it and the bricks with petrol and when that catches light – "

Matthew's face lost every vestige of colour.

"But I can't take the family outside front or back with all this stuff being hurled. What in God's name can I do?"

Gideon stared past him into the centre of the kitchen, looking briskly around him. "I'm telling you what you do. You get Julie, the children, Pamela, the whole household in here, at the double. That door over there leads to the garage, doesn't it?" He moved to the door, inspecting it and then continuing his instructions. "Looks solid enough to hold the flames back for quite a while. So the family should be pretty safe through here – and the steel doors on the garage will keep out anything the yobbos can fling. Then, as soon as the yobbos have gone, you can take everyone down to the end of the garden. Good job it's a long one. Knowing how this blaze was started, you should be okay down there. Is that clear?"

He might have been talking to the weedy, hesitant teenager that Matthew had once been: the lightweight shadow of his heavyweight father. And certainly, Matthew was showing no sign of being the smart, assured businessman now. He gulped as he struggled to grasp the situation.

"But supposing the mob *don't* go?"

Gideon dismissed this objection with a shrug.

"Don't worry about that. I've heard the sirens of the Riot Squad. They should be here any time now and as soon as they are on the scene they'll keep the yobbos far too busy to hurl stuff at anyone. Even you."

Matthew still looked afraid.

"Why – even *me*?" he asked.

Despite the strain and tension of the moment, Gideon felt a sudden wild surge of hope.

It was as if Matthew didn't know.

* * *

At that moment, there was a loud crackling from just outside the back door, coupled with the sound of raucous jeers and clapping. A flash, almost like lightning but far more prolonged, lit up the kitchen windows. It was followed by a Niagara-like roaring and belching and smoke pouring up past the window.

"That's your creeper going up," said Gideon grimly. "Better hurry and get the kids – " He broke off. A sudden change had come over Matthew, perhaps because of the reassuring presence of his father, perhaps the shock that had dulled his anger was wearing off, he no longer looked dazed and confused, but very, very angry.

"Those bastards! Who the hell do they think they are?" he roared and before Gideon could stop him he opened the back door, obviously intending to hurl himself at the marauders who laughed and cheered as they set his home ablaze.

All he hurled himself at, though, was a sheet of flame – and the next second he was staggering back, dressing-gown alight at the shoulder, his hair and eyebrows singed, his face blackened and his eyes streaming. Gideon slammed the back door, the wood already blackening, just in time to keep out most of a thick black cloud of acrid smoke and petrol fumes. Gasping and choking himself, he moved to the sink, seized a washing-up basin fortunately full of water, and hurled it over his son.

"Thanks Dad," Matthew gasped. "That was f-----g silly of me." Then he rushed to the door leading from the kitchen to the hall, and bellowed, in a voice slightly reminiscent of his father's roar: "In here. In the kitchen – everybody! At the double. Now! Oh Christ!"

The roar became a groan of total dismay as the lights went out.

Not that that, in fact, mattered. All over the house, lights were pouring in through every window – the red flashing light from the fires, small and great, that were now burning – everywhere. Upstairs, running footsteps sounded – then silence, and in a moment, the kitchen was packed with people. Through the smoke Gideon could make out a near-hysterical Julie carrying the three-year-old Debbie in her arms, but staggering so much that it seemed that at any moment she might drop her, and a calm, businesslike Pamela Carter, leading the four-year-old Richard with one hand and the five-year-old Sandra with the other.

Debbie, in her mother's arms, was bawling at the top of her voice. Richard had his thumb in his mouth, and looked close to tears. Sandra was surprisingly calm – so calm, in fact, that she seemed to Gideon to have almost the look of Kate as she tried to reassure her brother.

"Don't worry, Richard. We are all going to be all right. Look – your Grandpa Giddyman's here."

Richard was more impressed by the brilliant stream of sparks rising up from the burning creeper right outside the window, and lighting up the whole room.

"Pretty," he said approvingly. "Like golden rain."

Gideon had opened the door leading to the garage.

"That's right, Richard my boy," he said, "but better get in here, quick, before it rains on *you*!"

Richard ran across to him, almost leaving Sandra and Pamela behind him. A shaking Julie carried the bawling Debbie through next with Matthew bringing up the rear, a bedraggled figure with his eyes still stinging, his singed dressing-gown still dripping and making puddles behind him as he moved.

It was with profound relief that Gideon followed them into the garage, and slammed the door shut behind them.

God knew how many seconds away from death they had been in that kitchen. Here, at least, there was relative security . . . *If* the door held out against the flames; *if* the vandals were swiftly settled by the Riot Squad; *if* the fumes from that creeper weren't blown in the direction of the garage roof; *if* –

Gideon forced himself to forget about the "ifs" and concentrate on the immediate situation.

The garage was a big one, but since it housed three very large cars, there wasn't much room in it for the seven of them. Since it was also very dark – the tight-fitting steel doors admitted not a chink of light and the only illumination was from a small rear window, only two foot square – there was a lot of blundering about and bumping of shins. Then Pamela Carter found a torch, and with its help succeeded in ushering the whole family, including Matthew and Julie, between the cars and one of the garage walls. She'd really taken her police training to heart, thought Gideon: she might have been lining them all up to be searched. Her brisk efficiency seemed to be good for the children though. Neither Sandra nor Richard was crying, and Debbie had stopped that ear-splitting bawling – though that had more to do with Matthew than Pamela. He had moved alongside Julie, and taken Debbie from her. He had also slipped his free arm round his wife, and was doing his best to comfort her, which had left him too busy to take command himself.

Gideon eyed him approvingly. At least that showed he was human, he told himself – and then was appalled at his own thoughts. Human? Of course Matthew was human. He was his own flesh and blood, for heaven's sake. Hadn't he guided him along every step of his way all through his childhood –

He stopped thinking abruptly, and went to the little window which overlooked the back garden. What he saw was one of the most appalling spectacles of the night. It was impossible to see anything of the house from there, or for that matter, any of the other houses in Malibu Rise: but the whole scene was pervaded with an ominous flickering redness, reminding him not so much of the Blitz, as, going right back to his childhood, of that night of the Crystal Palace fire. The great fire must be blazing behind them. Probably 1, 2 and 3, Malibu Rise had gone up together: equally probably, other buildings all over the Heights were blazing too – that large hotel amongst them. Sparks and bits of blazing material were everywhere, a whirling myriad of flame. Smoke was gusting about like a mountain mist, one moment blanking out half the scene, the next being whisked away as though it had never been. In one clear moment he saw glimpses of several members of the marauding gangs in the garden. They were no longer cowering, half hidden. They were standing openly, staring in exhilaration at the blaze he could not see, light reddening their faces and eyes, even their glittering teeth, until they looked quite literally devilish.

No wonder they were grinning, thought Gideon bitterly. This was their moment, wasn't it – the greatest all-out triumph for mob lawlessness in the whole of his long experience. And, if the people down below didn't get their fingers out pretty damn quick, it would be by far the bloodiest.

It was at that darkest of all moments that Pamela Carter left the children, and came up to him. Suddenly, very much WPC Craddock, she whispered: "Commander, there's something I've discovered which I think you ought to . . ."

She seemed totally taken aback when Gideon interrupted her, and hissed: "Not now, WPC. For God's sake, not *now*!"

Before she could recover herself, and Gideon could get over his sudden fury, there was another interruption and a very welcome one.

A complex cacophony of sounds came from somewhere close by – the sirens of a dozen or more police cars; the drone of heavier engines – belonging perhaps to lorries, perhaps even to armoured trucks; and mingled with them, other bells and sirens, recognisable as those of ambulances and fire engines. Clearly the Riot Squad had arrived in force, and (Gideon guessed) was now reaching the burnt-out cars and improvised barricade at the end of the High Street, barely a hundred yards from where they stood. Behind them were the desperately needed emergency services – the fire brigade and ambulance men – but they could not begin to move up, of course, until the barricade was stormed, the obstructing cars pulled clear.

How long would that take? That was the question, every second counted –

There were new sounds now: shouts, defiant chanting, screams of rage, the banging, the crashing of metal against metal as objects were thrown at the police cars and lorries. There were also groans of pain, suggesting that not all the shots had missed, not all the missiles had been thrown at the cars . . .

Someone on the police side began bawling orders but the men in the lorries were being told to get out, and mount a charge. He thought he heard the words "hose them". That must mean they had a water cannon, though it had never been seen in combat before. Suddenly there was a prolonged burst of gunfire, though whether the police were doing the firing, or being fired at, it was difficult to tell. The shouting and jeering rose to a crescendo – and then was abruptly silenced by the roar of water, and the seismic spitting and hissing as it hit the white-hot cars. Screams of pain and panic followed, which could only mean one thing, Gideon realised, with an understandably deep satisfaction. The thugs at the barricades must be in full retreat. He glimpsed figures in the garden running for their lives, their expressions registering not gleeful triumph any longer but very great alarm.

Suddenly it was his turn to feel alarm. An ominous crackling sound from right above them, told him that the fire had caught the garage roof. Pamela flashed her torch upwards – and gulped as she saw a jagged line of cracks appear all over the ceiling with puffs of smoke seeping through them.

"That settles it!" roared Gideon. "Outside everyone, and into the garden fast!"

He spotted a black slimy object folded in a neat pile in one corner.

"Is that a tarpaulin? Then I suggest we hold it over us as we go. Should keep the sparks off our hair and faces, and if we run fast enough, it won't catch fire itself. Come on kids," he added as he advanced towards the pile. "Grandpa Giddyman will show you how to make a Chinese dragon . . ."

Within seconds he had unwrapped the tarpaulin and was hanging it over the heads of Matthew, Julie and Pamela and the children. The device worked beautifully. Under its cover, they were out of the garage and halfway down the garden within seconds – and without a scratch, burn or blister among them.

They could soon jettison the tarpaulin. The air was relatively free from the sparks and whirling debris, although that eerie cosmic redness was everywhere and looking backwards was like peering directly into the mouth of Hell.

Gideon saw that his fears had been well-founded. Numbers 1, 2 and 3, Malibu Rise were all blazing by now probably uncontrollably. And down all three gardens, across scorched grass, trees and shrubs reduced to blackened hulks, the fire was still creeping towards them. As he watched, a close-by stretch of fencing suddenly collapsed amidst a shower of sparks and on their immediate left, approaching flames licked at a small wooden garden shed.

"Keep going!" he shouted to Matthew. "We've got to get Julie and the kids right down to the end of the garden. They should be safe there. Please God, the brigade will be here soon. It won't take them for ever to clear the road."

He saw Matthew nod, then he and the whole family disappeared from sight in a thick cloud of smoke that abruptly descended from nowhere. Pamela did not disappear with them. On the contrary, she came looming out of the smoke and clutched Gideon's arm so fiercely that her grip was surprisingly painful.

"Commander, there's something you *must* see."

Before Gideon could stop her, she had opened the door of the little garden shed and dragged him inside.

"For God's sake, what is all this!" he began crossly – and then suddenly was too choked up to speak.

And it wasn't the smoke that was choking him.

Pamela had stooped and raised one of the floorboards of the shed, and was shining her torch through the gap – below was a pile of cardboard boxes. One of them, already singed and smoking, had broken open, revealing all too clearly what it contained: a dozen or more packages wrapped in polystyrene filled with a white powdery substance that was unmistakably heroin.

Each of the packages contained, he estimated, at least fifty thousand pounds worth of the drug. The total value of the haul he was looking at must run into millions.

The packets seemed to swim in front of Gideon's eyes, and Pamela's voice appeared to come from a great distance as she explained, in her best police-manual manner: "The looseness of the floorboards aroused my suspicions when I glanced into this shed earlier today, and so, when the Goddards were asleep, I took the opportunity to steal out and make a closer inspection – "

Suddenly her voice faded out altogether, as far as Gideon was concerned.

He heard a step behind him, and Matthew came in. Presumably he had taken Julie and the children to safety, and had come back to search for them.

Father and son stared down together at the boxes and packets, both looking equally aghast. The light of WPC Craddock's torch was barely needed now. The whole interior of the shed was lit up by the red glow of flames immediately outside the window. All three of them were in great danger, but for the moment, scarcely aware of it.

His face in fact a deathly white, but eerily flushed by the flames, Matthew turned to Gideon and began hoarsely: "Dad – you – you don't think – "

Gideon found his voice at last but it was so quiet as to be hardly recognisable as his own.

"What else can I think?" he said.

There was a long, terrible silence – broken by a scream, equally long, equally terrible, coming from somewhere close by: from the sound of it the garden of Fergus Atkinson's house, about twenty yards away.

There would be no trouble reaching it – both the retaining fences had collapsed, thought Gideon.

He shot out of the shed, and started running in the direction of the sound, so fast that anyone who didn't know him might have thought that he was running away.

16 Bonfire

Gideon, in fact, was not consciously running *to* or *away* from anything as he rushed along the black smoking scrublands which were all that was left of those once luxurious gardens. He was for the moment beyond thinking and feeling, but was functioning, as it were, purely on automatic pilot.

Someone was in trouble, even agony, and whether it turned out to be a marauding yobbo or a beleaguered householder, his overriding instinct was to be there and give what help he could. But the situation was far more complicated than that, as he realised as soon as he neared the garden of 3, Malibu Rise. The fence here had collapsed in a pile of wooden planks, that was now blazing like a bonfire.

A bonfire which, he could see as he drew near, was now a funeral pyre. A charred body was clearly discernible amongst the flames – and he could now make out the figure of a man standing over it, looking down in obvious incredulity and horror at what he'd done.

Which didn't make it any less a matter of murder, Gideon thought. If this man had tossed the other into the flames – as his guilty look seemed to suggest –

Slowing his pace, he stepped over the remains of the flower-bed bordering the garden and strode grimly up behind the man.

Not until he was a couple of yards away did it dawn on him that he was about to put his hand on the shoulder of Tom Riddell.

* * *

It took Riddell a long time to get out the whole story of what had happened to him that night – and during the last part of it, he was sweating, shivering and frequently retching.

After collapsing so dramatically at his enemy's feet he

had blacked out for only a few moments, and had recovered consciousness to find himself being dragged bodily across the patio and out on to the garden. It had been a painful progress but the bumps and bruises must have stimulated his brain and returned him abruptly to consciousness.

At first, he had assumed that Atkinson had had a change of heart, and decided that he simply couldn't leave him to die in a blazing house. But gradually the realisation dawned on him that a rescue was the last thing this evil monster intended.

The air grew hotter and hotter, as though he was being dragged not away from a blaze but towards one. Straining to glance round, he glimpsed the flames of two bonfires accidentally created by the collapse of the fence. They were so close that the heat scorched his face, his eyes started streaming, and it was the struggle of his life not to cough and splutter.

Then he heard, somewhere close by, the sirens of police cars and the clanging of fire engines, and saw in a flash what Atkinson was thinking. It was not safe to leave him in the house if firemen and the police could be here so soon. His chance of survival would be too high.

"But if he chucked me on to a bonfire like a bleeding Guy Fawkes, he'd be laughing," Riddell finished, his voice sounding less shaky as his anger rose. "What he didn't expect was that at the critical moment, I'd come to life and start struggling. He lost his balance and – well the next thing I knew, I was scrambling clear and being bloody near deafened by a god-awful scream from just behind me."

He stopped then, overtaken by another fit of retching. When he got his breath back, he spluttered:

"I know what you're going to say. I should have tried to pull him out, or something. But I couldn't make myself turn. Not until it was too late. I was afraid to look – Christ, that smell of burning – I'll remember it until my dying day – "

"Join the club, Tom," said Gideon, gruffly. "There are a lot of things about tonight that *I* shan't be forgetting for a long time, either."

He took Riddell's arm with a firm reassuring grip, but

Tom's shaking almost gave him the quakes, and he was obliged to let go. His voice became sharper. "There's nothing to feel guilty about. It's the clearest case of killing in self-defence I've ever heard of. For God's sake, pull yourself together – and don't you dare tell me you can't! There's no one in the whole Met who can pull himself together like you can. You've proved it time and time again – "

Suddenly his tone softened – "And never more so than tonight. You may as well know that to all intents and purposes I took you off this case on the grounds that you'd become a nervous wreck."

Riddell stuttered. "To – all – intents and . . ."

"Yes. By that I mean that I'd invited Lem to take over, but couldn't bring myself to spell the situation out to you. A clumsy, two-faced bit of administration that I'm far from proud of, I might tell you but at least it left you a loophole, and I'm thunderstruck at the thought of what you did with it. You came back on the case so late that there wouldn't even *be* a case by the morning. Everything was sewn up and you only had the small hours to work in. Any other copper in the force would have given up and gone home, especially after my warning that Fletchwood Heights was an unhealthy place to stay around in. But instead of that, you go doggedly on, obstinately taking all kinds of risks to save poor old Bertie's son from a life sentence.

"And you wound up by identifying and nailing, single-handed, one of the most cunning and conniving monsters I've ever come across . . . And without you, Tom, he'd have bamboozled us all along the line!"

He stared down unpityingly at the body, now just a featureless heap of glowing ash, and only just stopped himself from touching it with his foot.

"Yes, you're right, I do wish you'd yanked him out of this alive. His trial would have been a sensation – and you'd have emerged from it as the Copper of the City! As it is, what you've done is going to make a lot of headlines. I'll see to that, I promise you."

Riddell was still staring at him blankly. It was unusual, to say the least, for Gideon to be so profuse in his praises. But he not only wanted to make up to Tom for the rough deal he had given him: he wanted to boost the man's ego, once and for all, beyond the point where serious stress and self-doubt could deflate it.

It wasn't just a question of therapy. It was a matter of simple justice. Riddell *was*, in spite of himself, one of the most brilliant men in the C.I.D. and for proof of that, it was only necessary to see all that had been cleared up since he had arrived on the scene of the crime tonight.

The attempted frame-up of "Red" Benton had been exposed; the murder of Don Mitchell had been solved; that poor girl Suzy Nelson, he must check how she was doing in hospital, had been avenged; to say nothing of Tom's own wife, Vi.

Other problems were solving themselves now, all round him. The garden was suddenly crowded with firemen and riot-squad policemen who conducted him and Riddell to a safe distance while the blazing houses were tackled.

From the police, Gideon learned that the area was now free of rioters and that there had been as many as two hundred arrests.

"Glad to hear it," he growled. "Those hooligans don't deserve to be on any street for a long, long time. I don't know a word to describe people who set fire to houses – and then hang around to throw missiles at their occupants when they try to escape. Well if I did, I wouldn't use it. It might start another ruddy fire on the spot."

From the firemen he learnt that the thing he had feared most – an unstoppable blaze enveloping the whole of Fletchwood Heights – had not materialised.

Although attempts had been made to set upwards of fifty houses alight, less than half of these had succeeded. In some instances, the thugs had been tackled by security guards and fled. In others guard dogs had driven them away. The area's large gardens had also prevented blazes spreading too fast, and some had lawn-sprinklers powerful enough to stop the advancing flames dead.

"Not that there haven't been casualties," one of the firemen said. "Maybe a dozen of 'em. Like the poor devil back there . . ." He glanced towards the bonfire, "Probably knocked down by a missile when he was running for his life."

All trace of guilt vanished from Riddell's face as he realised what Fergus Atkinson's plan had been. Had his, Riddell's body, been found in that bonfire, that is just how it would have appeared that *he* had met death. Not the faintest hint of suspicion would have attached itself to the MP.

Gideon's heartfelt praises were now at last having their desired effect. The guilt gone, the nausea and retching past, Riddell was suddenly beginning to realise that this had been a night, not only of terror, but of triumph for him.

He turned to the leader of the Riot Squad, "I've got to get to the station," he said. "I've an important report to make. Is there a car available?"

"Will be soon, sir," he was told. "The road's clear – and once the ambulances are away – "

"Right. Lead me to it," snapped Riddell and vanished after him across the lawn.

A modest hero, and the most loyal man in the force, thought Gideon as he watched him go.

The houses behind him – or rather, the blackened shells of them – were already being hosed from five or six directions. No flames were in sight any more, but there was still smoke pouring out, some of it mixed with whitey-grey plumes of steam. High above them the moon shone. Her light made the plumes look eerie, witchlike, as though ghosts were literally rising from those houses where so much murder had been done.

He heard one of the riot policemen calling to him through the smoke and steam.

"Would you like a squad car too, sir?"

Just for a moment, Gideon was tempted to say "yes" – to have himself whisked away from Malibu Rise once and for all.

What conceivable good could he do for anyone by continuing to stay?

He dreaded to think what might be happening now in the garden of No. 1. Knowing WPC Craddock's dedication to duty, it was more than likely that she had revealed her identity to Matthew, and attempted to arrest him. If there were Riot Squad men in this garden, they would almost certainly have gone into Matthew's garden and would have backed Pamela up once she had shown them her badge. Gideon pictured Matthew, handcuffed, surrounded by policemen, waiting to be led to a squad car, with Julie and the children watching dazed, dumbfounded.

And Matthew would remember that he, Gideon, and WPC Craddock had worked almost as a team. He would probably think of her as his father's spy . . . And this arrest as his father's doing . . .

How would it help the situation if he turned up, to stand glumly in the background, providing positive proof that these suspicions were true?

There was every reason for him to absent himself from a painful scene – except one.

Something inside him was simply not going to let him stay away. Matthew was his son, and he had to know for certain what was going on.

In a voice, barely recognisable even to himself, Gideon shouted that he did not want a car, and the next moment, he was striding back towards the garden of No. 1.

He walked faster and faster with every step, his usual way of confronting mounting fear.

17 Man Hunt

Gideon's immediate fear, at least, proved to be groundless.

When he arrived at the end of the garden of No. 1, there were no policemen in sight. No one was there, except Julie and the three children.

In a strange, translucent moonlight, surrounded by plumes of steam and smoke, they all rushed towards him, Julie particularly glad to see him.

"Thank God you're back. What's been happening?" she asked. "What made that awful scream? And – and where's Matthew?"

She and the children had been right at the end of the garden, half-smothered in smoke, when Matthew had suddenly left them. The smoke had cleared enough for her to see him walk to the burning shed, and enter it.

A moment later, she had heard the scream, and seen Gideon go charging off across to the next door garden – *with Matthew close behind him.*

Gideon swallowed hard. He had heard no following footsteps, and had been far too intent on tracing the source of the scream to look round. And once in the next door garden, Matthew would have had every opportunity to slip away through the smoke and confusion . . .

"What else can I think?" was the last thing he had said to his son. That question had even more force now – if Matthew had simply fled from the scene.

Julie was suddenly not far from hysteria.

"If Matthew's not with you, where is he?" she asked. "And come to that where's Pamela Carter? She seems to have vanished too. For God's sake, what's going on?"

Richard was clutching at Gideon's sleeve. "Giddyman will tell you, Mummy," he said confidently. "I bet *he* knows."

Gideon knew all right – or could make a shrewd guess.

Matthew was obviously miles away from Malibu Rise by

now, and Pamela was at the police station, in a police car radioing a message to her drugs-squad superiors which could start an immediate manhunt, probably a nation-wide one.

Meanwhile, here was his brand-new daughter-in-law and her family lost, cold, shivering, and there was no word of hope or comfort he could honestly give them.

He did his best, though.

"I lost track of Matthew. Except he's giving a hand to the police or ambulancemen somewhere – probably Pamela's doing the same," he lied as comfortingly as he could. "The main thing is to get you all out of here. I'll rustle up a police car and you must all come back to my house. Kate and I will be delighted to put you up until . . . "

Until when? A voice inside him asked savagely. Until Matthew was caught, and the kids were virtually fatherless as well as homeless?

His fumbling instructions were almost immediately reversed. "We're not moving an inch until Matthew's back," Julie told him.

"Not an inch," said Richard and Sandra together and Debbie shook a defiant head. Gideon, his options as grey as the moonlight streaming around him, had no choice but to tell them all that Matthew might be gone for quite a while.

"Why!" said Julie and then had a flash of intuition. "It's something to do with that shed, isn't it? For God's sake, what did you find in there?"

At that moment Debbie began to bawl again giving Gideon a chance to say, in a whisper that did nothing to soften the bleak harshness of his words.

"If you want the truth – a multi-million-pound haul of heroin."

Julie's tone changed abruptly from near-hysteria to something far, far worse, as far as Gideon was concerned: simple, naked hate.

"And – and you think – you, his own father, think – "

He answered her as honestly as he could. "I'm not thinking anything – except that Matthew has a lot of questions to answer, and doesn't at the moment seem too keen on answering them," he told her. "Look, hadn't I better get that car now? These kids could end up with pneumonia. It's a miracle that they're not in a state of shock – "

The hatred in Julie's voice intensified.

"Thanks for your offer, Commander, but we have *friends* who will put us up," she said.

The word "Commander" came across with the viciousness of a slap in the face; a single-word announcement that as far as she was concerned he was no longer "family", and nothing but an enemy. What hurt most was that Matthew, wherever he was, was almost certainly thinking the same. Whether she realised this or not, she was speaking on behalf of them both.

Gideon did the only thing possible. He turned and walked away.

Heading this time in a different direction, he skirted the smouldering shell of No. 1 and found himself in Malibu Rise, now just packed with police, firemen and ambulancemen. He sent two policemen, and an ambulanceman with blankets, back to attend to Julie and the children. They couldn't be allowed to huddle there, shivering, for any longer, regardless of Julie's feelings about him.

This done, he commandeered a police car and asked it to take him straight to Scotland Yard. Once again he was following an instinct – that old instinct that told him to get himself at the centre of things, born of twenty-six years of being in high command.

It wasn't until the car had taken him halfway to Westminster that it suddenly dawned on him that, with a national man hunt in progress for his son, the further he was away from Scotland Yard the better.

He stopped the car, and told the driver to take him to Harringdon Street, Fulham.

Even as he gave the order, he was uneasily aware that even that might not, at this moment, prove the ideal place to be.

* * *

At Scotland Yard itself, Gideon's absence had been almost as devastating as his presence.

Thoughts of him had loomed large in the minds of senior men continually through the night, and especially in the mind of his son-in-law and immediate superior, Assistant Commissioner, Alec Hobbs.

Hobbs had been worrying about Gideon right from the start of the evening. He had known all about his and Kate's dinner engagement up at the Heights. Kate had rung his wife Penny, and poured out the news. On the phone Penny had been almost as excited about it as Kate. Matthew had been her favourite brother, and it was almost like learning that he had returned from the dead.

Fearful that if he went home Penny might get out of him the truth about Matthew, the massive tide of suspicions rising round him, Alec had decided to work late at the Yard. Not that he had got much work done. The thought of Gideon's predicament had continued to haunt him. It was, in a sense, his predicament too. If Matthew proved to be guilty, the lives of everyone in the Gideon family would never be the same again.

Then, at around midnight, the news had broken about the murder of Don Mitchell – in, of all places, the house next door to Matthew's – and the suspected involvement of the Oxfam Robin Hood. A TV celebrity apparently murdered by the favourite villain of the mass-circulation dailies, who had then shot down the maid of an equally big celebrity, Fergus Atkinson! The Yard had been flooded with enquiries from the media, and Alec had found himself suddenly desperately busy, issuing statements, receiving reports, and reporting on the situation himself on the phone to Scott-Marle.

Once again Gideon's name kept cropping up. George was down there, on the scene, in charge. Then it was learned that he had called in Lemaitre – and more sensational reports followed in quick succession. PC Benton's son Red was suspected of being the Oxfam Robin Hood. Lemaitre and Gideon were arresting him. Their car was besieged by thugs –

Hobbs was still at the Yard at 2.00 a.m. when Lemaitre himself had telephoned, on arriving home from Fletchwood station. He had been at his chirpiest, reporting that Red Benton was in the cells, that he would be charged in the morning with murder, that in fact, everything had been wrapped up "neat as a parcel on a Christmas tree".

"Can't honestly say Gee Gee seems too happy about it," he had suddenly added. "But then, Gee Gee's not too happy about anything tonight. For reasons you and I know only too well, Squire."

Alec had winced – not only because he never liked Lem's way of addressing superiors. If Gideon wasn't too happy about the situation, then neither was he.

To make matters worse, he had been all set to go home – Penny would be asleep in bed by now, and please God wouldn't wake up and ask a lot of questions – when he received the most worrying call of all.

It was from Kate, asking him if he knew what was going on at Fletchwood Heights. She had stuttered out something about George walking back there on foot – and that even from her house she could see the flames.

Alec had left his goldfish bowl of an office on the eleventh floor of the Yard – and found the whole place in turmoil: turmoil that concerned uniformed branch rather than C.I.D. which was why, as Assistant Commissioner (Crime) he hadn't been immediately notified. News was pouring in of a major riot developing in the Heights – arson, terror on a massive scale, the very scenario that Gideon had foreseen. And George was literally walking into the middle of it – right now.

Scott-Marle arrived, to take charge possibly at the very moment when a report was received that Gideon had been surrounded and very probably murdered by a lynch-mob. It put him in a "no holds barred" mood, and he immediately ordered the largest riot-squad operation ever known on the mainland: water cannons, riot shields, rubber bullets – everything was to be taken in.

"If George has gone down," he said to Alec, with a cold ferocity Hobbs had never seen in him before, "we'll get every last member of the mob that did it."

But Gideon had not gone down. A sergeant at Fletchwood station rang in to report that he had heard him radioing instructions from a car. "After which, Sir," said the sergeant in an awed voice, "he apparently left the vehicle and was proceeding on foot – in the direction of Malibu Rise . . ."

Malibu Rise? That was where the main trouble was

centred – where the fires were fiercest, the suspected carnage at its worst. But better news was soon coming in of the effectiveness of Scott-Marle's Riot Squad, the storming of the barricade, the mass arrests, the hooligans in full retreat. Still better news followed – of fire engines getting through, of flames under control.

It was around 4.00 a.m. when Hobbs received the most surprising call of the night. It was from Riddell who sounded, for once, almost as cocky as Lemaitre as he reported the Fergus Atkinson developments.

One thing that he said stood out from all the rest, as far as Hobbs was concerned. Gideon had been on the scene at the end, Riddell had spoken to him only a few minutes before. He was safe, alive, well – and (Riddell could not help implying) profuse in his praises . . .

"I'm not surprised," Alec told him. "It seems to me as though they were well-deserved, Tom. Very well-deserved indeed."

As he put down the phone, his sense of relief was overwhelming. But it was to be very, very short-lived. He looked up to see Scott-Marle himself standing in the doorway of his office, looking grave and stern. A quarter of an hour before, he had been telephoned by Naughton of the Drugs Squad.

"He was woken by a call from a WPC he's got doing undercover work in Matthew Gideon's household. It seems there's now water-tight evidence that Matthew *is* the drugs baron. Both she and Gideon have seen it – and Matthew knows they've seen it."

"Christ," said Alec softly. "What's Gideon going to do?"

Scott-Marle looked grimmer than ever.

"The point is what *I'm* going to do," he said. "I gather that Matthew has got away, vanished in the confusion and smoke. Naughton is quite rightly asking for an immediate all-out attempt to pull him in – headed by the Drugs Squad, but with support from all other sections. I've just been putting that in hand."

"Will it be needed?" said Alec. "Surely he can't get far – on foot, with the Riot Squad on the streets in such force."

"Slipping through even that squad during a full-scale emergency is child's play," said Scott-Marle. "And Naughton's guess is that he's probably not on foot any longer. Even if he hasn't got friends and contacts, there are such things as all-night hire firms – "

"Who'll ask no questions and roll out the red carpet once they see the wallet of cash he'll have with him," finished Alec.

"Quite so. If you haven't done it already, I'd better get the radio room to collate a description – and make sure it's sent to all media."

Hobbs raced across the room towards his desk and the battery of phones there – but he stopped halfway.

"My God," he said softly. "Do we have to use the name Gideon?"

Scott-Marle's expression was suddenly cold and bleak and his voice matched it, sounding harsh and oddly inhuman, as he snapped: "Of course we do. The usual format – Gideon alias Goddard and the very fact that you ask that question reminds me that you shouldn't be taking any part in this business. Do I have to repeat what I said yesterday afternoon? You are off the case, Hobbs, off it completely. My advice – no, my *orders* – are that you go home immediately, and away for a holiday until you have my permission to return."

It took Hobbs a moment to recover from this onslaught – a moment during which Commander Naughton suddenly appeared on the scene. As usual he looked like a hit-man, but now a hit-man in a hurry. His bald head gleamed with sweat. His clothes showed every sign of having been donned in haste: half the shirt buttons were undone, and the knot in his tie was in danger of being completely undone. His normally stony expression was replaced by the excited, eager look of a killer moving in for the kill.

"Sorry to barge in, sir, but they told me I'd find you here, and I reckoned this was no time to be kicking my heels in your office," he told the Commander. "There's something I think we need to put together now, if not sooner. It's – "

Scott-Marle held up a hand to silence him, and stared at Alec.

"*Goodnight*, Hobbs," he said, each word as sharp as a dagger.

He only allowed Naughton to resume when Alec was some way down the corridor outside, and then he stopped him after a few sentences while he slammed the door, cutting off all further sound from the retreating Hobbs.

This last gesture proved futile, in point of fact. Hobbs had sharp ears, and had already caught the gist of the request Naughton was making. It made him heartily thankful to be on his way.

The Drugs Squad Commander was asking for a warrant to carry out an immediate search of 12, Harringdon Street, Fulham – George Gideon's home.

* * *

It was at that very moment, a couple of miles away across London, that Gideon was asking the driver of his police car to turn around and drive him home.

And that Kate, at 12, Harringdon Street itself, was startled by a ring at the front door; a curious ring, almost a dot dot dash.

Her feelings a wild mixture of anxiety and excitement, dread and anticipation, she rushed to answer the summons, needing no telling who was ringing.

Matthew had always done a dot dot dash on that bell since he had learnt the Morse Code in the Wolf Cubs at the age of eight.

18 Matthew

Matthew was looking in a pretty bad way. It was hard to recognise him as the elegant man of affairs he had been earlier but Kate, of course, would have recognised him in any circumstances anywhere.

His face, hands, clothes – everything about him was blackened by the smoke of the fire. His eyebrows had been so singed that the left one was now invisible. His hair was streaked with dirt, much of it ash, so that it looked for a moment as if he had gone grey overnight. His hands were blistered and his trousers torn down both legs, so badly that socks and even a stitch of underpants showed through.

His voice sounded as if it had been as scorched as his eyebrows. In a harsh, dry crack, he muttered: "Sorry to bother you, Mum, but – but I need – "

"A drink, a bath and a change of clothes, in that order, from the look of it," said Kate promptly. "Come on in."

She did not ask any questions and, as if as a reward, promptly received the answer to the question that was uppermost in her thoughts.

"Dad isn't home yet, I take it," Matthew said. "But there's no need to worry – he's fine, and will be home before long – and to save you asking, Julie and the kids are fine too – thanks to Dad as much as anyone."

"Thank God," said Kate, her own voice just a little croaky. Matthew managed a lop-sided smile.

"Though something tells me nothing else will be fine," he added, "if I've not gone before Dad comes."

Kate's grey-blue eyes began to fill with tears.

"Don't tell me you've had one of those awful rows. If so it's my fault. I – I virtually forced him to go back and have everything out with you – never realising the danger he'd be running into. *Did* you talk?" Matthew's smile grew more lop-sided.

"On the subject of my alleged misdeeds, you mean? We had a few words – very few."

Then he was pushing past her into the house. "For God's sake, where's that drink? Don't you realise, I've *got* to be quick – "

Kate rushed into the dining-room, where the drinks cabinet was, and poured him out a glass of brandy. He drank it at a gulp, then went upstairs to the bathroom. While he was in there, Kate looked him out one of Gideon's weekend outfits – a tweed jacket and flannels – with a shirt, a pair of shoes and a tie.

In less than five minutes, Matthew was out of the bathroom, showered, clean, and dressed – though he could hardly have been called spruce. Gideon's jacket reached halfway to his knees; the flannel trousers touched the floor. Somehow, however, he managed to wear them with an air.

"I'll see Dad gets this back," he said. "Even if I have to send them with compliments from the nearest jail."

Kate was hardly able to see through her tears.

"Don't talk like that. I know you're not guilty of anything terrible. You *can't* be – "

Matthew put an arm round her. "Bless you, Mum. But try telling that to Dad."

"No," said Kate, suddenly pleadingly. "*You* try telling him. He'll be here in a moment, you said. Stay and talk to him."

Matthew guiltily let go of her and backed away.

"Sorry. But the mood he's in at the moment, I don't think that would be too good an idea."

"You don't believe he'd listen? That was why he turned back earlier tonight just to get to you, to hear what you had to say."

It was just as well Kate couldn't see Matthew too clearly. Bitterness twisted his mouth as he replied: "That's as may be. But in the end he seemed rather more interested in what that police spy he had planted on me had to say. Or, rather, in what she had to show him."

Kate stared at him, but her eyes were still not dry, and his face was a blotchy blur as she said, dazedly, "What was that?"

Matthew decided to be frank. "A hoard of heroin worth millions, hidden under the floorboards of my garden shed," he told her. "You may as well know it all, Mum. The police are after me in a big way – and since there's no way in which Dad can ever stop being a policeman, that means only one thing. Whether he likes it or not, he's after me too."

Fresh tears flooded into Kate's eyes, almost blinding her. "You know as well as I do, when it came to the point, your Dad would never – give you up – "

Her voice faltered even as she said it, betraying her own sudden doubt.

Matthew laughed – a sad laugh, without a hint of humour in it.

"Face it, Mum. Half of him would, the other half wouldn't. And believe it or not I happen to love the old devil too much to split him in two."

Before Kate could reply, there was the sound of a car drawing up outside.

"Cue for exit, if ever I heard one," Matthew said. "Do me one last favour, please. I've parked my car down the road. Give me the time to get to it before you tell Dad I've been here. For his sake as much as mine."

He kissed her on the cheek, and then was gone, heading in the direction of the kitchen and the back door. He would have no trouble getting away through the back garden without being seen from the front, Kate knew. There was a fence into an alley the other side of it – climbing over it had ripped his shirts many a time when he was a boy . . .

Kate had time to wipe her eyes before she heard a key turning in the front door – and Gideon was home.

He looked in a far worse way than Matthew had done. It wasn't only that his face, hands and clothes were blackened. He had a terrible look of combined weariness and anguish. It was as though he, not Matthew, was the hunted man.

Kate ran over and flung her arms around him. Perhaps it was partly a ploy to stop him asking questions, finding out about Matthew too soon – but it soon became much more than that. Relief at being with him again swamped all other feelings. She found herself violently trembling, which was very rare for the normally calm serene wife of the C.I.D.'s Commander.

"It's all right, love. Take it easy," Gideon found himself saying over and over again – though what was all right about the present situation he'd have given a lot to know.

The phone on the hall table rang, before he, or Kate, could say anything more. Releasing her very gently, he walked across to it, his normal purposeful stride reduced by tiredness to a lumbering slouch.

"Gideon here," he said, adding heavily, "by a miracle."

"George." It was Alec Hobbs, sounding very tense and half whispering, almost as though afraid of being overheard. "I'm ringing from the Yard. Kiosk in the foyer. Shouldn't be here really. Scott-Marle's ordered me off the premises." With a breathless rush he went on, "Listen, he could have my guts for garters for telling you this, but I think you ought to know. Naughton's asking Scott-Marle for a warrant to search your home."

Gideon's only reply was a grunt.

"Just what I'd do, in his place," he commented gruffly. "Well, as far as I'm concerned, he can search anywhere."

"I thought you'd feel like that," Alec told him. "But in case you change your mind, George, there's something else I think you ought to know. I only heard Naughton requesting a warrant. I didn't hear Scott-Marle's reply – and I strongly suspect that it will be negative. Sir Reginald would regard it as an insult to a senior man to sign something like that. 'If George can't be trusted who can?' – that's the attitude I reckon he's bound to take. So if Naughton should have the impudence to try pulling the place apart – and between you and me, I wouldn't put anything past him – just ask to see his authority for doing so. I'll lay any odds that he won't have any, and will be just bluffing. Okay?"

It was on the tip of Gideon's tongue to ask Alec what on earth he thought he was talking about. Naughton could pull the place apart for all he cared but he'd be a fool if he did. There simply wasn't the slightest likelihood of Matthew being here! Just in time, he realised what an enormous risk his normally cold and formal son-in-law was taking for him. If a word of this conversation got out, his job would be definitely on the line.

"Thank you, Alec," he said instead. "Thank you very much indeed." He replaced the receiver like a man in a trance. All this was so unlike anything he had ever had to cope with before in his career that he hardly knew how to begin. Still less did he know how to tell Kate that his son was wanted, on the run.

Kate, though, he suddenly realised, didn't need telling anything.

Those blue-grey eyes were dry now, and looking at him shrewdly, with almost a hint of mischief. Apparently she'd not missed a lot of what Alec had been saying, even though he'd been half whispering at the other end of the phone.

"So they are coming here to search for Matthew, are they? They'll be too late by half. He's already been and gone."

That woke Gideon out of his trance-like state with a vengeance.

"Matthew?" he spluttered. "Been and – "

"That's right," Kate told him. "I gave him a drink, and a bath, and a change of clothes – your tweed jacket and flannels. It was only after that, he told me about the man-hunt." Suddenly the mischief turned into something more like defiance. "Not that it would have made any difference if he had. I *want* him to get away. Don't you?"

It was a question Gideon didn't, couldn't, answer. Those packets of heroin haunted his memory. Street value: countless millions. Hidden cost: equally countless deaths and broken lives –

"What I want most of all, love, is a bath," he grunted. "I can't see myself facing Commander Naughton – and his merry men without one."

His weariness was such that he only made it up the stairs by clinging on to the banister. The hot bath did a lot to revive him, although all around him were visible reminders – blackened flannels, dirty soap, a massive dark-brown rim around the bath – of who had just bathed here before him.

Why in God's name had Matthew chosen to come here? As a drugs king, known to be inheriting The Big Four's empire, he would have inherited contacts. Once he was away from Fletchwood Heights, there must have been scores of venues where he could have got fitted up with clothes – and far smarter ones than his father's oldest jacket and flannels. And more than clothes could have been provided for him. A false passport with an assumed name – an airline ticket to any destination . . .

It simply didn't make sense that he should have driven, instead, to a home that had not been his for more than twenty years – and to parents he had hardly contacted in all that time. Especially since one of those parents was the father who he probably hated, feared –

Gideon's brain simply refused to reason any more. Even though he turned on the cold tap, and showered his face with freezing cold water, nothing remotely resembling an explanation occurred to him.

He climbed out of the bath, glad that his weary body was now relaxed enough to enable him to do it fairly effortlessly, dried himself and went into the bedroom to dress, by the light of a grey and misty dawn.

He noticed that his and Kate's bed had not been slept in – evidence that Kate had spent the night wandering around the house, waiting desperately for news of him. He began to worry about her heart. How much more of this strain and tension could it stand?

Just as the thought occurred to him, a crash sounded from the direction of the kitchen below.

He rushed downstairs – to find Kate staring dazedly by the back door, staring down at the remains of a teapot that had fallen from her hand.

"Nothing to – to worry about. I'm – just a bit tired," she said.

Gideon persuaded her to sit down while he cleaned up the mess and took over making the tea. As he worked, he kept glancing at her. There was a look on her face he couldn't understand – a look he could only describe as *guarded.*

There was something else about Kate that puzzled him. Although she was now sitting at the opposite end of the kitchen, she couldn't seem to take her eyes away from that back door.

The moment Gideon, following her glance himself,

turned to stare at the door, the wail of police car sirens sounded outside their front door.

It was followed by heavy footsteps and a strident knocking – signalling Commander Naughton's relentless determination to conduct a full search of the Gideon's home.

19 No Other Way

Gideon's feelings were a weird mixture as he strode to answer the summons.

Perhaps surprisingly anger was not among them. Alec – and even Scott-Marle – might feel it was an outrage to search Gideon's home, but Gideon himself didn't. He was above all things a practical policeman. As head of the C.I.D. he would unhesitatingly have asked for a warrant to search the home of the highest in the land, if the circumstances warranted it; and he felt no resentment against Naughton for taking the same attitude.

On the contrary, in a curious way, he sympathised with him. Searching a fellow policeman's home was the most unwelcome task that came a copper's way – as he had good reason to know remembering that terrible scene at PC Benton's earlier that night.

It was thoughts of PC Benton that haunted his mind as he reached the door, and found himself fumbling with the latch. Tiredness was making him clumsy for a moment, he couldn't seem to get the door open – Benton's face seemed to swim before him, and he could hear that legendary policeman, obstinately, defiantly insisting that his son was no murderer.

He heard another voice, from deeper inside him, whispering that that was how a father *ought* to be: how *he* ought to be, at a moment like this – no matter what the evidence against Matthew, no matter how high the tide of fear that was now rising inside him.

The fact that he couldn't, in all honesty, make such a stand made him feel not only sickened, but physically sick, and it was all he could do to stop himself shaking. Only one thing comforted him: the thought that at least he wasn't quite in as bad a spot as old Benton. He had known very well where the police could find "Red", whereas he genuinely had no idea where Matthew might be at the moment. He supposed that strictly it was his duty to admit that Matthew had been in the house earlier, but since that information would help so little, he felt there could be no harm in him suppressing it. That much at least he could do for his son . . .

Naughton kept on relentlessly knocking at the door, even though he could obviously see Gideon's outline through the glass: and when the door was finally opened, he wasted no time on pleasantries, not even so much as a "good evening", but came brutally to the point.

His face was as bleak as the grey dawn light behind him, as he announced: "Ten million pounds, Commander Gideon. That's the street value that's just been put on the hoard of drugs which our girl, Craddock, found in the shed in your son's garden. They weren't seriously damaged by the fire, being beneath the floorboards, and my men have just made a detailed examination of them. There wasn't only heroin there – there were several kilograms of 'crack', the swiftest and deadliest killer of them all. Do I have to spell out what that means?"

He thrust his bald head forwards, until his eyes were less than six inches from Gideon's, in the half light. "It means that all you suspected at the conference yesterday is true. Matthew Gideon *is* the most dangerous drug operator in the country, and we've got to get him quick no matter what it costs to any of us in human terms. I can see that you agree – "

Having delivered his verbal stomach punch, he went straight into what he no doubt considered the "knock-out blow" – "and will understand why I have a warrant here to search your house. Purely as a formality of course – but a formality I must insist on, I'm afraid."

It was a clever approach, carefully building an argument that seemed to squash all possible objections; but then Naughton made his first mistake. He tried to brush Gideon aside and stride on into the house, with his men behind him, three tough-looking characters who had "heavy mob" rather than "police" written all over them.

To his astonishment, he found himself being propelled fiercely backwards on to the doorstep, and Gideon's purple face leaning over *him*.

"So you're insisting on formalities, are you, Naughton?" said Gideon swiftly. "In that case, you won't mind if I do the same – and I'll see that warrant, if you please."

He was sure now that Alec's guess had been right, and that Naughton was equipped with no such thing. Only that would explain his extraordinary approach – bludgeoning Gideon with facts in the hope that this would leave him so dazed that he would let them in.

There was a long pause, while Naughton visibly struggled to find a reply. He ended by staring down at his boots, what little he could see of them in the dim light where he now stood as motionless as a puppet whose strings had been cut. There was no doubt that the victory was Gideon's but it was, for him, a hollow one. Never in his life had he been in the business of obstructing the police, and he didn't propose to start now.

"However," he grunted when the silence began to become unbearable, 'it's been a long night for all of us, and if you and your men want to come in and put your feet up, Kate and I have no objections."

"Very . . . kind of you," Naughton muttered, his tone almost comically different from what it had been the last time he'd spoken.

Gideon stood back, allowing them all to tramp into the cosy living-room. Kate invited them to sit down and began to serve beers, which were accepted gratefully. The "heavy mob" were now looking surprisingly human, smiles replacing glares everywhere, suggesting that their apparent toughness had been more to repress embarrassment than anything else. Even Naughton was lying back in an armchair, although his eyes were suspiciously glaring round the room.

Not that he could be blamed for his suspiciousness, thought Gideon. The facts that Naughton had delivered like a stomach punch had, in fact, left him mentally winded, reeling, lost for an answer. How could he possibly do a PC Benton now, and start defending his son? The only way in which Matthew could be innocent would be if the hoard of drugs had been "planted" in the shed by some enemy to frame him. Or if the shed had been used, without his knowledge, by some gang who found it a convenient storehouse.

These were unlikely possibilities even if the hoard of drugs had been a moderate one – but they simply had to be ruled out if it was worth ten million pounds!

It was inconceivable, surely, that any criminal on earth would throw away such a vast sum of money in an operation to frame somebody else. It was equally inconceivable that any drugs syndicate would store such an astronomically valuable hoard in the grounds of anyone who was not a member, or, most probably, a leader of the syndicate himself.

Everything pointed inexorably to the same conclusion. There wasn't the slightest chance that Matthew was innocent.

* * *

His fear now tinged with something far more terrible – a suffocating sense of anxiety that stifled all feelings except despair – Gideon shuffled into the room, and confronted Naughton with a faint, grim smile. The sooner he and his men were out of the house the better, he thought, but he didn't want him to go with suspicion still lying in the air.

"Right," he said, "as you might have guessed, Naughton, I'm not really the man to stand in the way of a copper with a job to do. If you're really set on searching the place, you and your men had better get on with it. But please be as quick about it as you can. Kate here can hardly remember when she last saw a bed – and for that matter neither can I."

He glanced at Kate as he said that – and saw her start slightly. He wondered why, but then put it down to strain. God knows there was no shortage of that about tonight.

Strain, though, was one thing that did *not* show on Naughton's face as he looked up from the armchair. His hard features suddenly relaxed completely, and he held out his hand.

"Thank you very much indeed, for that offer, George," he said, using his Christian name for the very first time. "But the fact that you've made it convinces me that there's no need to take it up. And between you, me and the gatepost, I'm bloody glad there isn't." He turned to his men, for once in his life on the point of smiling. "Finish your drinks, boys, and let's go. We've detained Mr and Mrs Gideon quite enough for one night . . ."

Gideon heard Kate give a tiny, involuntary sigh of relief.

He wished to God he hadn't heard it, but soft though it was, it was unmistakable – and it started something at the back of his mind putting two and two together.

In a flash, he was remembering that sudden start Kate had given when he had invited Naughton to go ahead and search the house . . . And then that guarded look she had put on in the kitchen . . . And then those glances at the back door.

The back door.

Gideon had a photographic memory for details – and despite his near exhaustion, that camera in his head was suddenly functioning.

He had glanced at that back door just once tonight, and yet he had only to close his eyes – or even half close them – to see every detail of it again.

He tried hard not to close them, not even to blink, but nothing could stop his mind's eye showing him that door and worse, moving in, as if with a zoom lens, on one particular detail.

He remembered having noticed that the middle bolt had not been fully drawn back. The significance of that had escaped him at the time. Naughton's banging outside on the front door had cut off his thoughts at that precise moment. But part of his mind had retained the memory, and was bringing it to his attention now.

In fact it was *forcing* it on his attention – and compelling him to face all the implications, which were now as clear to him as they had been to Kate.

Matthew could not have gone through that back door – but he had tried to make it look as though he had. Which could only mean one thing. He was here somewhere in the house – and Gideon didn't need telling where. He had discovered that loft hide-out of Matthew's in the long, long distant past – and still remembered how he had bruised his shins climbing up there. A forty-year-old Matthew wouldn't fit in there as well as the twelve-year-old had done but there would just be room and Matthew would of course consider that he was being very clever indeed, hiding in the shadow of his father's reputation for integrity and honesty.

Scott-Marle's voice seemed to ring in Gideon's ear. "*If Gideon can't be trusted, who can?*" He tried to quieten it, and with a massive effort, succeeded.

All his life he had been as straight as any policeman could be, and had always been merciless on any member of his staff who didn't conform to the same high standards. Yet here he was ready to throw, just for a minute, all those years of integrity away.

Less than a minute would probably do, he was showing Naughton and his men into the hall, and in forty-five, maybe fifty seconds they'd be gone: the car could be driving away its wailing siren fading, and he could be holding Kate in his arms, a warm glow filling him because he'd behaved like a husband and father, and not ignored that beseeching look which she was now throwing at him.

Yes, as usual at the moment of crisis, Kate was missing nothing. One glance at him had told her that he knew the truth, that the battle royal of his life was going on inside him. And the desperate appeal in her eyes left him in no doubt which side she was on.

And was she asking for so very much, after all?

He only had to pretend he hadn't heard that quivering gasp of relief – that the shutter in his bloody mental camera hadn't clicked – that his brain had simply been too exhausted to think.

He was at the front door, opening it for Naughton and his men.

In just fifteen seconds, they'd be away.

But suddenly he was reliving that moment when he'd roared at PC Benton, his voice filling the room, "If you think you know where we might find Red . . . it's your duty as a police officer to tell us – your plain and simple duty, which you've never shirked in all those years, and aren't going to start now. *Are* you?"

The words came back to him, searing and stabbing like so many red-hot knives. Could he, as the C.I.D.'s Commander, do less than he had expected a humble PC to do, just a few hours before?

There was only one possible answer. He *had* to play it by the book. For him, there was never going to be any other way.

Hating himself more than he had ever done at any moment in his life before, Gideon caught Naughton's arm at the very moment as he was going through the door, and pulled him back.

"Just a moment, Commander," he said gruffly. "There's someone in the house I think you ought to meet before you go."

Avoiding Kate's eyes – though there was no way of shutting out the little gasp of despair as he passed her – he strode to the foot of the stairs, and roared:

"*Matt* – "

His roar died away into a choke before he reached the second part of the name, but the single syllable rang round the house with the force of a cannon, and could not have failed to reach every part of it, including the loft.

Matthew, though, was obviously no longer in there, but had been on the landing eavesdropping. The echoes of the shouts had scarcely died away before he appeared at the top of the stairs, a ridiculous figure in his father's old jacket, so large that it flapped around him.

He descended the stairs in a strained silence. Naughton and his men too startled to say anything, Kate too shocked to speak, Gideon as motionless as though turned to stone.

When he reached his father, he took him aback completely by taking his arm and murmuring: "Don't blame yourself, Dad. I knew this would have to happen if you rumbled me. I was just hoping you wouldn't, that's all."

This was too much for Kate, who was suddenly openly sobbing. She was remembering what Matthew had said about loving the old devil too much to allow him to split himself in two.

* * *

Once Naughton and his men had left, taking Matthew with them, the house seemed cold and empty. Or perhaps, thought Gideon, it was simply that that was how he and Kate were feeling inside.

Kate had stopped sobbing now, but she resisted his

attempts to put an arm round her, and kept saying, over and over again:

"He's innocent, George. I just *know* it."

Gideon just grunted, as if in agreement, the first ten times she said it. But finally, he snapped back:

"You wouldn't say that if you'd seen what I've seen. Ten million pounds worth of crack and heroin. Enough to cause a good ten thousand deaths, I reckon. We've got to face it, love, though God knows how we can. That son of ours is the biggest – "

He broke off. It would be pointless, cruel, brutal to continue. And since, if he stayed in the house, it would be impossible for him not to, there was only one thing to do – to get out and go somewhere else, fast.

Kate made no attempt to stop him striding towards the door. It was almost as though she didn't care what he did; as if an invisible wall had sprung up between them. A wall of ice . . . .

In a desperate attempt to forget about it, Gideon charged round to the garage. A minute later, he was behind the wheel of his Rover, blasting off through the grey, misty streets at all of sixty miles an hour.

A crazy speed for someone who hardly knew what he was doing, scarcely aware of where he was going, and was simply driving nowhere.

20 Drive to Nowhere

Nowhere suddenly took on a strangely familiar shape.

Through the mists on his right loomed a large, rectangular building – red-bricked walls, though in the half-light it looked a ghostly grey – which he recognised instantly as Harringdon Comprehensive School. Long years ago it had been Harringdon High School, where Matthew and his other sons had attended for all their school days.

Wondering what weird impulse had brought him here, he slowed the Rover down to walking pace, eyeing the building sombrely as it slid mysteriously past him.

Memories seemed to be aroused by every brick of the place. Memories of the day Matthew had played truant; of the time he had been caught kissing a girl behind the bike-sheds; of that incident where he had fired air-gun pellets to try to knock off the cockerel on the weather-vane on the school's roof. The weather-vane was still there, he noticed, the bird still revolving.

There were proud memories, too: of the open day when Gideon had been told that his son was the brightest in the class in Maths: the moment when he had triumphed in the eleven-plus, and he and Kate had solemnly presented him with a whole ten shilling note as a reward . . . All of which he had subsequently spent on buying his music-mad sister a recorder for her birthday.

From all this, Matthew emerged as a boy who had always been in scrapes, but had been bright, hard-working and fundamentally good-hearted. What in God's name had happened to twist him, to turn him into Britain's number one drugs-pedlar? Was it that blazing row they had had which had led him to cut himself off from his roots; to become, as far as he and Kate were concerned, an almost total stranger?

And yet – and yet he had not really behaved like a stranger tonight had he? In desperate trouble, he had rejected all the opportunities he must have had to high-tail it out of the City, and had followed a schoolboy instinct – to come home.

The thoughts that had troubled Gideon earlier returned suddenly to haunt him now, persistent and pervasive as the rain which now splashed on the Rover's windscreen.

It didn't make sense for Matthew to have behaved like that – *if* he was, in fact, a major villain.

It was far more like the act of someone who was completely innocent, who feels himself being "set up" and possibly because there is no way out – that he could see – except to keep himself out of the hands of the police for as long as he could.

Gideon stopped the car, his head now aching with the struggle to think. The other side of his brain was taking over now; the stark police side, born of years of training himself to look facts in the face, however painful they might be.

"You're being sentimental," this side was screaming out at him.

"Pathetically sentimental . . . clutching at straws. Matthew could not have been set up for the simple reason that there's not a villain on God's earth who would throw away ten million pounds – "

The ache in his head became migraine-like, blinding. Just what Matthew had foreseen was happening. Gideon *was* being split in two . . .

* * *

How he had started the car again, or had driven with that blinding pain in his head, Gideon never knew, but suddenly he found himself miles away from Fulham, staring up at a building that was even more familiar than his sons' school – in fact, the place he knew better than anywhere else except his own home.

Above the Rover there now towered the office-block outline of New Scotland Yard. Most of its storeys were lost in the mist, which still showed no signs of clearing although the rain had stopped. The uppermost floor still visible was the seventh, and it was up there that Gideon found himself staring.

Why, he had no idea. This drive to nowhere had been a mystery tour in the deepest sense – dictated by mysterious impulses emanating from way beyond the level of his conscious mind. All his life, when everything else had failed, Gideon had followed his hunches – and he wouldn't deny that everything else was failing now.

The seventh floor . . .

* * *

The memories which the sight invoked were very recent ones, still dramatically sharp and clear.

Just a year ago, the entire floor had been set aside as the H.Q. for "Target Eighty" – the biggest operation in the history of the Met, designed by Gideon himself and planned to wipe out, at a stroke, the gangsters responsible for eighty per cent of London crime.

A lot of things had gone disturbingly wrong with that operation – leaks from a high level inside the Yard had almost caused the whole project to be abandoned at one point, and at another, he himself had been virtually buried alive by a bomb blast – but it had ended with the most triumphant moment of his career, when he had arrested The Big Four of London crime: the drugs king Jeremy Kemp, the gangster Barry Mayne, the bank-raid mastermind, Arturo Salvados and the rock star turned racketeer, Monty Marlowe.

He could see the faces of all four of them now – and the hatred in their eyes as they had stared at him: never before or since had he seen such concentrated venom. Any or all of them would do anything to get him, or get at him, to this day.

And – he suddenly remembered – he would be wrong to write any of them off. Their trial had not come up yet, and as he had pointed out to Naughton when they had been discussing Kemp, men in remand prison had special privileges. They have many opportunities to see associates, smuggle out messages, and, to some extent, continue to control what little was left of their criminal empire.

Gideon found himself stopping the car again – not this time because of a blinding headache, but because of an idea that had hit him like a blinding flash of light.

Supposing The Big Four had seen a chance of getting their revenge on him by framing his son?

They must have money hidden in bank accounts all over

the world. No price would be too high for them to pay. Not even ten million pounds . . .

* * *

Ideas were now exploding like fire-crackers all over his brain, forcing new connections between the facts and the theories which had filled it before.

There were activities not even The Big Four could do. It would be ridiculous to think that they could maintain their position as the major controlling force behind the Fletchwood drugs problem from the confines of prison. Quite obviously they had an agent – a master dealer, living somewhere in or near to the area, who so far had entirely evaded the police.

Gideon was inclined to think that he was probably *not* to be found anywhere in the Heights. The Big Four had always been masters at circulating rumours to suit their purposes, and would have taught the new man all the old tricks.

It followed that the "get-the-dealers-in-the-Heights" campaign could well have been started deliberately to deflect attention from the spot where the real drugs trafficker was operating. The Big Four had probably only discovered that Matthew was moving into Malibu Rise late in the day and of course they had promptly seen to it that the rumours circulating concerned him.

How had they come to know that Matthew Goddard was in fact Matthew Gideon? Even Scotland Yard had had no inkling of it until that photograph had been taken, and passed round at that nightmare conference, less than twenty-four hours before.

That problem did not deter Gideon for long. The men who had been responsible for so much of London's crime were bound to have almost limitless supplies of information. Added to that was the fact that his son bore a strong physical resemblance to him.

After all, if the police could take a snap of Matthew without him knowing it, why shouldn't The Big Four's agent have done the same – probably weeks earlier? And one glance at the Gideon family features would have been enough to start Jeremy Kemp and Co. instructing inquiries even as far away as New Zealand.

And once he had been identified, the attack on Matthew had been planned. Brutally designed to end either with him dying at the hands of a frenzied, rioting mob, or spending the rest of his life in prison, just like The Big Four themselves.

And he, Gideon, as a lifetime supporter of law and order, had actually been instrumental in making that second plan come true!

This was no time, though, for regrets and recriminations. This was a time for action – and Gideon suddenly realised that he knew just what action to take. The Big Four's agent had been supremely cunning at distracting all attention from himself – but he had made one big mistake. And he had made it in Gideon's hearing, when he had said –

At that point, Gideon's thoughts were abruptly interrupted.

A highly-polished Daimler was sweeping alongside and past his stationary Rover, with a solitary passenger in the back seat whom he vaguely recognised. A tall, solitary figure who looked tired and old and ill. He did not turn to right or left, but stared straight in front of him.

With a shot of disbelief, Gideon identified him as Scott-Marle, on his way home from one of the grimmest nights of his career. A night which had begun with a nightmare outbreak of violence, and ended with having to supervise personally a man hunt for Gideon's son . . .

A fanfare of angry toots from behind reminded Gideon that he had no right to be blocking the thoroughfare in Victoria Street, even at a quarter to six in the morning. He raised the clutch, and the Rover started forward. In seconds, he was overtaking the Daimler, startling Scott-Marle by smiling and waving as he zoomed past him.

He no longer looked like a man driving nowhere, but one with an urgent and challenging appointment to keep.

And, in fact, he had just that – in the heart of Fletchwood Vale, with Dr Ravi Gharad . . . who, above everyone else, had stoked up the hatred against the "Masters in the Heights" . . . who, as a doctor working on his own, was in the ideal position to distribute illegal drugs . . . and who, in rescuing Gideon from the mob, had told him that in his opinion, the sins of the children should not be visited upon their fathers.

Unless he was directly in league with The Big Four, and probably in the act of carrying out their orders to frame him, *how could he possibly have known that Matthew was Gideon's son*?

21 Sins of the Children

One thing became all too clear to Gideon as he reached the outskirts of Fletchwood Vale. Anger and violence still prevailed here, and all the blazes and spilt blood of the night had left the area's dark appetite for hate sharpened rather than appeased.

The sun was breaking through now, heralding another heat-bath of a day. Wisps of mist were still visible, but here they had a dirty brown look and an oddly sulphurous smell, as though the whole place was on the edge of a volcano which had just erupted, and could do so again at any minute.

One glance up – and this impression had redoubled force. No longer were there green trees and gardens of luxury up there in the Heights to offset the area of drab houses and litter-filled streets in the Vale. Nothing was visible now except burnt stubs and the blackened roof of the hotel, from which smoke was still rising as if the place had become a vast incinerator. Against this grim backdrop, the old-fashioned chimneys on the terraced houses all round him stood out like so many shaking fists, symbols of the explosion of anger that had reduced everything in sight to the level of Fletchwood Vale.

For evidence that this explosion was by no means over, it was only necessary to look at the people on the streets. There were quite a few about. Some were going to work, others were youths who had come out early out of curiosity to see what damage the night's activities had done. Everyone was peering up at the Heights, but in not a single face was there a hint of regret. Most had an expression of grim satisfaction.

Gideon glowered. Didn't these Fletchwood Vale people ever sleep? Crowds of hostile youths on the pavements were the last thing he needed.

His intention had been to go straight to Gharad's

surgery and confront the little doctor single-handed, almost in the way that Riddell had confronted Fergus Atkinson. But now he had to think again. Gharad was, after all, a hero to all the thugs of the area. Gideon would not get further than his doorstep where he would probably find himself surrounded, punched and pounced on by a bigger and more violent mob than before.

He did not want to have to rely on the doctor to rescue him once again! As a matter of fact, he still was not sure why he had done it on the previous occasion. Surely he must have realised that his masters, The Big Four, would have been delighted if he, Gideon, had been killed!

Then a chilling thought occurred to him. Perhaps The Big Four wouldn't have been so pleased and Gharad had known it. After all, if he had died at that moment, the whole ten million pound plan to frame Matthew would have been in vain.

Shivering in spite of the heat building up around him in the sulphurous haze, Gideon found himself regarding the little doctor in a new and very much harsher light. He had begun to think of him as a strangely divided man: half-healer, half-destroyer. But now it was possible only to see him as a singularly twisted one. God knows there was little enough excuse for anyone who earned money pushing drugs. But for a man who was in every day contact with drug-crazed victims, who knew every detail of the agony the pushers caused, there was simply no excuse at all. Behind all Gharad's passionate diatribes, apparently self-less crusade for the disadvantaged, there lay a cold sadistic killer, cunning to the point of being sub-human.

Just the sort of man The Big Four would enlist with the task of rebuilding a part of their criminal empire . . . and to be the instrument of their revenge over *him*.

Gideon was under no illusions now. He had a deadly and dangerous enemy – and all the odds were in Gharad's favour, every single one.

His instinct now was to go to Fletchwood Vale police station and order out a squad of men to support his raid. But there were endless difficulties there too. The presence of an angry mob outside the surgery would turn the raid into a battle, or even a blood-bath, unless he had Riot Squad support. But how could he ask for that, unless he had the authorisation for their use at the highest level? He doubted if he'd ever obtain a search warrant – and to get inside that surgery and search the place was what he most desperately needed to do.

He had a strong feeling that there would be a major consignment of drugs concealed on the premises – and probably not hidden all that carefully. Gharad had done such a clever job of deflecting suspicion that a search of his own property was probably the last thing he expected. This meant that it was theoretically possible to catch the evil little man red-handed – and clear Matthew at a stroke. The trouble was that between theory and practice there were so many obstacles that he couldn't begin to think how to bulldoze his way through them.

Not that this prospect deflected Gideon one inch from his cause. He would simply have to play things differently, and show a little cunning – as much cunning as his devious adversary. This decided, he was actually smiling faintly as the Rover pulled up in front of Fletchwood Vale police station.

The smile faded the moment he was inside the glass swing-doors. The entrance hall of the station was crowded with policemen. Some of them from the Riot Squad, others were ordinary constables, rushed here during the night from neighbouring areas to cope with the mounting crimes in the Heights. A few were on the normal strength of the station, looking red-eyed and weary after their long, rough night on duty. The inspector and the sergeant who had scoffed at the idea of impending trouble were both still there. To Gideon's astonishment, he also recognised the figure of PC Benton. Obviously the loyal copper had been living up to his legend and no doubt had heard trouble starting, and had simply donned his uniform and come in to see what he could do to help, regardless of the fact that his own son was in the cells.

At Gideon's appearance on the scene, all conversation stopped abruptly. He knew well enough why. Most of it would have been about *him* and the .man hunt for Matthew, probably believed by everyone here to be the real "Master of the Heights". He wondered if they had heard the news yet about Matthew's arrest at his, Gideon's, own house. He imagined that they had. A radio message would have been sent out to all stations, calling off the man hunt and probably those details would have been added. There was no point withholding facts from the police that would have to be released to the media a few minutes later.

So all these men knew, or had an inkling of the traumas he had been going through tonight. His long years as a father-figure of the force – affectionately regarded by most, if not all – had conditioned him to expect glances of understanding, maybe even concern. All he saw though on every side were looks of cold curiosity, thinly-disguised dislike. It couldn't have been plainer that he wasn't the great Gideon as far as they were concerned anymore. He was the father of the biggest drugs-pusher in the country – and had been harbouring him in his own house. It wasn't hard to imagine what comments had gone round. "Told you they were bent – up at the top. And Gideon's turned out just like the rest . . ."

In all the room, only PC Benton's hardy features were showing sympathy. And this was the man to whom he'd behaved almost brutally, this very night!

Instantly, Gideon walked across to him. As he went, the silence was broken by the sound of voices shouting from below. Clearly, Red Benton had a lot of companions in the cells, and being Red, was leading them in a roar of protest. Of course, thought Gideon, scores of yobbos arrested in the Heights must have been brought into the station – and few would have been allowed home . . .

To Benton he said: "Well, Bertie, you've one thing to be thankful for – God knows what your son would have got up to if he'd been on the loose tonight. As it is, all he's facing are reduced charges. Not of murder, but of simply being the Oxfam Robin Hood."

"I know that, sir." Benton's smile was suddenly fading away. "I reckon that means he'll get twelve or thirteen years instead of life. I might just be there to welcome him home before I die."

Gideon touched the constable's arm. "It should be a lot

sooner than that, Bertie. I'll tell you something. I've never in all my life known a criminal steal just to save others from starving. And I'll bet the judge and jury won't have either. So the verdict and the sentence are both unpredictable – and could be much better news than you think."

Relief lit up Bertie's face. "I hope to God you're right, sir," he said, almost as though beginning to believe Gideon could be.

The inspector intervened at that point. Plainly, he didn't like the idea of even a bent Commander of the C.I.D. stepping into his station, and talking exclusively to a mere constable. "Is there something we can do for you, sir?" he asked, almost like a supercilious store-detective asking a suspicious customer.

Gideon took a deep breath. It was time to begin – playing things differently. "There certainly is," he boomed. "I'd like four men, please, and a squad car. I'm organising a little raid."

"In Fletchwood Vale, sir?" the inspector fawned. "That could be a bit dicey. We've carried out so many arrests there through the night that the whole neighbourhood is up in arms, and the Riot Squad boys have advised us to hold off."

"How interesting," said Gideon, calmly. He had rarely been spoken to by an inspector like that before, and did not relish the experience. "Well, it so happens *I'm* ordering you to – to –"

He broke off there, clutching his head and groaning.

The inspector started.

"Are you all right, sir?" Genuine concern crossed his face at once.

"No, dammit, I'm anything *but* all right," choked Gideon, swaying and clutching at a nearby table. It toppled over at his touch, sending him crashing on to the floor. He fell with a thump that shook the room – and all of its inmates.

Policemen everywhere were suddenly springing to their feet, racing across to aid him.

As he was helped to his feet by half a dozen hands, PC Benton's among them, Gideon spluttered, "Can't you see, any of you? What I need is a doctor – "

"We'll – we'll get one here straight away, sir," yelped the inspector, rushing to the counter and a phone.

"No, no, there's no need for that," said Gideon. "You've a doctor here, already, haven't you – the one whose clinic never closes, so it says outside. Well, just drive me there, some of you – and *quick*."

"The Commander must mean Dr Gharad," said Benton. "Just down the road."

"That's the man," Gideon grunted and was suddenly interrupted by a spasm of agonising groans. Through them, he gasped: "That man's – saved my life once tonight already. Reckon – reckon he might do it again – "

With Benton on one arm and a sergeant on the other, and three constables and the inspector bringing up the rear, Gideon was swept out of the station towards a waiting panda.

Quite a visiting party, he told himself, and they'd get right inside the surgery before the mob outside could do anything. Just in time, he changed his chuckle into the most harrowing groan of all.

* * *

Gideon had been right in assuming that the hoard of drugs on Dr Gharad's premises would not be all that carefully hidden. At that very moment, they were hardly hidden at all – but contained in a plain leather suitcase waiting, with a load of other baggage, in a corridor leading off the surgery room itself. The doctor had spent the last hour packing, and was all set to leave on a vacation that he felt he richly deserved. "Richly" was the operative word: a cheque for a hundred thousand pounds would be on its way to him as a reward for having carried out The Big Four's wishes in respect of Gideon's son – sent via a Swiss bank to a special account which he had opened under an assumed name on the other side of London. His first task would be to go and check on this financial arrangement, and for the rest of the holiday, he would be living incognito in a luxury hotel, under circumstances that would help him to forget completely the years he had spent growing more and more disillusioned and bitter as a hard-up doctor in this squalid area.

He could not stay away too long, he knew. Questions

would be asked if he disappeared permanently from the scene at this stage. But there was nothing more for him to do here – it would be dangerous to continue distributing drugs now he could no longer deflect suspicion and when he returned, it would be purely for the purposes of selling the practice and clearing out. He had already closed the treatment centre – which he had been running for drug addicts in the attic, turning the occupants out with a contemptuous lack of concern that had astonished them. They had never seen that side of the caring Dr Gharad before . . .

His parcel of illicit drugs, then, was no longer needed in Fletchwood Vale. Moreover, he was going to take it with him for certain meetings with members of prime syndicates which had already been arranged for that luxury hotel. These were the only reasons why he was taking it with him. He had no fear that the surgery would be searched by the police when he was gone. Hadn't he just kept the place open all night as an emergency station, and worked non-stop treating burns, head injuries and even bullet wounds – with as many policemen wounded as yobbos? And as for his rabble-raising reputation, who could deny now that anything he had said had not been proved absolutely right. Thanks to his efforts, there was now proof that there *had* been a master drugs dealer in the Heights.

Convinced that after his night's work he was miles above all possibility of suspicion, Gharad felt not the faintest pangs of alarm when he heard the siren of a police car pulling up outside. Probably they were bringing him another casualty – someone else burnt or bashed up during the chaos of the night. Well, he had not put up his "closed" notice yet, so he supposed he would have to oblige them. The saintly Dr Gharad could do no less, he told himself wryly, if he didn't want a crack to appear in his halo.

His expression was a little less than saintly, however, when he opened the door, and saw who was being half-carried up the path to his front door. A glare came into his eyes which reflected many conflicting emotions – astonishment, wariness, amusement and triumph amongst them.

"I never expected, Commander, that we would meet again so soon," he began, but broke off as Gideon interrupted him with one of his most agonising groans.

The inspector hurriedly explained that Mr Gideon had been taken ill very suddenly, and had expressly asked to be brought straight here.

Gharad gave the Commander a swift glance of professional appraisal. His face showed all the traces of a sleepless night, of the relentless battle between will power and nervous exhaustion. The doctor's wariness began to fade – but didn't vanish altogether. Out of the corner of his eyes, he noticed a gang of thugs hanging around in the street – within hearing range if he needed their assistance.

He politely stood back and beckoned the police party inside – being careful at the same time to leave the door on the latch.

A minute or so later, the inspector and the others were seated uncomfortably in the dingy little waiting-room, and Gideon was in the surgery proper, with the door closed behind him, lying on a moth-eaten looking couch and having his blood pressure taken by the little doctor. He tried hard to put out of his mind all that he now knew about Gharad. If he allowed himself to brood for one half second on the fact that he was face-to-face with the villain who had framed his son, then in that instant he would probably explode.

As it was, Gharad's eyebrows raised as he read the figure being recorded.

"Tish, tish, Commander. Alarmingly high, I'm afraid – "

Gideon took the news with another low groan, then closed his eyes and lay motionless. It was odd, but Gharad as a doctor was evidently quite an artist. His touch was surprisingly gentle, his voice infectiously reassuring.

"But not, perhaps, unexpectedly high," he finished, "after such a night as you've been through." He put the apparatus away, adding, "There is really nothing I or any doctor could prescribe that would do you half as much good as ten hours' sleep and after that, several days of rest. You are suffering from extreme nervous tension, I would say, Commander, nothing more. Stay there for a moment and take several deep breaths then I think you will find yourself able to rise unaided and go."

Suddenly his voice changed dramatically, an indication of malevolence creeping in.

His dark eyes blazing, he added curtly:

"I can't pretend that I shall be sorry when you do. I have been listening to the radio, and I am astonished to learn that your son, Matthew Goddard, as he calls himself – is the man responsible for all the drugs abuse and suffering in Fletchwood. Still," he went on smoothly, clearly not beginning to realise what he was saying, "as I told you at our other meeting, in a bit of a misquote from your English Bible, where I come from, the sins – the sins of the – the children – "

He was realising his mistake now all right. The words came out as choked and squeaky as the sounds on an ancient gramophone record played at the wrong speed – and it wasn't entirely because it was dawning on him how completely he had given himself away. There was the additional shock of seeing George Gideon, no longer a groaning patient, but a terrifying adversary – standing, towering over him.

"Yes, doctor, it's pretty obvious you have secret information about Matthew, isn't it?" he said. "Just which of The Big Four gave it to you? Salvados? Marlowe? Mayne? Or Jerry Kemp?"

The names came out like successive cracks of a whip – and at each of them, Gharad took a backwards step. He might almost have been cowering, but in fact his immense reserves were telling now.

After the fourth step, he was suddenly close to a table, from the top of which he grabbed a knife – and as he brandished it, he started yelling: "Help!" at the top of his voice to the street mob outside.

Gideon replied by opening the surgery door behind him, and calling to his "raiding party": "There he is – the real master behind all the drugs in the Heights! Come and help me get – "

His voice trailed away – as, it was suddenly clear, what his police support had done. Evidently, when they had heard through the flimsy door that he was not seriously ill, the inspector and the others had decided there was nothing they could do, and had cleared off – leaving probably a car outside with a driver, but only one man in the waiting-room: PC Benton.

He stood up swiftly and advanced towards Gideon – just as the front door was flying back with a crash, and a crowd of Gharad's supporters burst into the waiting-room.

Great, thought Gideon angrily, the arrest of the most dangerous criminal in London backed by a vicious mob, had been left in the hands of just Bertie Benton and him.

He sprung back to face Gharad and saw that the doctor was laughing. "The odds seem to be just very slightly against you," he shouted. "I'd get out while the going is good if I were you. Though I can't promise to make it very good this time . . ."

His eyes looked as piercing as ever, and were flashing as fiercely as the knife in his hand. But there wasn't much perception evident in what Gharad was saying. He showed no awareness that he was talking to not one but *two*, legends of the force . . .

22 Freedom from Fear

Backing these legends was something still more forcible. Gideon and Benton, over their very different careers, had picked up between them a total of eighty years painfully hard-won experience of practical policing, sometimes at the sharp end of it, in dangerous situations. And this experience suddenly began to show results.

Benton, for example, might have looked as though he was proceeding ponderously across the waiting-room in answer to Gideon's summons. But he was inside the surgery, slamming and locking the door behind him, long before the mob was anywhere near him; and in the same second, he seized a chair and jammed it under the door handle, an old trick that would delay the door being broken down for valuable minutes.

Gideon, meanwhile, was advancing relentlessly on Gharad, apparently oblivious to the knife he was brandishing. In fact he was fully aware of it, and ready to duck at the first sign of a stabbing or slashing movement. But he had arrested criminals with knives before – homicidal murderers, some of them – and he had learnt that the trick was to stare them out and show no fear, and simply continue coming until one was close enough to kick out, dealing the most painful blow possible. In panic, the criminal would lash out wildly – and that was the moment to grip the knife-wielding arm . . .

Gharad, though, was not a man to be out-stared. The penetrating eyes looked straight back into Gideon's, seeming to read his thoughts in detail. He made one thrust with the knife, a long sabre-like instrument which he aimed with cold precision just below the heart. Gideon was forced to swerve a foot backwards out of its range – and instantly, the little doctor was through a door on the far side of the surgery and locking it behind him.

"Quick, Bertie," said Gideon.

He and the PC hurled themselves at the door together. Their combined weight, which must have been a good thirty-five stone, smashed it open in a single onslaught – and they found themselves, breathing heavily, in a small corridor leading to a side exit.

It was an exit which Gharad had not found the time to use – for a curious reason. On the corridor floor were a number of suitcases, and he had stopped to pick up one of them. He held it now, in his left hand, the knife still flashing in his right as he backed towards that door. "I warn you, Commander, that if you try and stop me again – "

Gideon scarcely heard him.

There was only one reason why Gharad should have stopped to pick up that suitcase at such a critical moment. It must contain something altogether too dangerous to the doctor to be left behind – and it was his betting that meant it contained a load of illicit drugs. That case there, in all probability contained all the evidence he needed to nail this servant of The Big Four – and get all the charges against Matthew dropped once and for all.

At that thought, Gideon was suddenly beyond practical policing. The menacing figure of Gharad, that still more menacing knife, slipped out of his mind and his field of vision simultaneously. He had eyes only for that suitcase. He had one impulse only, and that was to get his hands on it at all speed and at no matter what the cost.

That impulse carried him down the corridor at what seemed the speed of light, and before Gharad knew what was happening, Gideon was instantly on top of him, had grabbed the handle of the suitcase and was struggling to snatch it from the little doctor's grasp.

"Watch out, sir!" yelped a startled Benton from behind.

He could see how vulnerable Gideon was leaving himself. One single thrust from that knife – and Gharad's medical knowledge could direct it unerringly to the spot where it could bring instant death.

It seemed, though, that Gharad was almost beyond reason on the subject of that suitcase. It was as if it was more than his life was worth to part with it.

He would not let go of the handle, even though the

refusal to do so involved him in a virtual tug-of-war – a tug-of-war which, against Gideon's massive bulk, he could not hope to win.

His own left arm felt as though it was being wrenched out of its socket. He struggled desperately to bring his right arm round so that he could slash, thrust, kill – but that proved impossible, because his whole body was being dragged, left side first, half the length of the corridor in the wake of the suitcase.

Then Gideon gave the case a final savage twist, and Gharad's grip on the handle broke. He lost his balance and fell sprawling.

It took him a second to stumble to his feet – a second during which PC Benton quietly relieved him of the knife, and slipped handcuffs on his wrists.

"Sorry to have to do such a thing to a medical gent, like yourself, sir," he said, with the courtesy of a copper of the old school, and the firmness of one who had left it as Head Boy.

Gideon still hardly had eyes for Gharad. He picked up the knife and used it to slash open one side of the case. Some of the contents spilled out – packages so closely resembling the ones under the floor of Matthew's garden shed that no one could deny that they were part and parcel of the same consignment.

With this, and the other evidence he was sure now that he could collect against Gharad, he was certain that he could say that the horror was over. Matthew was in the clear.

For the first time in nearly twenty-four hours of nightmare, Gideon felt absolute freedom from that terrible, grinding fear.

The sensation left him so exhilarated that he was anything but afraid when a spectacular crash sounded from the direction of the surgery, and the angry faces of the street mob appeared at the end of the corridor.

They were the usual Fletchwood Vale mixture of whites, Asians, and blacks, armed with the inevitable flick-knives, coshes, chains. But it was suddenly clear that there was something different about them. They didn't have the look of arrogant, defiant hate – and it didn't take Gideon long to work out why. These boys who hung round Dr Gharad's surgery were probably, for the most part, the ones who were grateful to him for helping them to conquer drug addiction. It shattered them to see their saviour in handcuffs, with a suitcase beside him spilling out packages that were plainly heroin. They were obviously struggling to take in the situation, and Gideon was quite prepared to give them a hand.

"Want me to spell it out for you, boys? You're looking at the real master of Fletchwood Heights – and of the Vale too, for that – "

He broke off, realising that he and Benton faced the toughest bit of policing yet.

In the event they just succeeded in saving Dr Gharad from the mob.

* * *

Getting Gharad safely to the police station and into the cells was only the start of a hectic morning for the PC and the Commander, whose destinies had been so strongly linked all through the Fletchwood affair. Both of them had a sleepless night and hours of all that unbearable worry behind them, but felt strangely fresh and able to cope – because for each of them there was now hope where there had been nothing but despair. As though reflecting this, the sun was now strong and brilliant in the Fletchwood sky, and those sulphurous mists, the last remnants of the night of horror, had vanished, leaving nothing but faint, almost autumnal tangs of wood-smoke in the air.

At ten o'clock, PC Benton, dressed in a well-pressed Sunday suit, was sitting beside a calm but damp-eyed Grace in the public gallery of the magistrates' court, watching his son being brought in and charged with the string of burglaries he had committed as the Oxfam Robin Hood. The gallery was crowded, not with the public, but with representatives of the press. Their presence – and that of hoards of TV men outside the building – underlined the fact that the media limelight was being directed on Fletchwood as fiercely as the overhead sun.

Red Benton was not the boy to ignore that fact. Asked how he pleaded, he replied in his most oratorial tones:

"Guilty – but so is the whole Western World, in turning its back on the starving millions!"

The magistrate was completely non-plussed. He was about to call for that remark to be struck from the record, but the rustle of reporters' notebooks echoing from all directions made such an order rather pointless. So he just muttered: "Well. Yes – that's as may be, young man," and allowed the case to continue.

Benton, whose spirits had dropped at his son's reckless stand, suddenly found them rising. Could Gideon be right? If this magistrate was non-plussed, couldn't the judge and jury one day be the same?

Chief Inspector Superintendent Riddell now appeared to present the police case. Sometimes awkward and nervous in court, he seemed today supremely confident and in command. There were good reasons for that. His wife Vi was now over her nervous shock; Gideon's praising of the night before was still echoing in his head, and it was a major triumph, being back in charge of a case over which Lemaitre had seemed to be reigning supreme. Lem, in view of the changed circumstances, was keeping well away.

Riddell sounded almost like a spokesman for the defence. The prisoner, he said, was certainly responsible for the Oxfam burglaries, but had not kept a penny of the profits himself. Moreover, he was directly responsible for identifying the real murderer of Don Mitchell – his next-door neighbour, Fergus Atkinson, MP.

"Who," Riddell added in his best police voice, "unfortunately perished last night in the course of my attempts to apprehend him."

The magistrate could not avoid asking for silence in court this time. He had, in fact, to state it over and over again before the excited clamour died down and Riddell was able to resume. Aware that he had created one of the journalistic sensations of the decade, and was liable to be the hero of this and many hours to come, he continued with another surprise.

In view of the great assistance he had given them, the police would not oppose bail, and suggested that Roderick Benton should be released into the care of his father, one of the most respected policemen in the country.

Bertie and Grace could hardly believe their ears – or their eyes when, a few formalities completed, they found themselves ushered out of a side door of the court-house with a grinning Red alongside them.

A familiar figure came striding up to them, although it was hard to recognise him at first. Horace Nelson's bulldog features were sagging so much that they might have been a rubber mask that was melting. He had come straight from an all-night vigil at the hospital – Suzy was holding her own well after a six-hour operation, although there was no chance of saving her baby – and had arrived at the back of the court just in time to hear Riddell's revelation about Fergus Atkinson.

It was dawning on him slowly how he had wronged both Red and Bertie, and confusing the issue was the fact that he couldn't actually remember much about the events of the earlier part of the night. But he recollected enough for remorse to be paralysing him almost as much as the drink had done.

He caught hold of Bertie's arm, and spluttered something about how he would never touch a drop again; how he knew what trouble he'd caused; how he hoped that they'd be able to forgive him.

Red and Bertie assured him together that, as far as they were concerned, there was nothing to forgive. Red had a good deal to say.

"We've all of us been victims, don't you see? Power is in the hands of them, the capitalists, the villains of the Heights. You ask Dr Gharad. He'll tell you – "

Bertie was in the act of shaking hands with his old crony, and didn't want to spoil this magic moment by starting an argument with his son. So he just said quietly:

"I don't think you'll find he will, son. Not for quite some little time."

* * *

While all this was happening at the magistrates' court down the road, Gideon was in a tough battle at Fletchwood police station with Naughton.

The Drugs Squad Commander, with a sizable contingent of men, had rushed down there on hearing of Gharad's arrest. He seemed far from pleased to find Gideon interfering in a case from which he had been specifically banned, still less having the impudence to solve it. He took a lot of persuading that Gharad really was the man behind the whole Fletchwood drugs operation, and that the shady figures of The Big Four themselves had been behind *him*. He took even more persuading that Gideon had acted rightly in organising an early morning raid on the doctor, without so much as consulting him beforehand.

"Who said anything about me organising a raid?" said Gideon innocently. "I happened to be taken ill, Commander – and considering the way you and your men had treated me and my family an hour before, I think I can describe the disease as Naughtonitis." Menacingly he added: "And I happen to be having a dose or two of it now."

Naughton's bald head started to shine with sweat – a sign he was getting really angry. "There's no need to get personal."

Gideon was in no mood to relent.

"I think there is, Naughton." He pointed to the suitcase on the floor beside them, which had just been given the treatment by the fingerprint men who had arrived with Naughton to do a scene-of-the-crime operation on Gharad's surgery. "If you're too bloody thick to see that this evidence completely clears – Matthew – "

Naughton held his ground. "I'm afraid I *am* too bloody thick, as you call it, to see that," he yelled. "All this proves is that the two hauls of drugs are from the same consignment. It doesn't, in itself, substantiate your claim that Gharad planted the drugs under your son's shed. And it's a pretty wild claim, may I remind you. A plant of ten million pounds worth of – "

He broke off as one of the men came up to him and whispered something, and looked up, with his expression completely dazed.

"Fingerprints found on this suitcase match up with some that were found on those packets in the shed," he said slowly. "And they're both undeniably Gharad's. So it looks as though you win, Commander. All charges will be immediately dropped against your son."

There was a long, long pause, and then he added, as he reached for the phone, "And if you don't realise how glad I really am to be saying that, George, you're bloody thick yourself!"

Gideon hardly heard that. He was on his way to the door, his one thought to get home and break the news to Kate. He'd rather do it personally than phone . . .

A traffic jam on the way out of Fletchwood delayed him, though, and by the time he arrived home it was too late to break any news to Kate. Flushed, agitated, and smiling all over her face, she was standing on the doorstep waiting for him, with one arm round Matthew, who had been released a matter of minutes before and had rushed straight here to see his father and thank him.

"What made you think I had anything to do with it?" asked Gideon gruffly.

Matthew flung his arms round his father's neck and was giving him a great hug as he made the most appropriate possible answer. "Bless you, Dad. What else *can* I think?"

* * *

The next day, when she and Gideon had both had much more than the ten hours' sleep which Dr Gharad had so thoughtfully prescribed, Kate arranged the most spectacular event that had happened in the family for years.

At her insistence, Matthew, Julie and the children arrived to stay for an indefinite period while they found themselves a new home. Alec and Penny came round with their son, George, now a toddler, to make it an all-round family reunion.

For the first time in a long, long while, the old house in Harringdon Street came fully alive again with children jumping up and down the stairs, laughter and high spirits everywhere, and even the usually staid Penny, now a distinguished solo pianist, was tapping out "chopsticks" on the piano as she taught it to Sandra and Richard.

Best of all for Gideon was the sight of Kate, obviously in seventh heaven again, with the all-important difference that this time he felt he was up there with her.

That night when they were in bed, simply together as

though there had never been a wall of ice between them and never could be any such thing again, he summed it all up by saying softly, treating the darkness to one of his broadest-ever grins:

"Now that, love, is what you could *call* a day of days . . . "